D0201221

HIGH
STAKES

Books by Fern Michaels:

Fancy Dancer
No Safe Secret
Wishes for Christmas
About Face
Perfect Match
A Family Affair
Forget Me Not
The Blossom Sisters
Balancing Act
Tuesday's Child
Betrayal
Southern Comfort
To Taste the Wine
Sins of the Flesh
Sins of Omission
Return to Sender
Mr. and Miss Anonymous
Up Close and Personal
Fool Me Once
Picture Perfect
The Future Scrolls
Kentucky Sunrise
Kentucky Heat
Kentucky Rich
Plain Jane
Charming Lily
What You Wish For
The Guest List
Listen to Your Heart
Celebration
Yesterday
Finders Keepers
Annie's Rainbow
Sara's Song

Vegas Sunrise
Vegas Heat
Vegas Rich
Whitefire
Wish List
Dear Emily
Christmas at Timberwoods

The Sisterhood Novels:

Crash and Burn
Point Blank
In Plain Sight
Eyes Only
Kiss and Tell
Blindsided
Gotcha!
Home Free
Déjà Vu
Cross Roads
Game Over
Deadly Deals
Vanishing Act
Razor Sharp
Under the Radar
Final Justice
Collateral Damage
Fast Track
Hokus Pokus
Hide and Seek
Free Fall
Lethal Justice
Sweet Revenge

FERN MICHAELS

HIGH STAKES

KENSINGTON PUBLISHING CORP.
http://www.kensingtonbooks.com

KENSINGTON BOOKS are published by

Kensington Publishing Corp.
119 West 40th Street
New York, NY 10018

All Kensington titles, imprints and distributed lines are available at special quantity discounts for bulk purchases for sales promotion, premiums, fund-raising, educational or institutional use.

Special book excerpts or customized printings can also be created to fit specific needs. For details, write or phone the office of the Kensington Special Sales Manager: Kensington Publishing Corp., 119 West 40th Street, New York, NY 10018. Attn. Special Sales Department. Phone: 1-800-221-2647.

Library of Congress Control Number: 2017930993

ISBN-13: 978-1-4967-0314-9
ISBN-10: 1-4967-0314-6
First Kensington Hardcover Edition: May 2017

10 9 8 7 6 5 4 3 2 1

Printed in the United States of America

I'd like to dedicate this book to three wonderful, amazing, fearless women. To Julianna Triplett, who left us way too soon. Rest in peace, darling girl. To Julianna's mother, Suzanne Triplett, who truly is fearless, and to my dearest friend Claudeen Doll, who invented the word *fearless*. Thank you for being in my life.

Fern

Prologue

Dennis West thought it was going to be a beautiful spring day, even though it wasn't quite six o'clock in the morning. The dark night had turned the new day into a dizzying shade of pink and lavender. Plus, he'd gotten up at four thirty, which had to mean he needed to get started on what was sure to be a special day. Dennis believed in things like that. He took them as omens. Everything happened for a reason. Everything.

Now all he had to do was sit back and wait for whatever was going to happen to actually happen.

Carrying his morning coffee in one hand and the early edition of the *Post* in the other hand, Dennis made his way out to the postage stamp–sized courtyard of the Bagel Emporium to drink his first cup of coffee of the day. He was lucky this morning; one little bistro table was still available. He immediately laid claim to it, spread out the paper, and removed the lid from his coffee cup. He then settled his backpack under the minuscule table, rolled his shoulders, and stretched his neck. It was the same ritual that he practiced every morning. Now he was ready to drink his coffee. He took a healthy gulp, burning his tongue in the process. He ignored the temporary pain and scanned the headlines and everything above the fold. Nothing earth-shattering there. Nothing earth-shattering below the fold, either. He leaned back on the flimsy chair and settled in for some serious people watching. It was his absolutely favorite thing to do in the whole world. He loved, loved, loved coming up with little scenarios as people moved past him, some making eye contact, others so zoned out, they were like zombies. Sometimes he even gave the strangers names. Yes sirree, this hour was his favorite hour of the day.

Dennis was so intent on his people watching that he didn't hear his name being called. He did, however, whirl around when he felt a hand on his shoulder.

He looked up to see a tall, lanky guy around his age, with straggly hair, unshaven jaw and cheeks, and blood-shot eyes staring down at him.

"Dennis! Well, damn, this is a surprise! Never expected to see you here! Man, this is early! Great to see you!"

Dennis tried to see past the stubble, the red eyes, the straggly hair, and the dirty clothes. His eyes popped wide. "Toby! What the hell!"

"That's the best you can come up with? What the hell! I know it's been a bunch of years, but, damn, Dennis, am I that forgettable?"

"Jeez, no, Toby. I was doing what my mother used to call woolgathering. Watching people. It's kind of what I do. What brings you here to the nation's capital? When I saw you at our last reunion, you were working in New York, at some secret think tank, and making bookoo bucks. You slumming or something?" Dennis asked curiously.

"It's a long, sad story, pal," Toby said, sitting down on the spindly chair opposite Dennis.

Tobias Mason. Smart as a whip, highest IQ on the planet. The guy could discuss quantum theory but couldn't balance a checkbook. Not one ounce of street smarts. Not even half an ounce. They'd been study buddies back in the day. Two geeky nerds who never quite fit in. As close as they'd been, they had somehow drifted apart after graduation, Toby in demand for every think tank in the land and Dennis to find his way doing what he loved, gathering news to share with the world. As far as he knew, they'd both succeeded, he with a Pulitzer to his name and Toby doing all that top secret stuff no one would ever see or hear about.

"Ah . . . Toby, do you dress like that for work, or are you . . . what?"

"Actually, Dennis, I'm homeless at the moment. Gee, it's good to see you. What are you doing these days? At the last reunion, you were working at some small weekly paper in Maryland. This is Washington. Are you on vacation?"

"Whoa, whoa, whoa. We can discuss me later. Let's go back to your being homeless. What does that mean, Toby?"

"It means I have no home. I've been living in my car for the past week. I quit my job six months ago to follow my fiancée, who is no longer my fiancée, here. She kicked my ass out last week, saying I wasn't *earthy* enough for her. What does that mean, Dennis? Earthy? Does she want me to plow or dig in the earth? Plant stuff? Grow stuff? I asked her what it meant, and she said if she had to explain it to me, then I was truly hopeless.

"I paid for the move here, and we lost out on our lease in New York. I had to pay that off. Then there was the robust security deposit on the new place here, as well as first and last month's rent. Carrie—that's my ex-fiancée's name—wanted new furniture because, she said, our old stuff didn't go with the new place. I was flat-out broke when she kicked me to the curb. When I said I was homeless, I was until yesterday, even though I slept in my car last night. I called my brother for a loan, and I got a studio apartment in Crystal City. I can't move in until noon today, though. I'm going to be roughing it for a while, using a sleeping bag until I get a job."

"Why didn't you call me, Toby? I would have helped you. That's what friends do for each other."

"If I had known where you were, I probably would have, but I didn't know, so the matter is moot. Did I say that right? Anyway, maybe I wouldn't have called you. I was too embarrassed. She used me, Dennis. And then she just tossed me out like the trash. She did leave me six dollars in our checking account. I was going to marry her! Do you believe that?"

Dennis shook his head at that declaration to show he couldn't believe it, either.

"I think she's looking for a rich guy, one of those lobbyists. She was a hostess in a supper club back in New York and making squat. I paid for everything, even her credit cards, which she had maxed to the hilt, and now she's cavorting around town with fifty-year-old guys who travel in limos and wear wing-tip shoes. *Wing tips*, Dennis!" Toby screeched. "That's not even the worst. You want to hear the worst?"

All Dennis could do was nod.

"I love her. I'd take her back in a New York minute. How screwed up is that? Meaning I'm screwed up."

"Yeah, I get it, Toby. I'm no authority on women, even though I've had several relationships that haven't gone anywhere. I'm still out there looking for the right one, if there is such a thing as the right one. But I know a guy who is an expert on all things women. At least he says he is. I can introduce you to him. His name is Jack Emery. One of the smartest dudes I know. After you, of course. Maybe he can help you."

"Nah. Thanks for offering, though. This is something I have to work out on my own. . . . I have a job interview tomorrow. The pay is a hundred thou. Ginormous signing bonus, but I have to commit to two years. If I take it, I'll be good. Right now, I still have over a hundred bucks in my pocket, enough to get my good suit cleaned today, get a haircut, buy a new white shirt, get my shoes shined, and a few other things. I might even get my car detailed, because it stinks from my living in it."

"Can I help, Toby?"

Toby leaned across the little table. "Thanks, but no. Just be my friend. To be honest, Dennis, you're the only friend I ever had. I don't know why that is. I guess people just don't like me, or they can't relate to me."

"That's not true, Toby," Dennis objected, but he knew that it was. "I'll always be your friend. We don't have to see each other every day or be on the phone or texting to stay friends. Each of us has to live our life as we see fit. Friends, true friends, are a bonus in life. Here's my card, and my cell number is on the back. Call me anytime of the day or night, and I'll be there for you, Toby. Promise me you'll call if you need help. And don't go doing anything stupid, like calling your ex or begging her to take you back. That's a sign of weakness, and you are not weak. You weren't weak before, and despite everything, you are not weak now. You need to believe that. Real men do *not* grovel."

"But I am weak, Dennis. I love her. You should see her, Dennis. She's beautiful. She looks like an angel. I don't know if I'll ever get over her. I'm serious. That's how much I love her."

"*Used* to love her," Dennis said firmly. "From here on in, Carrie is someone you *used* to know. No more, no less. Repeat it after me, Toby, until you can't say it anymore."

Ten minutes later, his coffee cup empty, Dennis stood and shook hands with his old friend. Then he hugged him. "I mean it, Toby. Call me anytime of the day or night. I'll always be there for you. Good luck on the job interview."

"See ya, Dennis," Toby called over his shoulder.

"Yeah, see ya, Toby," Dennis muttered as he headed back

into the Bagel Emporium for another cup of coffee and something to eat. He needed to think about what had just transpired.

It wasn't until Dennis was back at the little bistro table, sipping at the scalding coffee and nibbling on a Danish, that he realized he hadn't gotten Toby's new apartment address or his cell-phone number. He banged his fist on the little table in frustration.

Five seconds later, his fist shot in the air. For crying out loud, he was an investigative reporter, wasn't he?

There was not a doubt in Dennis West's mind that by the end of the day, he would have all the information he needed in regard to Tobias Mason.

But it never happened.

Chapter One

Twenty months later . . .

The elevator on the newsroom floor of the *Post* pinged; then the door slid open for the Fearless Four reporters, as they had been dubbed, to exit. They were greeted with banners, streamers, and shouts of "Welcome home!" Leading the boisterous crowd was the owner of the *Post*, Countess Anna de Silva, who hugged the weary reporters one after the other and whispered her own personal greeting in their ears.

A mini-buffet and a table full of assorted beverages beckoned. Ted, Espinosa, and Dennis headed in that direction; Maggie stayed behind, which could mean only one thing to Annie. When Maggie Spritzer, with her incredibly whacked-out metabolism, ignored food, it had to mean that she was truly tired to the bone. Or sick. Or even homicidal.

"I just want to go home, shower, cuddle with Hero, who probably thinks I abandoned him, and sleep for a week. Can I have a car service take me home, Annie? Otherwise, I am going to fall asleep standing up right here. I need to sleep for a week. *A whole week*."

"Anything you want, dear. Anything," Annie said, putting

her arms around the red-eyed, frazzled reporter. "You all deserve the best the *Post* has to offer. You will all find a very nice bonus in your next paycheck by way of thanks."

"Just doing our jobs, Annie. Guess that means you're okay with the series on the shabby treatment of our veterans. I think we shamed the current administration to the point where they don't know what to do."

"When I read the last segment, I about went up in smoke. I had our lawyers go over it with a fine-tooth comb. They said we're spot on.

"Maggie, you know everything there is to know about me and know that I am no snob. But that man and I inhabit social and financial circles that, except for the Las Vegas casinos, are worlds apart. I did see that he was in the Babylon, once, and instructed Bert to comp him, a friendly gesture to a visiting fireman. But I also instructed Bert that under no circumstances was I going to meet with the Donald.

"The man has too much bluster for my tastes. I do, to be sure, admire the extent to which he has demonstrated an ability to accomplish his goals, though I am not sure I approve of some of the things he has done to get where he is today. Now, he does have a most beautiful wife. Third time is the charm, I suppose. That's about all I know of Mr. Donald Trump."

Maggie waved the comment aside. "Not a problem. All I said was that you were going to be calling on him and Warren Buffett to right this wrong that's being done to the men and women who give their lives for this country only to find themselves on the sidelines when they need help. I said you, *you*, Annie, would lead the charge and put your money where your mouth is. That's what people want to hear and see. They want to *see action*. What they don't want is meetings of committees that have to report to other committees that require more meetings. They want something *now*, not two years from now. Donald Trump says the same thing, and so does Buffett. And with Trump's presidential candidacy looming, there is no way he can back away from this once he gets started. It would look way too bad to his supporters. You will take their calls when they call, right?"

"My dear, I will run to meet them. I haven't exactly been sitting here idle while we waited for you all to get back. I've had my people calling all over the country for vacant buildings and recruiting doctors and nurses to help us out. We're going for a banner every single day in the paper. I won't rest until the White House is front and center on this. I don't give a fiddler's fart whose toes I step on. This political correctness has run its course, as far as I'm concerned. I even called Lizzie to ask her to check around for the biggest and best-known lawyers to join our cause. This country's warriors deserve the best of us all. Now, run along, dear. A car is waiting outside to take you home."

Annie offered up a bone-crushing hug, then walked Maggie to the elevator. "Don't come back till you're ready! That means next week!" she called as the elevator doors closed.

Annie turned to see Ted, Espinosa, and Dennis walking toward her, plates of food in their hands.

"You did good, boys. Real good. I'm proud of you. A month on the road, crisscrossing the country, and those wonderful interviews entitle you to as much time off as you need. You all made a difference. In case you don't know it, the paper and the media are calling you the Fearless Four. They tell me it's all Pulitzer material. Go home, children, and don't come back until you're ready. As I just told Maggie, that means next week. That's an order."

The boys nodded and Ted handed over his plate.

"I'm too tired to eat, Annie," Ted said. "You'll see me when you see me."

"Ditto," Espinosa said, also handing over his plate.

Annie looked at Dennis West, the youngest of the group, who was chewing on what looked like a shrimp egg roll. He held on to his plate.

"Before you leave, Dennis, I need to tell you that some young man has been trying to get in touch with you for the past two weeks. He's called the paper at least a few dozen times and even stopped by twice. He would never leave his name. If you check your extension, I think he left you some messages. Are you working on something? Is he a source or a snitch?" Annie asked curiously.

Dennis shook his head as he handed over his plate. "Nope. No clue. If he calls again, tell him I'm back and give him my cell-phone number. When he came by, did you see him?"

"No, but Adam in the mail room said he was a tall, really muscular guy. He also said the guy said it was urgent that he talk to you. Urgent, Dennis. Ian, our cub reporter, had a few meetings with him. Meaning he actually spoke to him."

"In this business, Annie, there is urgent, and then there is urgent. I'm going to sleep around the clock, and then I'll be back at my desk. This was a very nice homecoming. I wish I wasn't as tired as I am, so I could enjoy it more."

"Not a problem, dear. When we get notice of your Pulitzer, we'll really celebrate. Run along." Annie hugged the young reporter, wishing she had a son like Dennis West.

Dennis rolled out of bed three days after he'd returned to the small condo that he kept in town so he wouldn't face the long drive out to his mini-farm in McLean, Virginia, at the end of the long day. It was a one-bedroom, sparsely furnished and close to the *Post*.

It wasn't that he'd slept for seventy-two hours. He hadn't.

He'd periodically woken, eaten, and gone back to bed. Now, though, he was wide awake, his sleep quota fulfilled. He yawned as he looked at the digital clock on the little table next to his bed. Eleven o'clock. Other than now, the last time he'd slept till eleven o'clock was five years ago, when he had a bad case of the flu.

"Up and at 'em, dude," Dennis muttered to himself as he headed to the bathroom and a steaming-hot shower. He looked in the mirror and gasped. He looked ugly enough to scare small children. Three days of facial stubble, his hair standing on end, his eyes caked with something he'd never experienced before glared back at him. His mouth tasted like the inside of his winter snow boots. For sure, he needed to get back to the land of the living and get on with whatever this new day held for him. He grinned when he wondered what people would think if they saw him as he looked at that moment.

Forty minutes later, showered, shaved, his unruly hair slicked back, Dennis dressed in pressed khakis and a long-sleeved sky-blue Izod shirt. He sat down on the mini-stool and tied the laces on his new Nike sneakers. "Good to go, dude," he mumbled as he made his way out to the tiny area that pretended to be his kitchen, where he made a cup of coffee. He made a mental note to stop at the supermarket to buy some groceries. Being gone a whole month meant the larder was bare. As it was, he was going to have to drink his coffee black, when he preferred to douse it with *heavy* whipping cream and three sugars. Sometimes, he was worse than Maggie, with her whacked-out metabolism.

While he waited for his coffee to drip, Dennis checked his phone for missed calls and e-mails. Nothing worth getting excited over. He eyed the coffeepot and turned his head to make sure he could hear the last of the plopping sounds while he stared out the tiny window over the sink to see what kind of day it was going to be. It looked blustery. Well, that was normal for October and meant he would need his Windbreaker. The problem was he had no idea where or in which duffel bag the Windbreaker would be in. He hadn't bothered to unpack, and he wasn't going to do it now, either, which meant he'd have to wear one of his blazers. Not a problem.

Ten minutes later, Dennis closed the door behind him, vowing to stop at the nearest Starbucks for a real cup of coffee and possibly a Danish.

Forty minutes after consuming not one but two delectable pastries and two coffees, Dennis literally raced to the *Post*. He could hardly wait to get inside his home away from home. God, it was good to be back. So good, he felt like dancing a jig. He managed to control himself as he high-fived his colleagues and humbly accepted all their congratulations and praise on the veterans series he, Maggie, Ted, and Espinosa had worked on.

"Has anyone seen the rest of the Fearless Four?" Dennis called out.

A young cub reporter named Ian Smith shouted that they hadn't even called in. Dennis felt his eyebrows shoot up. For sure he thought Ted would be at his desk. Oh, well. The other three were getting older, so that probably accounted for their absence. For some weird reason, it pleased him that of the four of them, he was the only one who had shown up to work.

Dennis turned on his computer and waited for it to boot up. Once he was up and running, he stared at the screen, wondering what he was going to do. Maybe he should have checked with the EIC to see what, if any, assignments were available this late in the day. He was saved from making any decisions when Ian Smith ran over to him with a sheaf of phone messages.

"And, Dennis, some guy has been here three times looking for you, but he wouldn't leave his name."

Dennis rifled through the pink slips. Nothing that needed his attention. "What guy? Did he say what he wanted? Did he leave a number to call?" He surmised it was the same guy Annie said the mail-room clerk had told her about.

"No to everything. I asked, Dennis. Heck, I even followed him the last time he was here. I figured you would want to know, being an investigative reporter. All I can tell you is he was a tall, buff, good-looking guy. He probably weighed around one-eighty. Great suntan, bright blue eyes, and he was sporting a two-hundred-dollar haircut. Drives a Beemer. I was on foot, so I lost him. He looked jittery and nervous. I will say that. I figured he was one of your sources and was looking to get paid or something. Or that he had the skinny on something for you to work on."

Dennis squinted at the cub reporter as he tried to remember if he knew anyone who fit Ian's description. He couldn't come up with anyone. "When was the last time he was here? I know all my sources and snitches, and the way you described the guy doesn't come near to anyone I know. Well, if he shows up again, tell him I'm back. You have my permission to give him my personal cell-phone number."

Ian scampered off, leaving Dennis staring at the home page on his computer. He squeezed his eyes shut, trying to conjure up someone in his life—friend, foe, acquaintance—who fit Ian's description. Absolutely nothing came to him. Therefore, it must be a stranger who had some kind of news for him or needed help of some kind. A mystery, to be sure. One that was going to drive him nuts if he didn't figure it out.

Dennis knew sitting here at his desk with nothing to do was also going to make him nuts. He shut off the computer and headed to the EIC's office. He stuck his head in the door and asked if there was anything for him to do.

"Annie said to tell you to go home and not come back till Monday," the editor in chief replied. "I told Maggie, Ted, and Espinosa the same thing when they called in earlier this morning. So hike your tail on home, Mr. West, and don't let me see you till seven o'clock Monday morning. You guys did a super job, so rest on your laurels. If anything earth-shattering happens, I'll send you a text. Go on now. Git!"

Now what was he supposed to do? Monday was days away. Dennis dragged his feet as he headed back to his workstation, grabbed his backpack, then made his way to the elevator. He felt lost, homeless, for some reason. He couldn't even visit the rest of the fearless group, since they were under the same orders as he was. Well, crap!

He supposed he could use up some time by going to lunch. Or he could hang out in the lobby and hope a big news story walked through the doors. Like that was going to happen. Not. Maybe he should head out to his farmhouse in McLean to check on things. But if he did that, he'd rattle around like a bean in a seven-thousand-square-foot warehouse. He nixed that idea immediately. He needed to do *something*. Something meant going to the supermarket to fill his larder. He could also stop to pick up his dry cleaning and his shirts at the dry cleaners. Usually, he did things like that on the fly, but it was a way to take up some time.

Dennis moved through the revolving door, stepped aside, and looked around, across the street, up and down the street. Nothing caught his eye. Just another ordinary day. He wondered what, if anything, would happen if he went to the BOLO Building and pestered the guys. If they were even there. He could have lunch outside at the Bagel Emporium. The weather had cleared since he set out earlier. The wind had died down, and the sun was out. He should take advantage of the day since it was coming up to the end of October and the weather would turn too cold to eat outside.

His decision made, Dennis started walking. Georgetown wasn't all that far. The exercise would be good for him, and his reward would be a hot pastrami on one of Ding's perfect bagels.

As he made his way to Georgetown, Dennis let his thoughts turn to the mysterious stranger who had been trying to get in touch with him. *What, who, where, and why?* As hard as he tried, he could not get his brain around who it could possibly be. Letting his imagination run wild, he went from one scenario to another, trying to fit each one to the mysterious stranger. He came up dry each time.

Forty minutes later, Dennis checked out the BOLO Building, only to find it uninhabited. He shrugged and made his way down the alley, pressed in the security code, and left the area. Out front, he waited for a break in traffic before he sprinted across the busy road to enter the Bagel Emporium, where he waited in line to place his order. The delectable, tantalizing aromas made him realize he was truly hungry. He explained to the waitress that he would be eating outside. She handed over a numbered card, which meant his bagel, coffee, and brownie would be brought to him.

Dennis sat down at a table and prepared to do some serious people watching until his food came. His cell rang. He looked at the caller ID. Ian from the paper. His heart clicked up a beat as he pressed the TALK button. "What's up, Ian?"

"That guy just called again. The one who has been calling. I told him you were back. He asked how he could get in touch with you. I gave him your cell number, Dennis. I hope that was okay. Is it okay?" the cub reporter asked anxiously.

"Absolutely. Thanks, Ian. He hasn't called yet. I guess we should hang up and give him a chance."

After ending his call with Ian, Dennis held his cell phone in front of him, willing it to ring. All thoughts of food or people watching had disappeared. "Ring, damn it," he muttered.

The waitress appeared with his food. She set it down and picked up the numbered card and left. Like he could really eat now. His eyes never leaving the cell phone, Dennis reached for the bagel, which was cut in half, and bit down. Tasty. He slurped at the hot coffee. Ding made really exceptional coffee. Delicious. "Ring, damn it."

An elderly couple with a golden retriever sat down two tables away. Dennis was just about to attack his brownie when two Georgetown college girls loaded down with books took up another table. He took a moment to realize they were cute but too young for him to get any ideas.

Ring, damn it.

Dennis gathered up his trash. How long should he wait? He'd finished his coffee and brownie. If he was going to stay until the phone rang, he'd have to go inside to get another cup of coffee. *Stupid is as stupid does.* Of course he was staying. He deposited his trash in the trash can that stood off to the side and walked back inside, then returned to his table with a double latte. The golden retriever barked to welcome him back.

"Ring, damn it."

Thirty minutes later, Dennis's cell still hadn't rung. He finished his double latte and tossed the cup in the trash as well. He patted the golden's head, smiled at the owners, and left the Bagel Emporium. He stepped to the curb and hailed a taxi and told the driver to take him to the market that was a block from his home. He felt high and low and everything in between. A hair away from finding out who the mysterious stranger was who wanted to get in touch with him.

"Well, here I am, buddy, so where the hell are you? Whatever it is you want from me can't be very important, or you would have been in touch by now. So, Mr. Mysterious, screw you and the horse you rode in on," Dennis mumbled under his breath.

In the neighborhood supermarket, Dennis zipped up and down the aisles, picking and choosing as he went along. Total time spent perusing the aisles: twenty-two minutes. He loped back to his condo at a fast clip and was putting away the last of his groceries when his cell finally rang. He was so ticked off, he almost didn't answer it, but the reporter in him wouldn't allow for a phone to ring without being answered. He barked a surly, snarly greeting and waited.

"Dennis?" He didn't recognize the deep timbre of the voice.

"Speaking. Who is this?"

"It's me, Toby. I need to see and talk to you. It's urgent, Dennis."

"Do you have a cold, or did you have throat surgery? Doesn't sound like you. Are you the guy who has been stopping by the paper and calling but not leaving a name?"

"Yeah, yeah, it was me. It's the lessons. You know, the voice thing."

Dennis didn't know, but he let it slide. "Look, I'm sorry I never called you after we met up two years ago. Life just got in the way. What's up?"

"Are you busy? Can we meet somewhere? Off the grid."

Off the grid. Spies and federal agents went off the grid. He had read enough and watched enough television to confirm that "off the grid" was spook talk. The fine hairs on the back of Dennis's neck moved slightly, an indication he needed to go on high alert. "I'm home. I've been on the road for work. Just got home this past Friday and slept the past few days away, until today. You want to come by my place? I gave you the address on my card the last time we met."

"Yeah, well, in the move and the shuffle, I lost the card. We need to meet someplace in the open, where there are people around. It needs to look like we met up by chance. Listen, I usually run in Rock Creek Park around four. I end up at the zoo, so how about we meet up there? Just wear running clothes and sneakers. I'll find you. Don't worry about watching out for me. And don't tell anyone you're meeting me."

Dennis swallowed hard. The fine hairs on the back of his neck were doing their dance of anxiety. "Are you in trouble, Toby?"

"Hell, yes. What I mean is, right now I am not in trouble, but I will be very shortly. Why else do you think I would be calling you and going through all this bullshit?"

"Well, to be honest, I thought we were friends and were going to stay in touch. That's why I thought you were calling, to stay in touch."

"It's complicated, Dennis. So, are you going to meet me or not?"

"Sure." Dennis waited for Toby to say something, but the call ended. He stared at the phone in his hand for a long time before he placed it gently on the little bistro table in his small kitchen. He could barely take his eyes off the small square. The fine hairs on the back of his neck were still doing their dance.

Dennis looked at the clock on the range. An hour to go. Time enough to find his running gear and grab a taxi to take him to the entrance of the park.

And he needed time to *think*.

Chapter Two

Dennis climbed out of the cab at the entrance to the zoo. He walked over to a bench and sat down as he settled his baseball cap more firmly on his head. The wind had picked up in the past hour. Colorful leaves swirled with gay abandonment as children shrieked, trying to catch them, their mothers shrieking right along with them as they chased after the laughing children. Dogs on leashes tugged their owners along. It was the end of the day; it was beginning to darken earlier these days.

Toby had said he would find him. Maybe he was supposed to find a path and run. Toby's instructions were less than specific. Now that he was here, he was rapidly becoming annoyed at what was going on. He started off at a slow jog. He glanced down at his watch as he wondered what time the zoo closed. *Five? Six? Probably five*, he thought.

As he jogged along, Dennis grew more and more aware of the strange zoo sounds. It made him feel creepy. "C'mon, c'mon, Toby. Let's get this show on the road," he mumbled under his breath.

He almost jumped out of his skin when he heard a voice behind him say, "Sit down on the next bench you see."

Dennis did exactly as he was told. He waited. He reared

back when Toby Mason approached him. At least he thought it was Toby Mason. "Toby?"

"Yeah, Dennis, it's me. Who'd you think it was?"

Dennis eyed the six-foot hunk of sinewy muscle who was doing leg stretches. He even sounded different, all deep timbred and modulated. "What . . . you look . . . What's up with you? What happened? How did you . . ."

"My new job. Working out three hours a day. Voice lessons, dance lessons. Listen, this really isn't a good place to talk."

"Well, damn it, Toby, you picked this place. What? We're going someplace else now? No! Sit your butt down and talk to me, or I'm leaving."

"My bad. I didn't think this through. I'm sorry. The zoo is going to close, so this is what we're going to do. There's a sports bar right off Dupont Circle where I go on Mondays and Tuesdays. Today is Tuesday, so no one will think anything out of the ordinary if I show up. I'll be in the back. Food is decent. My treat. Don't go all hard-ass on me now, okay? This is serious and right up your investigative alley. Give me a five-minute head start and head that way."

"It would help if you'd tell me the name of the sports bar."

"It's called Mac's Shack," Toby called over his shoulder.

Dennis kept his eyes on the digital numbers on his watch. He was on the run the moment his five minutes were up, his mind boggling at his old friend's appearance. Working out. Dance lessons. Voice lessons. What the hell was Toby into?

Outside the zoo, he lucked out when he spotted a cruising cab. He hailed it, hopped in, gave up his destination, then sat back and closed his eyes. The fine hairs on the back of his neck were still tickling his neck. Try as he might, he could not come up with any scenario that spelled trouble for his old friend. He simply could not wrap his mind around the Toby Mason he'd just seen and talked to. How and why had he morphed into the person he was now, who might or might not be in trouble?

Now he had a headache. Dennis massaged his temples. His only consolation was that soon he would know what was going on with his old friend. He bit down on his lower lip. Toby needed his help. That was the bottom line.

Dennis pocketed the taxi receipt and sprinted against the wind to the entrance to Mac's Shack. It was just like all seafood eateries that called themselves sports bars. The place featured a long, horseshoe-shaped bar that was polished to a high sheen. It was full, with three bartenders hustling to accommodate all the first-on-the-scene patrons. The four walls held televisions of every size and shape, the sound muted. He looked around to see where the back of the bar was. He spotted Toby in the last booth. Dennis picked up his pace and slid into the booth.

"Talk, damn it, or I am out of here."

"Dennis, I don't really know where to start. I'm sorry about all this cloak-and-dagger stuff, but I've never been in a position like the one I find myself in now."

"Try starting at the beginning, when we last saw each other. You were getting ready to move into an apartment, because you'd been living out of your car. You borrowed money from your brother because the woman you were engaged to kicked you to the curb, took all your money, and you had quit your job in New York. Start from there," Dennis said through clenched teeth.

He looked up to see a waitress set two Bud Lights on the table, along with a huge platter of fried shrimp and chips.

"I'll eat and drink. You, Toby, talk!"

Toby sighed and leaned closer into the rough plank table. "That job I told you about, the one that was going to pay me a hundred thou? Well, I lied. I was too embarrassed to tell you that I had gotten a job at the Earth Market. I bagged groceries. I stocked shelves. When they were shorthanded, I did cashier duty. You might say I was a jack-of-all-trades. It was a job, and it paid my bills. About four days into my new job, I was helping a lady with her groceries out to her car. No big deal. Then every day for, like, the next two weeks, this same lady would come in every day and ask for me to take out her groceries.

"Finally, she got around to asking me if I was dedicated to my job, or would I be open to another offer that, she said, would pay me fifty times what I was making? Right off the bat, I didn't say yes, but I didn't say no, either. I told her to make me an offer. We agreed to meet at a coffee shop when I got off work. I showed up, and she introduced herself as Pilar Sanders. She said that she and her husband, whose name is Gabriel, own the Supper Clubs. You know what they are, right?"

"Actually, I don't think I do. What are they?" Dennis popped a delicious shrimp into his mouth and chewed.

"They own nine of them. A few in Arlington, one in Alexandria, and the rest in the District. They go by number. Supper Club One, then two and so on. The chefs are all five star. I know your paper did articles on them. Maybe that was before your time. Not sure. Anyway, after the dinner, there is entertainment. That's where I come in. I'm a dancer. You know, like the famous Chippendales."

Dennis felt his eyes start to pop. "No shit! You do that . . . you know . . . ?"

Toby laughed in spite of himself. "You mean jiggle around so women can stick money in my G-string. Yep, that's what I do. And if you think it's easy, think again. I had to go to school. I had to go to a gym. I had to take voice lessons. Hell, I was reworked from top to bottom. You are looking at the new me."

All Dennis could do was nod. Of all the things that could possibly account for this new Toby, this was never in any way near his list. No way. His head kept bobbing up and down for Toby to continue.

"The perks were over the moon. Each Supper Club comes with a string of dancers. Six, to be exact. We all live in the same house. For free. We have a housekeeper and a cook. They're free, too. We work only four days a week. Thursday, Friday, Saturday, and Sunday. We're allowed to do private parties on Wednesdays if we get a call. You know, bachelorette parties. It's a thousand dollars a night. I get sixty percent, and the Supper Club gets forty. For three hours' work. I do one or two a month. Actually, we can do the private parties on Mondays and Tuesdays, too, if we want. I don't, because those are my days off."

"So you're making money," Dennis said. *Where is this all going?*

"The answer is yes. From the day I started, I've banked close to four hundred thousand dollars."

"What?" Dennis yelped.

Toby smiled, but it was more of a grimace. "And I pay taxes, so don't go getting bent out of shape over that. I am, at this moment in time, waiting for a check for my calendar shoot. I was Mr. April. I got one hundred fifty thousand dollars for that. But it's the Christmas calendar where you really make the money. We already did the shoot for that but won't get paid until after the first of the year. That's an easy three hundred thousand dollars. Easy-peasy. But I won't be here to collect."

Dennis licked his fingers and reached for another shrimp. His eyes narrowed. "Where are you going?"

"As far away as I can get. That's why I got in touch with you, Dennis. I need you to help me make a successful getaway so that I don't spend the rest of my life looking over my shoulder."

Dennis raked his hands through his hair, then threw them up in the air. "I'm not getting this. Did you do something wrong? You said you weren't in trouble . . . yet. What does that mean, yet? Be explicit, Toby."

"Pilar and Gabe take the show on the road twice a year. July and December. In July we go to Los Angeles and in December to Miami. We have contests. Each Supper Club has its own PR person, who grooms us for the coveted top-dog position. Big, big bonus to the winner. Women turn out in droves. They pay to vote for their favorite dancer, twenty-five bucks a pop. You can vote for your favorite dancer as many times as you want as long as you pony up your twenty-five bucks. If you're in the top three, you can take home a quarter of a million dollars. Before taxes. The number one gets a half million."

Dennis gasped for air and reached for his Bud Light. He wondered if he looked as shocked as he felt.

Toby grinned. "The months we're on the road, we do private parties, in addition to the shows and contests. One big part of it—to show the legitimacy and that we aren't all about bumps and grinds—is the costume show we put on for kids. 'Fairy Tales.' We donate *all* the money to various charities. We get a lot of exposure and play to a full house each and every night. It's classic Pilar and Gabe. When we hit the town, we are met by the mayor and every town dignitary there is. We get the keys to the city, crap like that. The Sanderses soak that up like a sponge.

"While in town, we travel by bus. The last week we travel to outlying towns and cities and perform. When we leave, the lead dancer and winner is presented with a gift. The winner is photographed out the wazoo. His name is splashed everywhere. You couldn't buy that kind of publicity. Think boot box in size, silver paper, big red ribbon. A gift that is turned over to Gabe and Pilar. That gift is never seen again. This happens at each and every stop. Different-sized boxes, different gift wrap.

"It's drugs, Dennis. The Sanderses are moving drugs.

They've been doing it for years would be my guess. I just can't prove it. That's where you come in, with your investigative skills."

"Holy shit!" was all Dennis could think of to say. "Are you just guessing here, Toby, or do you know for certain?"

"A little bit of both, actually. The winner retires once we get back to home base. At least that's what the Sanderses say. No one has ever seen a winner again. No one, to my knowledge, ever questions it, either. Don't rock the boat. The money is too good. That's why Pilar is constantly on the prowl for new recruits. You know me, Dennis. I am not a joiner. I don't have friends to confide in. You are the exception. I've always been a loner, but I do listen. I hear things. Any lamebrain could put it together and come up with what I did. LA is the perfect place for the Mexican drugs. Miami is the same. They've been doing this for years, Dennis. And getting away with it."

Dennis struggled to take a deep breath. "I think I'm getting it. Why don't you just . . . you know, quit?"

"No one quits. No one. Those contests I just told you about—they're rigged. What got my knickers in a knot is I heard it whispered that I'm up for the number one spot this December. I have to be honest with you, Dennis. I am *not* cool under pressure. I'm jittery as all hell. Pilar has spoken to me twice about my timing onstage. She said I was throwing the others off. It's true. She wanted to know what was bothering me. I tried to laugh it off and said, 'Women problems,' but she keeps close tabs on all of us guys, and she knows there are no women in my life. I'm almost ashamed to admit that, but right now, I'm all for full disclosure.

"I don't have all that much time. It's already coming up to the end of October. That leaves November, and then we go on the road December first. Someone is following me. It's not something I can see. More like I feel eyes on me. That's why all the cloak-and-dagger stuff today. I was being careful when I stopped by your paper. I did it only on my days off. I also have a burner phone, in case they have a way to check my calls. I don't leave anything in my room at the house. I carry everything in my rucksack.

"Then I got nervous and rented a safe-deposit box. I've been spending a lot of time at different libraries and use only their computers, being careful to erase all traces of where I have been online. So, can you help me or not?"

Chapter Three

Dennis looked at the depleted shrimp platter, startled that he'd eaten so much. Next, he eyed the Bud Light bottle, which was now almost empty. He held it aloft for a refill. "Eat," he said so he could stall for time. "How come you're so bronzed? This is October."

"Tanning bed. It's a requirement. We have to be tanned, and we have to glisten."

"Uh-huh."

Toby raised his hand to get their waiter's attention, then pointed to the shrimp platter for a refill. He looked directly at Dennis and said, "That's another thing. Lately, maybe the past three months or so, I started having these highs and lows. I'm a pretty even-keeled kind of guy. I don't have ups and downs. Then I got to thinking, and now I'm convinced that they're putting something in my food. Don't look at me like that, Dennis. I'm not crazy. Once I figured it all out, I stopped eating at the house and started eating out. Guess what? No more highs, and no more lows. Hell, I won't even drink the coffee in the morning. I just barrel out of bed, put on my running clothes, and head for the park. I eat breakfast on the way back. I rarely eat lunch, and dinner has been on the fly. I do consume a lot of PowerBars, though. So, pal, say something."

Dennis massaged his chin, his eyes worried. "I would, Toby, if I knew what to say, but I don't. Why don't you just leave? Go back home. At least for a little while, until . . . well, until you're ready to come back. Money isn't everything. Listen, a while back, I inherited a boatload of money, so I can help you out. I just want you to be safe."

"Here's the thing, Dennis. If Pilar and Gabe are doing what I think they're doing, if I walk away, they just continue to get away with it. Where are all those guys who won the contest? There have to be dozens of them. Where the hell are they? I can't just turn my back on all of that. It simply is not in my DNA."

"Can you pick a time or date when you think things changed? Something you said or did that threw up a red flag, or maybe something happened that alerted them?"

"April, beginning of May," Toby snapped without missing a beat. "We were gearing up for the calendar and the trip to LA. I was kind of jittery. We were in the dressing room, me and the guys. We were oiling and bronzing up, but I heard the twins—that's Kevin and Kyle, who live at the house with me—talking. They're, like, joined at the hip, and one finishes what the other one says, that kind of thing. They creep me out, to be honest. I call them Frick and Frack.

"Anyway, one of them said something about Tony and how he loved LA. Then the other one said he wondered if Tony would show up for the show, you know, to congratulate us. Tony was last year's winner. Then they laughed and looked straight at me. It was one of those deer-in-the-headlights moments. Then they walked away. My brain went into overdrive, and my timing was really off that night. Pilar laced into me big-time. The other three guys shunned me the rest of the trip. I know it's not much, Dennis, but it's all I have to go on. I need you to believe in me and to trust me that something is really wrong here."

Dennis leaned back in his chair. He was aware of the clink of silverware and crystal, because they were seated almost on top of the wait station. Music was coming from somewhere, something with a fast beat to it. Chatter was everywhere, making it hard to think. He really needed to say something to his friend to wipe the miserable expression off his face. *What to say?* "You were always the smart one, Toby. Tell me what I can do. Do you want me to find a place for you to stay? Do you want me to contact the authorities and use fake names? Do you want me to sneak you out of town? Like, what can I do?"

"All the above, plus more. I have to be honest. I don't really know if I should leave now or wait and hang on a little longer. And to be *brutally* honest, I'm scared shitless, Dennis."

Dennis read the fear in his friend's eyes. He fought the urge to look over his own shoulder. *What to do?* "If you're ready to walk away now, I can take you to a secure place. But first I have to call my . . . my team and a few other people. I'm not . . . On my own, there is no way that I can give you the kind of help I think you're going to need, but my team and my friends do . . . well, they do stuff like this all the time. I'm just a cog in the wheel. What do you say? Should I alert them?"

Toby's head bobbed up and down.

It was all Dennis needed. He whipped out his phone and sent off a blizzard of texts. "Now we wait. Order some more of those shrimp, since they were very good."

Toby raised his arm and waved it in the direction of their waiter. He pointed down at the second empty platter. He called out for two coffees to replace the Bud Lights. "Two is my limit," he said to Dennis.

"Mine too," Dennis mumbled as return texts started to appear on his phone. When he read the last one, his fist shot high in the air. "Eat up, buddy, so we can be on our way."

"I'm not really hungry, Dennis. Let's take them to go and get the hell out of here. I hate being in one place too long. Where are we going?"

"Someplace as safe as Fort Knox. Remember Ding's Bagel Emporium, where we met the last time? My friends and I own a building across the street. We conduct business there when I'm not working at the paper."

"What kind of business?" Toby asked.

"That's NTK. If the others want you to know, they'll vote on it and either tell you or not tell you. You okay with that? You do realize you can't go back to that house you were living in, right?"

Toby nodded as he poked at his rucksack. "I have everything I need in here, right down to spare underwear. There really is nothing back at the house except some books and junk. I carry my life with me."

Dennis reached for the check and counted out some bills while Toby gathered up his rucksack and the bag of food. "You want to walk or take a cab?" Dennis asked.

"Let's take a cab. Less exposure, if you know what I mean."

Dennis did know what he meant. From time to time, along with the others, he'd operated in the shadows when they were on a mission. The only difference was, he hadn't been in fear of his life the way Toby was.

"Let's do it, then." Dennis slid out of the booth and began making his way through the milling crowds, jostling and apologizing at the same time.

Thirty minutes later, Dennis paid the cabdriver and waited for Toby to slide out of the cab. "This is the front of the building. If you look across the street, that's Ding's, where we met. Even though this is the front and has a door, we never use it. We have to walk around back. I don't see anything out of the ordinary, do you?"

"No. What does BOLO stand for?" Toby asked as he stared at the polished brass plaque under the coach light.

"BOLO is a law-enforcement term. It means 'be on the lookout.' That's sort of, kind of, what we do here."

Toby stuck to Dennis like glue as the reporter hiked around to the back of the building, where he pressed in a code that opened a monster iron gate that then closed within seconds after they had slipped through.

"Other businesses also use this alley, because they are all located in one structure. Our building is a stand-alone. There's a gate at the other end, too. No one can get in or out without the code. Like I said earlier, you'll be safer than Fort Knox here."

At the massive special door, Dennis leaned over the retina scanner so his eyeball could be photographed. The door beeped, and a small light turned green at the bottom of the scanner. Toby's eyes almost popped out of his head. He took a moment to wonder if he'd jumped from the frying pan into another fire. *What the hell is this place?* He shivered when he heard the special hydraulics lock into place when the door closed behind them. There was safe, and then there was safe.

Dennis adjusted the thermostat, removed his jacket, and started to prepare the big Bunn coffeemaker, explaining that the guys and one girl did like their coffee. "If you aren't going to eat that shrimp, you should put it in the fridge. Then make yourself at home. It's going to be at least an hour before Jack, Fergus, and Charles can get here, since they have to come all the way from McLean. The others will be here shortly."

"Ah . . . Dennis, aside from reporting the news, is this some kind of . . . vigilante group? Like those women a few years ago who turned this town upside down? I don't care if you are, and don't worry about me ratting you out. I would never do that. Never. I'm loyal to the core. I mean that. That guy Jack, the one you said lived in McLean, is he the one you told me about who knows everything there is to know about women?"

"Yep, that's the one. He's a great guy, even if he is a lawyer. Just so you know, there are eleven of us. Including one woman, my colleague. She earned her place here. We have another member, but at the moment he's in China, helping to build a new casino in Macao, so he's off the grid for now. So that means we're down to ten."

Dennis slapped at his head. "Crap. I forgot one of our most important members. Cyrus. Smartest damn dog in the universe. German shepherd. He's smarter than some people I know. He can answer the phone, fold towels, make his bed, and he can even buckle his seat belt. As if that isn't enough, Jack taught him to unset the alarm so he can let himself out in the morning. We all defer to Cyrus, because he's one of a kind. Well, not really. There's Cooper, but we won't go into Cooper right now. Cyrus can spot a bad guy a mile away and lives for the day Jack lets him bite someone's ass. If he doesn't like you, Toby, you are toast. Someone is at the door."

The door flew open to admit Ted Robinson, Joe Espinosa, and Maggie Spritzer. Dennis made the introductions.

"Jack's on his way with Fergus and Charles, but they'll be last men in," he announced. "No point in going through Toby's plight until everyone is here. I made coffee."

"And I brought doughnuts," Maggie chirped. "Did I understand you right, that Jack Sparrow is attending? I thought I saw him pulling out of his driveway when Ted picked me up."

"Yep. I think he *needs* to be in on this," Dennis responded.

"Isn't that the . . . ?" Toby asked, his eyebrows shooting almost to his hairline.

"Yep, the director of the FBI. You're associating with some heavy-duty company here, mister."

Toby gave Dennis his deer-in-the-headlights look.

"It's okay. He's a friend and . . . um . . . associate," Dennis said between clenched teeth.

The retina scanner beeped. Company.

The door opened to admit Abner Tookus, Harry Wong, and Jack Sparrow. Introductions were made again.

Toby, a dazed look on his face, nodded at Harry and said, "Isn't he . . . ?"

"Yep. The number one martial-arts expert in the world," Dennis said.

Toby slumped in his chair. *What have I gotten myself into?* They all looked so . . . *normal.* And yet . . .

"What? I'm chopped liver?" Abner growled.

"I was saving you till last, Abner." Dennis looked over at Toby and said, "Abner is CIA, and he can't tell you what he does, because if he did, then he'd have to kill you. You okay with not knowing, Toby? Speak up now, or forever hold your peace."

"Yeah, yeah, you bet I'm okay with it." *Definitely from the frying pan into the fire. Oh, shit.* Toby just closed his eyes and didn't move. He wished he could make himself invisible.

Small talk continued. Maggie said she was going to go by Yoko's nursery to get some pumpkins for her front stoop and asked the group if they wanted her to pick one up for them. Everyone raised his hand.

"Okay, then, I've been thinking about having a Halloween party this year. Full costume. I think we all need some fun for a change," she said. "You guys up for a party?"

Again the group's hands shot in the air.

Toby winced. *Halloween party?* He was dying here, and they were talking about a Halloween party. Maybe they were just trying to get him to relax. He risked a glance at

Jack Sparrow. He looked so . . . ordinary, just like a regular guy, but the power behind him made Toby break out into a hard sweat.

Then there was that kung fu expert, or whatever he was. The kind of guy who could kill you with a flick of his pinkie finger. To Toby, he had the look of a killer. Then, shit, there was that CIA guy, who didn't say much but was capable of killing. Man, he'd really stepped into it. Already, he could feel his blood starting to freeze in his veins. He could hardly wait to lay eyes on the expert on women, and his dog who could fold towels. The urge to bolt was so strong, Toby felt his feet start to itch.

Harry wiggled his fingers in the air. "Jack's here!"

Toby couldn't help but notice that no one disputed the comment. He hadn't heard a thing. The knot in his stomach tightened.

The massive door opened, and all Toby could see was the huge dog that bounded into the room. He barked so loud, Toby thought his eardrums were going to burst. He sat rigid in his chair, waiting for the big dog to notice him. He looked kind of playful as he made his rounds to each person, getting a tickle and a treat. The big guy, the expert on women, was pouring a cup of coffee. The two older gents stood next to him, waiting their turn at the coffee urn. Scotland Yard and the other guy so British he made his eyeballs stand at attention. He didn't know why, but he sensed that the geriatric duo was the brains of this outfit.

And then the monster dog was staring up at him. All Toby could think was this dog knew how to fold towels. He blinked. He felt a treat being slipped into his hand by someone. Damn. This was one fearsome-looking dog, who could also make his own bed and answer the phone and buckle his seat belt. He believed it all implicitly.

"Ah . . . I'm Toby." Tentatively, he held out his hand. Cyrus raised his paw and slapped it down onto Toby's palm. Toby handed over the treat. Cyrus backed up and moved over to where Jack was standing, his eyes never leaving the newcomer. Dennis made the introductions.

"Any friend of Dennis's is a friend of mine," Jack said.

Fergus and Charles nodded.

"Welcome to the BOLO, Toby. Let's get to it. Conference room, everyone!" Jack said, exuberance ringing in his voice.

It was a nice room, Toby thought as he plopped down on a chair next to Dennis. While he waited for the others to settle themselves, he looked around. He liked and recognized the Jackson Pollock prints on the wall. Someone obviously had a green thumb, because the two ficus trees in the corner looked lush and full. There were no computers in here, no fax machines. The only digital appliance was an elaborate telephone console sitting on a credenza, next to a twelve-cup coffee machine. A mini-fridge was nestled under the credenza. Dennis did say this group, whatever the hell this group was, did like their coffee.

Yellow legal pads, pens, and tablets appeared out of nowhere, along with a crystal bowl of dog treats. Obviously, the monster dog was an important member of this group. Toby made a mental note not to forget that little fact.

"Looks like we're all here, so let's get started and yield the floor to Dennis, who called this special meeting," Jack said. Cyrus barked to show he was on board.

Dennis cleared his throat. He hated being the center of attention. "I'm going to go with the quick version. Then you all can question Toby. For starters, Toby and I go way back. We've been friends for many years. We lost touch for a while, until a few years ago, when we met up by accident across the street at Ding's. We promised to stay in touch, but that never happened. Life got in the way, as they say.

"Toby is Dr. Tobias Mason. He's an economist. He worked in New York, at the American Baylor Institute. He was engaged to be married, but his fiancée wanted to relocate to Washington to be a part of the political scene. Toby gave up his job, and they moved here. Shortly afterward, to his chagrin, his fiancée decided she didn't want to be his fiancée any longer. She booted him out, took all his money, and hooked up with a rich, middle-aged lobbyist. Toby was living out of his car when we met up at Ding's. That was the last I heard of Toby until today. Here we are.

"Toby met up with me today. He'd been trying to get in touch with me, but, as you all know, Maggie, Ted, Espinosa, and I were out of town on an assignment," Dennis said. He pointed to Toby. "This guy is not the old Toby. I have a picture on my phone for you all to see the old Toby." Dennis worked his thumb over his phone until a picture of Toby and him at Ding's appeared. He passed it around the conference table.

Toby wished he could fall through the floor.

"This is the new, buff Toby. He has a job. He is a dancer at the Supper Club. The *flagship* Supper Club. The Supper Clubs are owned by a couple named Gabriel and Pilar Sanders. The wife, Pilar, discovered Toby at the supermarket where he was working. He said after more than a week of carrying her groceries out to the car, she approached him and offered him a job. He's worked as a dancer for a little under two years now and is paid extremely well. He had to learn how to dance, had to work out at the gym, take all kinds of classes. The man you see sitting here is the new Toby. And, by the way, he is scheduled to be Mr. December for the Supper Clubs' yearly calendar.

"A while back, possibly two or three months ago, Toby said he felt like he was being watched and followed. I'll let him explain what he thinks is going on. He got in touch with me because he knows I'm an investigative reporter. My gut is telling me my friend needs our special brand of help. And he does not want to go back to the house he's been living in. He fears for his life. That's why I brought him here and called this meeting. We have to keep him safe. That's my side of it. Toby, you up for some questions?"

Toby took a huge, deep breath and exhaled in a loud swoosh of sound. "Ask me whatever you need to ask. Just be mindful of the fact that I probably won't be able to answer most of them. The Sanderses run an extremely tight ship, and by that I mean they tell us nothing. They do not confide in any of us. They pay extremely well. Their rules are stringent, and if you don't obey them, you are *out*."

Charles nodded. Pen in hand poised over his yellow tablet, he asked the first question and all the rest. Toby answered as best he could until Jack called a halt a full hour later.

"It's not enough. At this point in time, the case does not qualify for a mission," Jack observed.

The others nodded, with the exception of Dennis.

"What isn't enough?" Dennis queried.

"Just because someone thinks he is being followed does not mean he really is being followed. Ever hear the word *paranoia*? So the December winner receives a gift at the end of the pageant, or whatever it is, but that doesn't mean there are drugs in said package. There is no proof that the Sanderses are drug traffickers. The winners, as you stated, are never heard from again. Can you prove that? You said yourself there were no friendships among the dancers. How do you know the Sanderses didn't arrange for other jobs for the winners? Have any missing person reports been made? You don't know. We don't know. Before we can even consider taking on this mission, we would have to run all kinds of background checks, and that takes time. All of you who agree with me, raise your hand."

Every hand in the room shot in the air except for Dennis's. Cyrus barked his vote.

Toby looked around at all the faces staring at him. His last hope, and they had just shot him down. Now what was he supposed to do? Even the damn dog was against him. He looked over at Dennis, his only ally. Whatever he saw in his friend's expression caused a knot in his stomach. "I'm not paranoid. I take my life seriously, and I know what I know and feel. I am damn well in danger!" Toby was surprised at how strong and forceful his voice sounded.

Jack Sparrow stared at Toby. "I think what Jack is trying to say is we can help you, but not right this instant. We don't work that way. We strategize, we make plans, and we cover our asses up one side and down the other. That means you have to cooperate with us. I know Charles has something he wants to say. Are you willing to listen?"

"Of course I'm willing to listen. This is my life we're discussing here. That's why Dennis brought me to all of you." Toby wished he didn't sound so belligerent, but what the hell? This was his life these people were talking about.

"I want you to think about something, young man," Charles said in a voice he would have used to discuss the weather. "How do you feel about going back to the house where you live tonight? We'll arrange security for you. We need to create a legend for all of us so that we can help you. We have a top-notch security detail at our disposal twenty-four/seven. Off the top of my head, I'd say we can come up with a young lady who will pretend to be your new girlfriend to drive you home. This will account for any lapses in time where you shook your tails today, if you are being followed, as you suspect. If your people really are stalking you, it won't take long to get a handle on it. With what Dennis has told us, you seem pretty adept at eluding anyone following you. Would you be agreeable to going back and pretending all is well? I can personally guarantee nothing will happen to you. You will also have the entire FBI watching your back."

Toby looked over at Dennis, who nodded. "Yeah, sure. Just tell me what I need to do." Oh, God. Did he just agree to go back to the lion's den?

"Right now, nothing. We will get to work and see what we can come up with. While we do that, perhaps you could take Cyrus out for a walk in the alley."

The moment the shepherd heard his name, he was on his feet, then at the door, where he stopped to wait.

"Uh, does he bite?" Toby asked.

"Only if you bite first. He's good for fifteen minutes. Cyrus, watch this guy."

At Toby's look of horror, Jack hastened to explain. "No, I didn't mean you were going to do anything. I meant for Cyrus to protect you. You might not know the difference, but Cyrus knows, and that's all that is important."

The moment the hydraulics locked into place, the group got down to business, with the first order of the day being a call to Avery Snowden to show up with a young, attractive operative who would, over the following days, play the part of Toby Mason's main squeeze.

"So, then, we'll take Toby's case?" Dennis asked.

"Once our due diligence is complete, if it warrants our help, then of course we will take it on. For starters, tomorrow night or the night afterward, I want all of you to hit the Supper Club to observe."

"We can't do that, Charles. Those Supper Clubs are for women. We'll stand out like warts on a baby's behind. You need women for that, and Maggie is out, because someone might recognize her picture since it's always in the paper. Ditto for me and Espinosa. I see that look on your face, Jack. Don't go there. We are not going to go disguised as women," Ted said.

Jack laughed out loud because that was exactly what he

had been thinking. "Well, Mr. Intrepid Reporter, if we don't go in disguise, then that means we have to call in the girls to do it for us. Who wants to make that call?" When there was no response to his question, Jack smirked and said, "I rest my case."

"We'll work on that," Charles said. "Avery said he would have someone here within the hour, and his operatives are all on standby. That was our first immediate hurdle. Now for assignments. But before I get to that, a thought just struck me. What if we have Bert Navarro get in touch with the Sanderses and invite x number of dancers to Macao for the big grand opening, which is just around the corner? That would be the big time for the Supper Clubs. Tons of free press, thanks to Maggie and the *Post*. And everyone knows what China has to do with drugs. If young Toby is right, and they are onto him, it might take some of the pressure off all of that if they think they're on to bigger and better rewards. As I said, let's let it simmer for a bit and get back to it."

Chapter Four

Toby leaned against the BOLO Building's wall as Cyrus prowled the alley until he found the exact spot he was looking for. One eye on the massive dog and the other on the gate to the alley, Toby let his thoughts run rampant. How in the hell had he allowed himself to get into this predicament? He wasn't stupid. He immediately corrected the thought. Sometimes the things he did were stupid, and this was about the stupidest thing he'd ever done in his life, but it didn't necessarily mean he was stupid as in *stupid* stupid.

What he should have done after Carrie dumped him was go back to New York, set up shop on his own, and get his old job back. Why hadn't he done that? Because he'd hoped against hope that Carrie would change her mind and want him back. Well, that hadn't happened, and now, a little more than two years after moving to the District, it was obvious that it was never going to happen. Not now, not ever. Yet here he was, in this strange place, with equally strange people. The term *mercenary* floated around inside his brain.

Cyrus meandered up to the gate, pawed the ground, lifted his leg, then meandered back down the alley.

Toby fired up a cigarette. That was another thing. He'd taken up smoking. So that was another stupid thing he was guilty of. He didn't smoke much, maybe three or four cigarettes a week. Cyrus growled as the cigarette smoke wafted his way.

"You just do your thing, dog, and let me do mine," Toby growled in return.

Cyrus offered no response to that declaration.

So here he was, in the clutches of some very strange dudes who were probably mercenaries and were taking his situation under advisement. Among those strange dudes was the director of the FBI and some goddamn spook from the CIA. Dennis . . . Dennis wouldn't let anything happen to him. His old friend wouldn't have brought him here to this Fort Knox hideout if he didn't think he could be helped. Then again, how well did he really know Dennis West? *No one ever really knows anyone*, he thought. The realization did not make him feel one bit better.

Toby shivered in the brisk October wind rushing down the alley. Leaves were blowing from somewhere. How weird was that with not a tree in sight? Just as weird as everything else going on in his life right now. He crushed out the cigarette under his foot, then picked it up and stuffed it in his pocket. "Hey, dog, anytime now would be good, okay?"

Cyrus ignored him.

It suddenly occurred to Toby to wonder how he was going to get back into the BOLO Building, since his eyeball wasn't recorded with the retina scanner or however one gained admittance. Maybe he was doomed to spend the night out here, shivering, while all the strange dudes inside decided his fate. He looked at the numbers on his watch. One minute to go, and the fifteen minutes that the dog was good for would be up. He looked down the alley and saw the huge dog sprint to where he was standing. Man and dog eyeballed one another until Toby dropped to his haunches. He could feel the dog's warm breath.

"We should talk . . . ah . . . Cyrus. I get the feeling you're really high up on the totem pole here. I respect that. You, that is. I'm new to this. And to be honest, I am scared shit-less. You also scare me shitless. See how honest I'm being? I have no clue how we're supposed to get back inside this fortress. I should know that, but I don't. They said to walk you, and here I am, but any fool can see you walk your-self. Damn, you are one big dog. I have to give you that."

Cyrus let loose with a soft woof of thanks for the com-pliment. He cocked his head and appeared to be waiting for Toby's next declaration.

"Are you, like, some kind of special dog? A mutant of some kind?"

Cyrus growled.

"Okay, okay. You're just a really, really big dog. Scratch that mutant part."

Cyrus woofed his acceptance of Toby's apology. Sud-denly, one big paw slapped at Toby's wrist.

"My watch, right? Yeah, yeah, your fifteen minutes are up, but I have no clue how to get back in. If you recall, no one gave me instructions. Unless you know how to get in, we're stuck out here. I have no clue as to how to get back in-side. Of course, you know. How silly of me to think other-wise. So, do whatever you have to do and get us back inside."

Cyrus waited a moment, then stood on his hind legs as he tilted his head to the scanner. The hiss of the hydraulics was music to Toby's ears. Gentleman that he was, Cyrus waited until Toby walked through the door, then followed him inside. He stood perfectly still until he heard the massive door lock into place. Then he barked loudly to announce their arrival. He nudged Toby to the kitchen counter, where a jar of treats rested. He barked three times.

"Okay, I get it. You get three of these things, right? Here you go, sport," Toby said as he handed over the treats. He stuck an additional two in his pocket, just in case. In case of what, he had no clue. With no idea of where to go, Toby

opted to follow the shepherd, who led him to the conference room.

Toby looked around, but no one even bothered to look
in his direction. He finally settled himself in the same chair
he'd been sitting on earlier and waited for someone either
to notice him or speak to him. When nothing happened,
he leaned back and closed his eyes. He wouldn't sleep; he
was too wired up. He shifted into what he called his neutral zone, the way he had trained himself to do before
every performance onstage. It was the only way he could
rid himself of his inhibitions and do what was expected of
him in front of a bunch of howling, yowling women bent
on attacking his body. Right now he could tune in to the
mutterings, the key tapping, and the sounds of the grease
pencils scribbling on the whiteboards hanging on the far
wall. A question was thrown out, and three or four an-
swers were forthcoming. He was jolted back to awareness
when he heard his name called by the portly British guy.

"Toby, do you dancers take steroids?"

"I don't. I can't answer for the others. Our contracts say
if you're caught taking any, it's cause for immediate dis-
missal."

"When you're in the green room prior to a performance,
do you guys have lockers? How do you know no one goes
through your things?" Toby sat up a little straighter when
he saw it was the director of the FBI posing the questions.

"In the beginning, I never gave it a thought, but a few
months ago I started to think about it, so I bought a new
laptop, a tablet, and two burner phones. The original ones,
which I leave in my lockers, I just use for playing video
games. I don't even use them for e-mails. As for my regular
cell phone, I just use it to call home, to call my parents, my
brother, the dry cleaner, the video store, that kind of thing."

"What about your car? What do you keep in your car?"
the director asked, continuing to probe.

Toby laughed out loud. "Here's the thing, Mr. Director. Several months ago I sold my car and bought a new one from the FBI vehicle auction. To me it was new, but it wasn't *brand-new, off-the-lot new*. I got a Beemer from your impound lot auction for half the price of a brand-new one with the sticker still on the window. After I filled out all the paperwork and forms and paid cash for the car, which is a requirement, one of your agents told me the car had belonged to a big-time drug dealer. And the drug dealer had had the car outfitted with all kinds of compartments for smuggling drugs. Your guys, of course, found all those compartments, and your agent showed them to me.

"From that day on, I started to stash all my stuff in those compartments. You would actually need to know where they are to find them. No way are they visible to the naked eye. I'm good in that respect."

Sparrow squinted at Toby. "I remember that auction. I remember that car, too. You got yourself a hell of a deal. If I recall correctly, the Beemer had only eighteen hundred miles on it."

"Actually, Mr. Director, it had one thousand eight hundred thirteen miles on it," Toby said sotto voce.

"I stand corrected." Sparrow laughed just as Cyrus reared up and raced from the room. "Sounds like Snowden is here."

It wasn't just Avery Snowden. Cyrus led a parade of five people into the conference room and was rewarded with a handful of treats from Jack's pocket. His job done, the big dog resumed his place at Jack's feet under the table.

Introductions were made. Toby's jaw dropped as his eyebrows shot up to his hairline. *Well, okayyyy*, he thought as he stared at a bevy of beautiful young women. The women smiled, completely at ease, shaking hands, making eye contact with everyone.

Maggie Spritzer winced. On her best day, after getting the

"works" at a day spa, she knew she couldn't even come close to looking like these women. And they weren't models or show people; they were all operatives working for Avery Snowden off his roster of employees.

Refreshments were offered and declined.

Charles took to the floor. "It's getting late, and we want to get Toby back to his digs. Which operative have you assigned to him, Avery?"

"Sylvia. Did you create a legend for her?"

"I did. From here on in her new name is Mia Grande. She's an heiress to a fortune built on a Brazilian hot pepper sauce called Grande Hot Pepper Sauce. She's worth millions. She's been in the States for a few years, finishing up some grad work at Georgetown. She's a party girl. But that's okay, because she carries a four-point-oh GPA. We've arranged for a candy apple–red Ferrari F12tdf edition to be delivered momentarily. She resides at the Watergate. We backstopped everything. When and if Toby's people check her out, everything will clear. Toby will say they met at a museum a while back, then met up again, and the rest is history. She will drive him home and meet up with him at six a.m. tomorrow morning. They will go for a run, have breakfast. Toby will never be out of her sight. When she is out of his sight, these other ladies, friends of Mia, will step in. Toby's residence will be under surveillance as of"—he looked at Snowden, who mouthed the words, "One hour ago"—"one hour ago."

He gazed at Toby. "Avery will give you a special watch that you are to wear at all times. It's even safe to shower with. You can talk to him on it. When he wants to speak with you, you will feel a soft buzz on your wrist, at which point you will press the stem on the watch and will be able to converse. Mia also has one. It's been programmed, so you shouldn't have any trouble."

Toby thought it was all a bit too cloak and daggerish,

but he had committed, so he was in for all he was worth. He simply nodded that he understood and agreed. Dennis gave him a thumbs-up.

Toby continued to watch and listen as the new group clustered around what he thought of as "the mercenaries," being briefed on *the mission*. That had to be spookspeak for what he was going through. He half closed his eyes and pretended not to look at what he considered his babysitter. He wondered if she packed a gun and, if so, where she kept it, since she was covered in formfitting spandex. He liked the cowboy boots and the pearl-white Stetson that sat on top of a glorious head of shimmering strawberry-blond curls. The killer smile certainly didn't hurt anything. All in all, one hell of a babysitter, all things considered.

Toby was jolted from his thoughts when he heard Joe Espinosa volunteer to do a makeover so they could attend tonight's dance session. He heard him say amid groans that someone named Alexis practiced on him all the time, and he had the red bag of tricks at his disposal. Whatever the hell that meant. He was right on the edge of the rabbit hole, and he definitely knew it. *Kick back. Go with the flow.* Dennis said these people would help. They were into it. That was for sure. Along with the director of the FBI. How cool was that? *Pretty damn cool*, he decided.

Charles looked down at the phone in his hand. He waved his free hand for silence. "It would appear your ride is here, Toby. The car is parked in front of this very building. You and Mia are now free to go. Be sure to take some selfies—I believe that is the term you young people use—in case anyone wants to see your new...ah... squeeze. One last thing. Be sure you all take a boatload of pictures tomorrow evening at Toby's, um . . . recital. Maggie, it would be nice if some of those pictures could find their way to Page Six. I'm sure you all have sources who can make this happen. And, Maggie, play up the heiress part and how smitten Mia is with Toby. So smitten, her parents are on the way from Brazil to check him out. The publicity alone will put Toby front and center, and if the people he works for have devious thoughts, they will have to shelve them with all the notoriety that is coming his way. Any questions?"

There were no questions.

Ten minutes later, Toby settled himself in the passenger seat of the candy apple–red Ferrari. "Now, this is one sweet set of wheels," he grunted as he strapped himself into the low-slung seat, his long legs stretched out in front of him. "My surrey with the fringe on top can't come close to this hunk of perfection. Can you handle this baby, Mia? There's a lot of horsepower under that gleaming hood."

Instead of answering what Mia thought was a stupid question, she stomped on the gas. The Ferrari went from zero to seventy in a nanosecond.

"You just gave me whiplash!" Toby bellowed.

"That will teach you to ask stupid questions. This car is not meant to be driven the way your grandma drives. It's built for *speed*."

"Yeah, well, listen, sweetie. The Georgetown police frown on anything over twenty-five miles an hour. You want to go head-to-head with them, go for it," Toby snapped.

Mia eased her foot off the gas pedal and stopped for a red light. The engine growled like eighteen monsters belching fire. "Well, *sweetie*, there is that," Mia said, pushing the Stetson back a smidgen, and smiled at him, her pearly whites lighting up the interior of the car. Toby just knew somehow, someway, some orthodontist had retired to some pricey beachfront property on his fee for that smile. "I think I can talk my way out of a ticket if it comes to that. By the way, this might be a good time for you to tell me where we're going."

Toby punched in the address on the GPS.

Mia shifted gears and moved ahead at a sedate twenty-five miles an hour, the horsepower under the hood protesting mightily. "So tell me how a brainiac like you ended up stripping for a bunch of howling, yowling women."

Toby's back stiffened. "I don't strip. I dance. What? You want me to apologize for having a brain? That's not going to happen."

"We need to be on the same page here if I'm going to protect you. You have to admit, that hour back there at Fort Knox was just a teaser. Talk to me. Tell me what I need to know."

Toby clamped his lips shut and closed his eyes. As far as he was concerned, this discussion was over and done with. Like this 110-pound piece of fluff in her cowboy hat and boots was *really* going to protect him. More like the other way around.

"Okay. Be like that, then. But just for the record, one does not get a job with Avery Snowden unless one qualifies and measures up. In case you are interested, I am a third-degree brown belt. I trained under Harry Wong. I came in first at sniper training. I always hit what I shoot at, double tap to the head, center mass, you name it. I came in first at the endurance trials. I can scale the mountain at the training base in the time it would take you to buckle up your gear. I chewed off the ear of a man who somehow caught me off guard. That's my résumé. Any questions?"

Jesus. Toby didn't like what he was feeling. This cowgirl sitting next to him had actually chewed off someone's ear. He fought the urge not to cover his ears. He knew in his gut she wasn't making it up to entertain him. Man, this was right up there with that damn dog knowing how to fold towels.

Toby sucked in his breath. What the hell. His life wasn't exactly a secret these days. "You're right. I am . . . was . . . a brainiac. I have two PhDs, two MBAs." He went on to tell Mia about the past few years of his life, up to when he got hired at the Supper Club. "So that's my background. Now we're even, and that's the house two doors up."

The Ferrari slid to the curb, making enough noise to wake the dead. Toby reached for the latch to open the door.

"No, no, no. We need to sit here for a little while. Remember, we are smitten with each other. Someone might be looking out the window. This car just alerted everyone within a ten-mile radius that you are home. And remember, when you go inside, you need to look dazed, like you just scored with the best cheerleader for the football team. In other words, you need to look sappy. *Dreamy*, if you like that word better."

Toby felt like he had one foot over the rabbit hole. "Am I supposed to kiss you good night or what?"

"That would be nice."

"I don't kiss on a first date," Toby mumbled.

"Well, there's a first time for everything, right? This is a game. Even a brainiac like you should realize that, right? You want to win, you play by the rules. You're a real stiff, you know that? Loosen up. Nothing is going to happen to you on my watch. I guarantee it."

Toby almost believed what she was saying. In spite of himself, he asked the question he swore to himself he wasn't going to ask. "How'd you get into this . . . line of work?"

"Lean a little closer. I see someone at one of the windows. Well, it's like this. I was one of those darling debutante girls. Mummy and Daddy had some rich guy all picked out for me. A banker. You know how deadly dull those guys are. That's what my life would have been like. I didn't want any part of that."

Suddenly, Toby found himself in a lip-lock that threatened to expel his tonsils. He felt hands yanking at his hair as 110 pounds of girl mashed her face against his. *Holy Jesus.*

When he came up for air, all he could do was stare at the young woman sitting across from him.

"Someone came out on the front porch. I wanted to give them an eyeful." Without missing a beat, Mia continued. "As I was saying, I had a friend who was taking martial-arts lessons because she had been mugged. I joined to keep her company. One thing led to another, and then Mr. Snowden came into the picture via Harry Wong. He pays exceedingly well. Lots of perks. Okay, you can go now. I'll be here at six on the dot. Do. Not. Be. Late. Go now!"

Toby barreled out of the car like his pants were on fire. *Holy shit.* He swallowed hard to make sure his tonsils weren't swirling around in the back of his throat. He was supposed to do something. *Shit.* What was it? *Look dazed. Sappy. Dreamy.* He knew he already looked like all of the above. *Well damn, and damn again.*

Inside the well-lit, well-appointed foyer, Toby leaned against the door the moment it closed. Out of the corner of his eye, he saw Martha, the housekeeper/warden, coming down the hall. Mia's warning ricocheted inside his head. *Look sappy, dreamy.* He closed his eyes and started to hum under his breath to the count of ten, at which point he pushed himself away from the wall and sauntered through the foyer to the staircase that led to the second floor. He pretended to notice Martha for the first time.

"Well, helllooo, Marthaaa. Beautiful evening, isn't it?" he singsonged as he did a little twirling jig in his effort to look like a love-struck fool.

Martha was a motherly-looking, bosomy, middle-aged woman with graying hair, pink cheeks, and a penchant for wearing a ton of jewelry that tinkled and clanked as she moved. "Are you all right, Toby? You look . . . um . . . out of it. As usual, we missed you at dinner. Do you need help? You aren't drunk or high, are you? You know the rules."

"I am, I am, I am. Drunk on love, that is. I am sooo in

love. I met this gorgeous, beautiful young woman in a museum, of all places, and she cannot keep her hands off me. We just hit it off perfectly. I met her a while back and kept bumping into her at the most unlikely places, and today we both just stood there looking at each other. I invited her for coffee, and she said yes. Do you believe that?" Toby squealed. "Her name is Mia Grande. Isn't that the most beautiful name you've ever heard in your whole entire life? It's like music when you say it out loud. Meeaaa Grandeee. I'm going to be dreaming of her all night long." He squealed again.

Martha's eyes narrowed. "Just like that you're in love! What do you know about her? You have to be careful out there, Toby," Martha said in her most motherly voice.

"Martha, Martha, Martha. I knew the moment I met her, she was for me. She said the same thing. It was meant to be. You should see her car. Man, that is one impressive set of wheels. She's doing some grad work at Georgetown, and she carries a four-point-oh. Now, that I respect. Plus . . . plus . . . are you ready for this? She's *rich*. She's an heiress to some Brazilian hot sauce fortune. She's really, really rich. Not that money is important, but it does help. She's from Brazil, and she is runway-model beautiful, and her body is smoking hot. Did I say I'm in love? I am. God, I am sooo in love!"

"Uh-huh. Well, it's late, Toby, and you should be in bed by now. Unless you want me to fix you some warm milk or hot chocolate."

"No, no, no milk or chocolate. Oh, Martha, you're right. You are so right. Mia. That's her name. Did I tell you that?" he continued to gush. "She is picking me up at six so we can go running together and have breakfast. I won't have any trouble sleeping tonight. Besides, I promised her I would dream about her all night long. She promised to do the same thing. This is so great. I can't believe how wonderful I feel."

To prove his point, Toby grabbed the housekeeper, hugged her until she squealed, then kissed her on the cheek. "See ya," he bellowed as he bounded up the stairs, taking them two at a time.

Inside his room, Toby locked the door and dived onto the king-size bed, his heart pounding so hard he thought it would burst right out of his chest. "I pulled it off. I know I pulled it off." The gang, the mercenaries, would be proud of his performance. He was almost sure of it. Even the damn dog would be proud of him.

Chapter Five

The ten-thousand-square-foot penthouse in Crystal City, Virginia, was tomb quiet at five o'clock in the morning, as it should be. It wasn't that the penthouse was empty, because Pilar and Gabriel Sanders, the owners, lived in the luxurious quarters. They were a quiet couple even when they were together. Now, though, only Pilar Sanders, who was five feet ten inches tall and weighed 120 pounds soaking wet, moved about the blinding white and stainless-steel state-of-the art kitchen. She moved silently, pressing buttons that would activate the quiet built-in coffee machine. The machine was so high tech, it didn't even make the plopping sound common to all coffeemakers when it finished brewing.

Pilar Sanders wasn't beautiful, though she was reasonably attractive, thanks to Botox injections, contact lenses that were changed daily depending on their color and her mood, pricey dental work, a sculpted nose job to the tune of eight thousand dollars, a chin tuck to erase the turkey wattle that seemed to attack most women when they hit the magic five-oh, along with a plethora of hair extensions. The breast implants that threatened to spill from the satin dressing gown had been a must-have no matter what, as had the tummy tuck. Then there were the acrylic nails, the dyed hair to match the extensions, and the tattooed brows and eyeliner. The end result was Pilar Sanders. As her husband, Gabriel, put it, she was a walking, talking hundred-thousand-dollar bill with a five-thousand-dollar-a-month maintenance tab.

It was all true, and in private she had no problem admitting to it when fighting with her husband, which was a constant, ongoing part of their lives.

Gabe, as he liked to be called, had wondered countless times what his wife looked like under the heavy makeup she was never without. Even this early, at five o'clock in the morning, Pilar was perfectly made up, perfumed, and powdered, every hair in order, the hair extensions perfectly placed. "How," he'd asked thousands of times, "do you sleep?" Pilar's answer was simple. She didn't sleep, getting by on catnaps and perhaps an hour or so of actual sleep here or there. Her favorite saying was she would have plenty of time to sleep when she was dead.

Pilar glided in satin slippers across the exquisite floor tiles, poured her coffee, and settled herself in the cozy breakfast nook she'd designed for just these early morning alone times. She flipped open the laptop on the table and brought up the nightly reports from all nine Supper Clubs. Then she checked her e-mails, fully expecting nothing of interest since she'd checked them around eleven last night, before shutting down her computer. She frowned when she recognized an e-mail address belonging to Martha Howell, the housekeeper/spy at the Supper Club One residence. She bit down on her lower lip. An e-mail from Martha could mean only that something was up with her number one dancer, Toby Mason.

She childishly crossed her fingers that the e-mail wasn't going to pose a problem and disrupt her plans. She delayed the inevitable by sipping the dark French roast coffee she was addicted to as she concentrated on what she considered to be real and imaginary problems where Toby Mason was concerned. The main problem was that Toby was too smart for his own good. It was entirely possible that Toby was her first and only mistake since she and Gabe had embarked on what she called their Supper Club Adventure. It wasn't that Toby was asking questions or doing something he shouldn't be doing. It was more that he wasn't doing anything.

When a routine of several years' making was the rule of the day, and then that rule was bent or ignored, it threw up a red flag. Pilar was constantly on the alert for red flags. Her gut had warned her months ago that Toby bore watching. She'd hired a top-notch investigative firm, which had proved to be not so top-notch, because they kept losing Toby and filing reports that simply said "The guy is onto us." She didn't believe that for a minute and had fired the firm and hired a new one, which hadn't fared any better. Like it or not, she finally had to admit that Toby Mason was smarter than she'd given him credit for.

And now this e-mail.

Pilar clenched her pricey dental work and clicked open the e-mail. She scanned it, then read it word for word. Then she smiled. So the young man was in love. Well, that certainly explained things. Or did it? No, not really. Toby had been acting peculiar for months now. According to this e-mail, he'd fallen in love virtually overnight. She read the e-mail again, noting this time that Martha had gotten the license plate of the fancy sports car that had dropped him off last night.

Without stopping to think, Pilar sent an e-mail to the second investigative agency, asking for an in-depth check on one Mia Grande. She added an ASAP in bold red letters. She was confident that by ten o'clock, she'd be reading the in-depth report she had requested. There was a lot to be said for young love. A lot.

Pilar finished her coffee and was about to refill her cup when she looked up to see her husband standing in the doorway. She cringed at his bed hair, which was standing out at all sorts of crazy angles, at his dark stubble, and the potbelly pressed against his pajama top. She said what she always said when she saw him like this. "Gabe, you really need to get that fat sucked out of your stomach."

To which he replied, "Not going to happen, babe. You're the beautiful one on this team." Pilar shook her head.

"So, anything going on?" Gabe asked as he scratched at his chest as if he were digging for gold.

Pilar winced again. Where, oh where, was the buff, muscled man she'd married so long ago? "Not really. There was an e-mail from Martha. She said Toby is in love. Check the e-mail for yourself."

Gabe did just that as Pilar refilled her coffee cup and also filled one for her husband.

"Well, guess you feel pretty foolish now, don't you? The guy is in love. That explains everything. You were stewing and fretting over nothing and spending a fortune on those private detectives."

"No, Gabe, it does not explain *everything*. Toby was acting peculiar months ago. He wasn't in love then. In fact, I doubt he knew this girl back then. Martha said they'd met just recently. I requested an in-depth background check on the woman. I should have it by midmorning."

Gabe nodded. "How did the club do last night?"

"Stable. You know that revenue is down when it's just dinner. I think we should start having the guys dance on Wednesdays now, until the holidays are over. Carlie told me yesterday that people are already calling for Christmas reservations." Carlie Fisher was the Sanderses' business manager and the person responsible for all the scheduling of the dancers.

"Works for me if it works for you. Did you sleep at all last night, Pilar?"

"Actually, I did, Gabe. Don't I look fresh and rested?"

Gabe snorted as he eyed his wife. "Someday, I'm going to drag you through a car wash so I can see if you look anything like the young girl I married all those years ago. You've been nipped and tucked, sliced and diced to the nth degree. And those pillow lips! What the hell is up with that? Believe me when I tell you they look slutty. Don't you care that people whisper behind your back? What you really look like under all that war paint is still a mystery to me these days. What happened to that bright-eyed girl I married?"

"You mean that scrawny, knock-kneed, ugly duckling with the space between her front teeth, the crooked nose, and the thick glasses? That bright-eyed girl?" Pilar asked with a warning bite in her voice.

Gabe shrugged. "Yes, that's the one. The one I fell in love with. Look at you. You look like you've been shellacked and lacquered from head to toe. You don't even look real anymore. You look like one of those plastic mannequins you see in department stores."

Pilar sighed. They had had this same talk so many times that she'd lost count. Well, what was one more time? "Look, Gabe, the time before we picked up and left that trash heap back in Alabama and made our way up to this place is not something I like to dwell on. How many times do I have to tell you the past is past? I don't want to remember wearing rags and going hungry and looking like a starving refugee. I like where I am, and if you don't like how I look now, just say so and be on your way. No hard feelings."

As always after this little speech, Gabe backed down. In his heart, he knew he would never be happy unless he was with Pilar, because somehow, someway, she was ingrained in his DNA.

"What's on the schedule for today?" Gabe asked as he rubbed at the stubble on his face. He asked the question, not caring if Pilar answered or not. Anything to keep the conversation moving in this overly bright, institutional-looking kitchen. He took it a step farther and said, "You should get some flowers for the table. This place needs some color. It would also be nice if from time to time we could smell something around here besides air fresheners. Like frying bacon or cinnamon."

Pilar stared at her husband over the top of her laptop. They'd had this same conversation just as many times as the one where they discussed her physical appearance. Secretly, she had herself convinced that somehow Gabe had programmed himself. Not that she cared. "That's why they have restaurants and coffee shops. When we moved in here, I told you I wasn't going to do any cooking. You said it was okay with you. And if you want flowers, go out and buy some."

Gabe felt his insides start to shrivel. He didn't like his wife's tone. She was always nasty, but today he was hearing something strange. Worry? If Pilar was worried, that had to mean it was time for him to *panic*. He swallowed hard. This whole past year he'd been warning his wife that it was time to downsize, time to pack up and head to the islands, like they'd originally planned when they started out in this crazy-ass business.

"Pilar, we need to talk seriously. It's time to shut down Supper Club Five, Eight, and Eleven. They are deadweight. Supper Club Eleven is a black hole. We moved too fast on those. We should have stuck with the nine, but oh, no, you got greedy. We also need to think about clubs three and six. Breaking even isn't worth it."

"I know, I know. But I think we should wait till after the holidays. Carlie seems to think things are picking up. They always do during the Christmas season. If we stay open until the first of the year, we can recoup some of our losses."

Gabe stood up and leaned over the table so he was eyeball-to-eyeball with his wife. "Listen to me, Pilar. I want out of this business. Out, as in all the way out. My gut has been warning me for a year now. I'll be honest with you. I can't imagine going it alone without you at my side, but I will, because I cannot handle this any longer. So far, we've been lucky. That luck is not going to hold forever. We both know that. We have, at last count, fourteen million dollars in our accounts. That's more than enough to keep to our plan and head for the islands. If we shut down totally the first of the year, sell off everything, we'll end up, if we're lucky, with three or four million dollars more. If we invest wisely—and I think you have to agree that I've done a good job so far—we can live just the way you want for the rest of our lives. I do not want to be a drug dealer, Pilar. I *can't* do it anymore. I don't *want* to do it anymore. We're pushing our luck, honey. Can't you see it? I know how fearless you are, but that's what is going to do you in, in the end."

The pillow lips puckered up in a pout. Pilar nodded ever so slightly to signal her agreement with her husband. "I thought we both decided never to use that hideous term. I hate it. We need the score this year to even things out. I know we've been lucky, and now is the time to get out, especially with . . . well, whatever it is that's going on with Toby Mason. For now, let's plan for a retirement party for New Year's Eve."

Gabe was stunned at how easy that was. When Pilar agreed with him, though, it was always suspect. He looked at his wife and struggled for a smile. He knew he wasn't pulling it off, because he saw his wife narrow her eyes.

"I mean it this time, Gabe. Relax."

Like he could really relax with what they were doing. He tried to remember the last time he'd truly relaxed and simply could not remember. He hated looking over his shoulder all the time, hated wondering when he would be hauled off to jail and be separated from Pilar. Maybe she was finally seeing things his way. Maybe. But he didn't believe it for a minute.

"Why are you looking at me like that, Gabe? You don't believe me. Is that it?"

Gabe stared at his wife for a very long minute before he turned and walked away. He had to stiffen his spine, make a decision he could live with. Stick around or go it alone without his wife at his side. A no-brainer really when it came right down to it. Going it alone was a hell of a lot better than living in a nine-by-six cell alone. He turned and said, "No, Pilar, I don't believe you. I'm tired of preaching to you. Do what you want, but don't count on me for anything other than keeping track of our investments, which, by the way, will be split right down the middle if you back-water come the first of the year."

Pilar stared at the spot where Gabe had been standing. A small worm of fear crawled around her stomach. He had sounded so . . . so final. Was that an ultimatum she'd just heard? They were a team; they'd always been a team from the time they were youngsters. Surely, Gabe wouldn't kick her to the curb. They were just words to scare her, the way she used words to scare him when she wanted things to go her way. Teamwork was all well and good when it was just business, with each member pulling his or her weight, but when you were involved in drug running, there was only one rule, and that was "Do not get caught." With Gabe watching her back, she hadn't worried too much, but now that he was turning on her, she knew she was going to have to alter her plans. Especially with Toby Mason being front and center.

Pilar looked around the kitchen. She saw what Gabe had seen, the starkness, the shiny appliances, the white light. He was right; it looked like no one lived here. He was right about the flowers, too. Clutter bound you to a place. She'd tried numerous times to explain that to him. With clutter, with doodads, junk, stuff, you couldn't cut and run. While Gabe said he understood, he didn't, not really.

Pilar rubbed at her temples. She was getting a headache. It would turn into a migraine if she didn't nip it in the bud. Migraines were her curse in life. She got up and walked into the foyer, where she'd dropped her purse. She picked up her purse and rummaged around until she found the prescription bottle she was looking for. She shook out three yellow pills and dry swallowed them. She was back in the kitchen moments later, filling her coffee cup.

Now all she could do for the moment was wait for the investigative report to show up in her e-mail.

Pilar looked around the stark kitchen again and tried to imagine what it would look like with *stuff* in it. Colored place mats. Colored cushions on the futuristic-looking chrome chairs, flowers on the table, bowls of fruit and some green plants on the counters. She didn't know if she could live with that, because *stuff* meant *home*. This penthouse was not home. Just the word *home* conjured up too many ugly memories she was not prepared to deal with. Not now, not ever. That was all behind her. This penthouse was the place where she slept, showered, dressed, and applied her makeup. A stopping-off place. An investment. Nothing more. Why she was even thinking about such things was beyond her. Why? Because of her suspicions about Toby Mason. This new information from Martha the housekeeper, the failed investigative report? *December?* The second month of the year when she broke the law to fatten her and Gabe's bank account. Yes, it was dangerous, but she was careful and smart. She had a handle on it all.

Or did she? Gabe was really antsy. She had to pay attention to that. While her husband was mostly docile, he did have a stubborn streak, and he'd aired it just a little while ago. If he wanted out, then he would do just what he said. She needed to be mindful of that stubborn streak and start to play nice. Really nice.

Pilar looked at the watch on her wrist, the tiny diamonds surrounding the bezel winking in the bright overhead light. She opened up her laptop again and proceeded to do what she did every morning, check everything that went on the night before and prepare for the coming night. It always took a full two hours. By the time she was finished, the report from the investigative agency should be in her in-box, and Gabe would be back with toasted bagels slathered with butter and cream cheese. After eating, she would get dressed and head out to check on the Supper Clubs. The rule was that she would take six and Gabe the rest. They never missed a day, which qualified them both as hands-on owners. Then they would do a nice leisurely lunch and head back to the penthouse so Gabe could take a nap and she could do whatever she wanted, which was pretty much nothing other than watching reruns on television or counting the money in their various accounts.

Pilar shifted into what she called her neutral zone and went to work. When she was finally finished, the clock on the Wolf range said it was three minutes to ten. She leaned back and waited. She hated that she was feeling jittery, because it just proved that something in her immediate world was not right. And Gabe knew it before she did, so she really had to pay attention. She squinted as she watched the digital numbers on the range go past the twelve, then the one, then the two. Finally, her computer dinged at the number three, alerting her to an incoming e-mail with an attachment. She clicked it on and read slowly. She sighed heavily when she got to the end of the report. She couldn't see any immediate cause for worry, unless Toby decided his dancing career was over. She didn't think that would happen anytime soon. He would need money to squire the wealthy young woman around town. She would have a certain lifestyle, and he would have to step up to the plate. No fast food and walks in the park for an heiress with a robust trust fund, a Ferrari, and a Black American Express card. Even Pilar didn't have the Centurion Card.

Pilar clicked on the icon that would allow her to view the pictures of Mia Grande. She was beautiful. Gorgeous, actually, with a body to die for. Designer clothes, just the right amount of jewelry. The girl had bedroom eyes, all soft brown and dewy. She also had a magnificent head of shimmering, glossy hair, which she could just see Toby burying his face in. Men loved long hair for some reason, and this girl didn't have extensions. One close facial shot showed eyelashes Pilar would cheerfully kill for. A real beauty.

Now, what did this all mean? Why would someone like Mia Grande pick someone like Toby Mason to hang with? Was she slumming, was she playing with him, or did she really see something in him that she could love? According to the report, Mia Grande was a party girl. Toby was not a party boy. Where was the common cord? What attracted them to each other? That was what she needed to know.

How was she going to find that out? Go straight to the source and ask, of course. She had a good relationship with Toby, had always had, from the very beginning, when she found him bagging groceries at that supermarket. While she knew she didn't exactly project a motherly image, she could still talk a good game and offer advice on love. Toby would listen. She was almost sure of it.

Pilar was so deep into her thoughts she almost jumped out of her own skin when Gabe set a white bag down in front of her. Her daily bagel. With her emotions as bundled up as they were, she doubted the bagel would stay in her stomach. She pushed the bag away. "I'm not really hungry this morning, Gabe."

"I wasn't either, but I forced myself to eat," Gabe said, sitting down at the table, across from his wife. "We really should talk. I mean really talk, the way we used to."

Pilar nodded. "Say what you have to say. I promise to keep an open mind. I will fight you only if I think you're wrong."

"Look, honey. Right now we are in a fairly good place. We're running on nothing but suspicion. We can change that all right now simply by canceling Mr. December. We can say we are getting ready to restructure the Supper Clubs, and that it is going to take up all our time. We can pay off Toby, because he will lose out on the calendar. You can notify your . . . your sources and tell them we're off the grid until next July due to circumstances beyond our control. Say whatever you want, since you know those people better than I do. It might not be a bad idea to throw some worry their way so they don't make waves. We need to get out from under, and the sooner we do that, the better off we are. The longer we're in the picture, the more things can go wrong.

"I know your gut and all your feminine instincts are telling you that Toby and his new love are not what is on the surface, and I think you are right, which just makes my point more valid. Forget about the money and think in terms of the rest of our lives. If we go out now, we go out clean. If we hang around another year, the odds we'll make it to next Christmas are iffy at best. Please, Pilar, listen to me."

Gabe was shocked senseless when his wife reached for his hand across the table. "You're right, Gabe. You've always been the voice of reason. I'm sorry I'm the greedy one. I just don't ever want to go back . . ."

"Don't go there, Pilar. This is now. We need to make a plan. Like now."

"Okay. You get started on how you want to proceed

while I get dressed. Let's take a walk around the Tidal Basin, the way we used to. Bring a notebook, so we can write everything down. Like we used to. We can sit on a bench and talk and formulate a plan. Like we used to. Remember how, back in the day, once we had a plan and put it on paper, it was a go and we never looked back? Back then we trusted ourselves and each other. We need to do that now, so it is official."

"Works for me," Gabe said happily. When Pilar was out of sight, Gabe's shoulders slumped. That was way too easy, was his first thought. His second thought was that Pilar had a plan, and he wasn't going to like it. His third thought was that his wife loved money too much to cave in the way she just had. He corrected his thought. Pilar didn't just love money; she *worshipped* money.

Chapter Six

It was three minutes shy of seven o'clock when Jack Emery opened the door of the BOLO Building. He stepped aside to let Cyrus enter first. He waited for the massive door's hydraulics to fall into place before he headed to the kitchen to turn up the heat and make coffee. He'd been up since the crack of dawn because he had to drive his wife to the airport. Nikki was headed to Boston, where she and Alexis were scheduled to talk to a group of surgeons concerning a monster malpractice case. She'd said her best guess was that they would be there for a week at the beginning, and then they would have to commute to and from Boston for another month to six weeks, getting home for weekends. He missed her already, but the possibility of this new mission would take the edge off being alone because he knew he'd be spending most of the next week here at the BOLO Building.

Cyrus barked, a reminder that he'd had no breakfast. There had been no time, so now he had to make do.

"Tell you what. I'm going to call Ding and have our breakfast sent over."

Cyrus barked again to show he approved of his master's decision. Five minutes later, their breakfast of scrambled eggs, hash browns, extra-crisp, snap-in-two bacon, and raisin toast was in the works. If Ding ran true to form, in fifteen minutes there would be a knock on the front door, and he and Cyrus would be chowing down.

"Conference room, big guy. Bring your gear. I need to tidy up before the others get here." *Gear* meant his security blanket; his one-eared, no-tail rabbit with only one eye; and a stuffed duck whose beak, when pressed, played "Rock-a-Bye Baby."

Jack eyed the messy conference table. He winced, wishing he'd had the energy to clean up before he left last night, but he'd been too tired. He and Cyrus had been the last ones to leave, at ten minutes to two. Then the forty-five-minute ride out to the farm before he fell into bed, only to get up two hours later for the drive back into town and the airport.

Jack gathered up the yellow legal pads and pens. They were all old school, preferring to write, as opposed to keeping notes on their tablets and laptops. He was the biggest Neanderthal of them all, followed closely by Maggie and Ted. All the trash went into the shredder. He looked at his watch. Three minutes until Ding's son, his main deliveryman, banged on the front door. Always in tune with his master, Cyrus beelined for the front door, where he settled down on his haunches to wait.

"Someday, I want you to tell me how you know exactly when something is going to happen," Jack grumbled as he fished around in his pockets for the money to pay the tab.

From his position at the window, Jack had a clear view of the Bagel Emporium across the street. The moment the door to the establishment opened and young Ding stepped out, Cyrus was on his feet, tail quivering a mile a minute. Seconds later, Jack had the door open before the young man could bang the brass knocker. Money changed hands.

"Dad said to tell you the rest of the order will be delivered at ten sharp, piping hot." Jack pretended not to see the treat young Ding handed to Cyrus.

Jack closed and locked the door. Cyrus was patiently

waiting for his food, which Jack fixed before he sat down to eat his own. Cyrus always came first. Always.

Jack's thoughts were all over the map as he worked his way through his breakfast. His adrenaline was pumping through him at an all-time high. Dennis was onto something; he could feel it in his bones. The kid's intuition was something he'd learned to pay attention to over time.

On his way to the massive coffee urn to refill his coffee cup, he heard the hiss of the back door. He made a silent bet with himself that it was Dennis, the intrepid reporter.

"Morning, Jack, Cyrus! Didn't expect to see you here this early. I thought I was the only early worm," Dennis said so cheerfully that Jack had to fight the urge to smack him.

"I had to drop Nikki off at the airport for an early morning flight to Boston. No sense going back home just to have to turn around and come back at ten. Did you hear from your friend last night?"

"I did, and he said he pulled it off to perfection. He also said he's a nervous wreck for more than one reason. Seems Mia Grande kissed him like she was in love with him. All part of the act, of course, but he said he felt strange things." Dennis giggled to show what he thought of *that*.

In spite of himself, Jack laughed out loud.

"I sent him a text before I got here, but he hasn't responded yet. He was to go running with Mia early this morning. If we're sticking with her legend, she will have to go to Georgetown for a class or two to keep it all straight. The other female operatives will swoop in. He should have responded by now," Dennis said, fretting. "I just keep worrying he's going to blow it somehow. What we do is not even close to the way Toby thinks or does things."

"Well, he's going to have to learn real quick. I think he'll be okay, Dennis."

"Has anyone else checked in this morning?" Dennis asked as he stared down at an incoming text from Toby.

"Not yet. I just told everyone to be back here at ten this morning. We were all whipped when we left last night. Ding is going to be delivering bagels shortly. Is that text from your friend?"

Dennis let his head bob up and down. "I'm thinking we might have a wee problem here. At least Toby thinks we might. He says he got a phone call—not a text, mind you, which he says is Pilar Sanders's usual method of getting in touch—to tell him to meet her at the Dog and Duck for lunch. He is telling me this is a first, so, of course, he is jittery now. He wants to know what he should do and say. And he wants to know if Mia should go with him. Seems Pilar did not specify if he should come alone or bring his friend. He is certain that the house mother has notified Pilar of his performance by now. What should I tell him, Jack?"

"Nothing right now. We need to talk to the others first."

"Someone is here," Dennis said just as Cyrus got up and ran from the room. "How does Cyrus know, Jack? I didn't hear a thing. Do you think my hearing is going?"

"All dogs have extraordinary hearing and a keen sense of smell. I think Cyrus got an extra dose because of his size. We'll never know, so don't stew and fret about it, kid."

Abner was in the lead, followed by Avery Snowden, Charles, and Fergus. All looked tired and cranky but somehow still alert. Just then, the front door knocker sounded so loud, Jack clamped his hands over his ears as he tried to outrun Cyrus to the front door. He lost the race.

It was Ding at the door delivering the rest of the bagels from Jack's earlier order. By the time Jack and Cyrus made it back to the conference room, the rest of the team was in place, seated and talking over everyone else to be heard.

Cyrus barked, and Jack whistled sharply for silence. "While I set these bagels out and make fresh coffee, Dennis has a bit of an emergency he needs to discuss with all of us.

One at a time, people, so we can actually hear what everyone is saying, okay? Dennis, the floor is yours."

Dennis rushed right into it, reading Toby's texts in a firm, hard voice. "Toby needs to know what we want him to do. Remember now, he's not an operative, he's new to this game, and he is not as fearless as we all are. Always remember that about him, okay? He is not a person we want to traumatize. So, let's hear it!"

Jack smiled to himself as he measured coffee into the giant urn. The kid had some chutzpah, and he valued loyalty, which was understandable where his friend was concerned.

"I've already taken care of that, people. Our story is that Mia had a class she didn't want to miss. Her friends, my operatives, will be waiting at the Dog and Duck before Toby and his boss arrive. They'll play it by ear. Rest assured, your boy will be fine. We have his back," Snowden volunteered.

Dennis nodded as his fingers tapped out a response to Toby's last frantic e-mail.

Jack took his place at the head of the conference table. Maggie settled the plate of bagels, which were fully loaded, along with napkins, in the center of the table. Ted filled coffee cups, which everyone gratefully accepted.

"We can't stay, Jack. Ted, Espinosa, Dennis, and I have to be in Alexandria at noon. Myra and Annie's orders. They want a full-court press on the temporary VA clinic that opened to the veterans this morning. Media will be all over the place. We stand a chance of getting a Pulitzer for our reporting on the VA. Make sure you guys turn on the TV so you can see it all going down. Annie sent me an early morning text saying that the White House is really miffed at her for taking matters into her own hands. Not that she cares. When Annie and Myra set their mind to something, there is no changing it, as you all know," Maggie said.

"Man, they got that up and running quickly," Jack said. "How did they do that?"

"Do you know anyone who can say no to those two women?" Abner asked. "Plus, they used a very large portion of the Sisterhood's *black funds*. They ordered top of the line, the best of the best in medical equipment. They paid double time, triple time to people to set up the lab and the MRI and CAT scan machines. Then they shamed people—doctors and nurses, physician's assistants and nurse's assistants—into volunteering. Annie has got four full-time doctors, four full-time PAs, and seven nurses to help the vets. No one is going to get turned away. Everything is going to be done in-house, and they're going to be open round the clock until every last vet sees a doctor. The doctors, the PAs, and the nurses are being paid, and Myra said others are standing in line to help.

"Forty thousand square feet of help is how Annie explained it when she bought that old warehouse in Alexandria. The owners cut her a deal when they found out what she was going to use it for. Oh, one other thing. You remember that Medal of Honor–winning dog? His name was Gizmo. He's appearing at noon to welcome the vets. Like I said, a full-court press."

"None of us can top that. Rest assured we will have the TV on at noon. Now to business," Charles said as he withdrew a sheaf of papers from his briefcase. "On the drive here, Bert got back to me via text. He is on board and even thanked us for our sterling idea. He immediately accessed the Supper Clubs' Web site and sent them an e-mail, then sent his offer via overnight mail. What he meant by 'overnight mail' is this. A guy he knows who works at the Wynn was flying back to the States via private jet, and he gave him the envelope to deliver. His friend promised to deliver it in person when he landed in D.C. The Sanderses should get his personal invitation by the time the clubs go live tonight."

"Wow!" Maggie said.

"You know what I always say, Maggie. It's not what you know. It's who you know," Ted said, cackling. "Hey, where's Sparrow? Isn't he supposed to be here?"

"He called Charles and me early this morning to say he got a last-minute call to be at the White House this morning. He said there is no way he could blow that off without causing a ruckus. He thinks it might have something to do with the VA thing. We'll have to make do without him and clue him in later," Fergus said.

Jack looked around the table. His gaze settled on Abner. "Any luck with the couple's finances?"

"Yes and yes and yes again. I'm double-checking it all. I'll have a printout for you soon."

"Espinosa, what did you dig up from the archives on the clubs?" Jack asked.

"I have a whole parade of pictures for you all to view. On the surface, it looks just like what they are, supper clubs with live entertainment, with a few sidelines, like the shows they put on in California and Miami every July and December. There's a ton of their 'do-gooder' projects. There are some pictures of the guys, the dancers, but not what you would expect. You know, normal, everyday pictures as they go about their lives. Most of them look pretty preppy. Blazers, pressed khakis, no jewelry, no piercings. Normal young guys. I have to admit, that in itself was a bit of a surprise."

Ted said, "I'm beating a dead horse here with the background checks on the dancers. As dancers, do they use their real names, or do they give themselves names? We forgot to ask Toby. They get paid by check, so they pay taxes and have health insurance. But under what names? I didn't have a master list to go by. Abner is going to have to hack into their records before I can get anything else."

Then it was Snowden's turn. "The boy was right. He does have a tail. I even know who the agency is. Third rate at best. Obviously, they lost Toby yesterday and, with no other recourse, staked out the house he lives in, waiting for him to get home last night. Mia said two guys were already staked out when she picked Toby up at six this morning. The boy was spot on. He is definitely under surveillance. He is not paranoid."

"Then that has to mean we now have an active mission, right? We're taking Toby's case, right?" Dennis asked, his eyes sparkling with excitement.

"It's good enough for me," Charles said. "We can vote on it to make it legitimate if you like. Raise your hand for taking on this new mission, people."

Every hand in the room shot upward.

"It's okay to tell Toby, isn't it? I know he's anxious." Dennis was already pulling out his phone before Charles even nodded.

A few miles away, in Rock Creek Park, Toby and Mia walked hand in hand up one path and down another, speaking softly to each other as they continued their pretense of being lovers.

"They're behind us, pretending they belong. How stupid is that? Who wears sweats and leather-soled shoes? They must be new to the game. You didn't notice that, did you, Toby?"

"No, I didn't, but I'm not a trained investigator, so why would you expect me to notice something like that? Does that mean you probably won't be chewing anyone's ear off today while in my company? Was there a lot of blood? How did you handle that?" Toby asked in a jittery voice that somehow stopped short of being angry sounding.

"None of your business. Trade secrets. Pay attention to your surroundings. Look. There's a bench up there. Let's fake them out and sit down and pretend to make out."

Pretend. He planned to give it his all to see if he was

man enough to rock her boat. Carrie said he'd rocked her boat a few times before she went all *earthy* on him. He immediately knew it was a bad idea. He had to remember that none of this was real. This was his life, his safety he was dealing with. Getting it on had no place under the current circumstances. She was a hottie, though, he had to admit. He wanted to ask her if she was involved with anyone, but knew that was also a bad idea. *Just go with the flow, Toby.*

Once they were seated on the bench, facing each other, Mia leaned in and whispered, "Nibble on my ear like you mean it."

Ear? Oh, man, that was so not going to happen. "How about I just lick your nose or something? I'm . . . um . . . um . . . not into ears."

"Then, damn it, do it *now*. Here they come. Remember to paw me."

"You want me to do that all at one time? Lick your nose, grope you? What are you going to be doing?" Toby gasped as he tried to comply.

"This!" Mia giggled as she plunged her hand onto his crotch.

"Oh myyy Goddd!" Toby bleated just as two joggers in mismatched sweat suits and leather-soled shoes whizzed by. He almost rolled off the bench when he saw one of the joggers look over his shoulder and shout, "Get a room already!"

Toby retaliated like any red-blooded twelve-year-old would. "Up yours, buddy. You're just jealous!" He made sure his tongue was securely locked behind his teeth before he muttered, "Too much, huh?"

Disgust ringing in her voice, Mia said, "What was your first clue?"

Toby squirmed from side to side, hoping his junk would at least go to half-mast. "The business with the ear. Look,

I know you're a real smart-ass, and you think I'm a dumb ass, so let's just leave it at that. What do we do now, o fearless leader? Do we sit here and wait for them to come back, or do we split, and I head to the Dog and Duck to meet up with the Dragon Lady? What?"

"We're going to sit here, hold hands, and stare into each other's eyes like we're in love. Trust me, those two yahoos are just around the bend, probably hiding in the bushes, waiting to see what we're going to do. Eventually, they'll head back this way. So we talk. Tell me about your ex-girlfriend, the one who dumped you. You still in love with her?"

"I have a better idea. Why don't we talk about you and this business you're in?"

"See, now, that doesn't work for me. In order for me to protect you, I need to know everything there is to know about you, so I can anticipate trouble on the horizon. I already told you I am razor sharp and can take care of myself and you, too. So talk! How does it feel when all those screaming women are staring up at you when you bump and grind. Is it a turn-on? How many have you hit on? Or are you still true blue to the one who dumped you for some gray-haired lobbyist with major money? That is so not good, if that's what you're doing. You need to move on with your life."

"My personal life is none of your business, and I do not need any advice from you. I've decided I really don't like you, Mia Grande, or whatever the hell your name is. You are too full of yourself. Oh, one last thing. I know in my gut that when push comes to shove, and it will happen, I'll be the one saving your ass, not the other way around. We're done here. I'm going to the Dog and Duck. Do whatever the hell you want. Like report me to that scary-looking dude who is your boss. Go for it. Then I'm going to report you to . . . to *Cyrus*. Just so you know, that monster dog can fold towels."

Before Mia could blink, Toby kissed her full on the mouth, putting on a lip-lock, and screamed, "Race you back to the car!"

Mia was on her feet a second later, but she was too late. Toby was so far ahead of her, she knew she'd never catch up. Avery was not going to be happy with this turn of events. A dog that folded towels. That was a new one on her, and she thought she'd heard it all. She decided right then and there that she liked the brainiac, even though he'd said he didn't like her. That was now. Later . . . Who knew what the future held?

Chapter Seven

T he Ferrari growled its way to the curb and stopped.
  "You sure you can handle this, Toby? You seem a little
too jittery to me. I need you to calm down. Like now. Take
deep breaths. The girls are already inside, so they have
your back. Keep your eyes on them and follow their cues if
they offer any up. Nothing is going to happen in a public
place like this. Watch Pilar's eyes. No matter how hard
you try, your eyes always give you away. I know you're
smart, Toby, but you're out of your league here. The girls
and I know how to play this, so don't try anything on your
own. We talked about this on the way over here. You are
not going to be all gushy mushy with Pilar. That was all
okay last night. Today it's a different story. This morning
your feet are firmly on the ground. Yes, you are in love. Yes
to all the stuff you spouted last night to the housemother.
Today, with your boss, you're just happy and willing to
share your happiness with Pilar, your boss. You got it?"

"I got it. I am jittery. Once I'm inside, I'll be okay. Oh,
am I supposed to know the girls inside?"

"Yes. I introduced you to them a few days ago. My
friends. You don't have any background, just that they're
my friends and fellow grad students on lunch break. Don't
volunteer anything. Like I said, just react to their cues. Be-

fore this is over, you'll be as suave and debonair as Sean Connery. You know, the original James Bond character. Think of it as a plus on your résumé next time you send one out."

"I don't send out résumés. They come to me," Toby said through clenched teeth. Like he could even come close to Sean Connery. Not even within a mile. He sighed and turned to open the door.

"Aren't you forgetting something?" Mia said.

"No. What?"

"You're supposed to get me in a lip-lock. A little squeeze here or there. I need to see some sparkle in those baby blues of yours. You're supposed to be in love, remember? People are watching. It might be this fancy car, but they also want to see who is in this fancy car. For all I know, your boss already passed us and is inside or is watching from someplace. You're an actor, so, damn it, start acting."

Toby felt his eyes narrow. She wanted acting. Well, then, he'd give her a first-class performance worthy of Sean Connery. Before Mia could draw a breath, Toby had her in a clinch as he smashed his lips against hers. He knocked off her pearly-white Stetson as his fist grabbed hair that smelled like lilacs, forcing her even closer to him. He swore later that he could feel the beat of her heart, or maybe it was his heart, or then again, maybe it was both their hearts. *Sean Connery, eat your heart out.*

And then he was outside the low-slung sports car, leaning in the window, a wicked grin on his face. He thought his heart was going to explode right out of his chest, but somehow he kept his cool. "I'll be available for an encore in about ninety minutes, if you think you can handle it. See you, sweet cheeks!"

For the first time in her young life, Mia Grande was left totally and completely speechless. "Uh-huh," was the best she could manage before she clamped the Stetson on her head and peeled away from the curb to head toward the Georgetown campus. *"Uh-huh."*

Toby entered the Dog and Duck on trembling legs. Inside, it was neither dark nor light, just dim, with music blaring from somewhere. Toby tried to remember if he'd ever been here before, but nothing came to him. *Probably*, was his best guess, or someplace that looked just like this one. It was, after all, a sports bar of sorts, with television screens on every available wall. Wall-to-wall people, waitresses and busboys scurrying back and forth with platters of fast food, mostly finger food, held high to allow them to maneuver through the crowds. The noise level was deafening. He could feel a headache coming on. He looked around. How the hell was he supposed to find Mia's operatives and Pilar in this mass of humanity?

Toby looked down at the phone clutched in his hand. He felt the vibration and looked at the incoming text:

Back of the bar. We're here, and so is your boss.

There was no signature. He jammed the phone in his pocket as he pushed and shoved and elbowed his way to the back of the room, where there were six booths and five tables. He saw Pilar immediately, taking up a table for four. He had to wonder how much that table cost her.

"Right on time." Pilar smiled up at him. "I took the liberty of ordering for us. You might want to think about wiping that lipstick off your cheek, honey."

Toby hated it when she called him honey. He flushed a bright crimson as he reached for the tissue Pilar was holding out to him. Then he remembered his instructions. He shrugged and grinned, just as Mia's friends erupted in a loud greeting. He turned and bolted from the table to the booth to be hugged and squeezed. *Eat your heart out again, Sean Connery.*

Five minutes of playful, happy banter followed before Toby turned to Pilar and said, "I'd like to introduce you to Mia's friends, but I can't remember their names. So, girls, this is my boss, Pilar Sanders. Pilar, meet . . ."

One by one, the giggling girls introduced themselves. The last young woman, who introduced herself as Mandy Lee, looked at Pilar and brazenly asked if she was a cougar.

Pilar laughed, but it was a forced sound. "Sorry, no. I'm happily married to a wonderful man." She waved her left hand to make her point, at which point people started pointing at all the televisions on the walls and yelling for quiet. The room went totally silent.

Toby looked up and almost blacked out when he saw Dennis and his fellow reporters standing next to two elderly ladies. *What the hell . . . ?* He looked over at Pilar, who was reading an incoming text, her eyes wide and disbelieving at what she was seeing. The thought that entered his mind was that whatever she was reading was good news, and she was delighted. But whatever it was she was reading couldn't possibly be as interesting as what was playing out on the big-screen television sets. He watched, his jaw dropping, as someone named Countess Anna de Silva welcomed what looked to him like several hundred veterans holding up placards and pointing to the large building behind where they were patiently lined up. Doctors in white jackets and with stethoscopes around their necks stood next to a group of nurses in white, who were smiling into the cameras.

The young woman named Mandy looked at Toby's puzzled expression and hissed, "You do know who Countess de Silva is, right? If she isn't the richest woman in the world, then she is the second richest, after that lady standing next to her, Myra Rutledge. Those ladies have taken on the current administration and the VA to get our veterans the help they need. It's been all over the news for the past month. This is the result."

Toby frowned. He knew he was missing something here. He also knew that Mandy was trying to tell him something, but he was too dense to figure it out.

"I wish my boyfriend, Avery Snowden, was here," Mandy said. "He donates all his free time to VA centers."

Toby nodded. He finally got it. It was all falling into place for him now. He stepped back from the edge of the rabbit hole and fixed his gaze on Pilar, who finally started to pay attention to what was happening on the screens all around her.

Pilar eyeballed Toby and smiled. She waved away what was playing out on the giant screens, which meant "Let's get down to business." The group of young women made their way back to their own table, still watching the TV screens. "So, tell me your good news."

Toby forced a grin that he didn't feel. "I think I found my soul mate. I can only hope she feels the same way. I guess Martha told you, huh?"

"Well, yes. That's her job as housemother. She told me how deliriously happy you were last night, when you got home. Now, I don't want to seem like one of those helicopter mothers, but this happened so quick, Toby, so naturally I'm a little concerned. What do you really know about the young lady, honey?"

"All I need to know. I love her sense of humor. She's kind, caring, and she loves animals. She does a lot of volunteer work for the elderly. She comes from Brazil. Actually, she's an heiress to a fortune derived from some kind of hot sauce her family makes. She told me she has a trust fund that will never run out. Whatever that means. She's going for her MBA at Georgetown and carries a four-point-oh GPA. It's not the money. She didn't even tell me that until last night, because she was afraid it would scare me away. She wants to be loved for herself, not her money. I don't care either way. She wants her parents to come here to meet me. We plan to Skype tonight so she can introduce me to them. She's in class right now but is picking me up after our lunch is over. I'll introduce you to her." Breathlessly, Toby picked up a crispy wonton and popped it into his mouth. He hoped he didn't choke on it.

"What does this mean in regard to your job, Toby? Are you planning on leaving us? You wouldn't bail out on me this close to the end of the year, would you?" Pilar's tone of voice clearly warned him he better not even be thinking about it.

"Of course not. Mia is fine with what I do. She says she likes that I can express myself onstage. Nothing is going to change, at least for now. When she finishes up her studies in the spring, it might be a different story. For now, it's the status quo. Don't tell me you're worried about me. Oh, there is one thing. She wants a ringside table the nights I dance. I said no problem. That won't be a problem, will it, Pilar?" Toby asked, a definite edge to his voice. "A whole table for six so she can have her friends with her."

"Of course that's not a problem. For now. However, I'm calling a meeting tonight, before the first performance. An offer has come to us from Hong Kong that I want to discuss with my lead dancers. A very lucrative offer, I might add. So, Toby, tell me more about your new love," Pilar said as she broke an egg roll in two, one that she never bothered to eat.

I pulled it off. I think I really pulled it off. Damn. Toby, you are good.

They talked for another half hour, until one of the operatives in the booth gave him a nod and held up her cell phone. Mia was waiting out front. Time to go.

Toby looked up to see the girls sliding out of their booth. Then he looked up at the TV screens in time to see a dog named Gizmo offer up a snappy salute to the veterans making their way into the new clinic. He took a moment to wonder if the amazing dog could fold towels. His phone buzzed.

"My ride is here, Pilar. Gotta go. What time is the meeting?"

"Seven o'clock in the second-floor conference room at Supper Club One. You cannot bring your girlfriend. Understood?"

"Understood," Toby said.

"You did say you were going to introduce me to your new love. Let's do it, honey. I can't wait to meet her." Pilar laid some bills on the table, then set a bottle of hot sauce on top. She blinked when she read the label. GRANDE HOT SAUCE. If she weren't in such a hurry, she might have noticed that the Grande label had been affixed over a Pico Pica label.

Outside, the day had turned gray and blustery, leaves swirling in all directions as Pilar focused on the candy apple–red Ferrari whose engine was purring at the curb. She felt Toby's hand on her elbow as he guided her to the curb and the purring Ferrari. The window slid down.

He leaned in and said, "Mia, come around. I want you to meet my boss."

Fascinated, Pilar watched as the young woman slid out of the car, adjusted the pearly-white Stetson she was wearing, and walked around the front of the car. She stepped up onto the curb, a huge smile on her face. Pilar took it in all at once, the Stetson, the beautiful smile, the perfect teeth, the wealth of gorgeous hair. The designer jacket, the long legs encased in black tights with a miniskirt and, of course, the cowboy boots. She felt a flash of envy and sadness all at the same time. She would kill to be this young woman, even without the trust fund. When the woman moved closer, she caught the wink of light from her earrings. Three carats each at least. Hidden by her hair. Understated. As were her nails. French manicure. Pilar was aware of her own bloodred talons, which suddenly looked tacky to her eye.

"How nice to finally meet you, Ms. Sanders. Toby has

told me so much about you. Not to worry. It was all very flattering."

"Then you have the upper hand on me, Miss Grande. I just found out about you. I don't want you stealing my prize dancer away from me now, you hear?" Pilar teased in a light voice.

Mia smiled, her teeth glistening on this gloomy day. "It won't happen. My little sweetie here is very loyal."

Pilar worked her tongue over her own veneers and felt cheated. "I am so glad to meet you. I would have been terribly offended if my prize here, meaning Toby, didn't see fit to introduce us. I try to be a stand-in mother to the boys. Sometimes it works, and sometimes it doesn't. This time, it did. I'm sorry, but I have to cut this short. I have a meeting I need to get to, and I'm already running late. I'll see you tonight, Toby. Please don't be late. Again, nice meeting you, Mia."

Her body ramrod straight in her Jimmy Choo shoes, which couldn't hold a candle to Mia's cowboy boots, Pilar walked away to the parking lot and her four-door Mercedes sedan. Suddenly, she hated the high-end, family-looking car. Compared to the candy apple–red Ferrari, the Mercedes was a Volkswagen Beetle. Right now, right this minute, all she wanted was a pair of cowboy boots. For a moment, she was tempted to call a cab so as not to be seen in this drab black vehicle, but in the end she opened the door and climbed behind the wheel. She sat for five minutes as she let her thoughts go from Toby and Mia to the text that had come through earlier from Carlie Fisher, the club's business manager. She wondered if Carlie had sent the same message to Gabe. Evidently not, or Gabe would have called her by now.

What did it all mean?

Jack clicked the remote, and the room turned silent. Everyone looked at everyone else in disbelief. "Charles, did you know about all of that?" Jack said, pointing to the over-head screen.

"Not really. I knew they were working on it from the day Maggie, Ted, Espinosa, and Dennis left to start the series. I guess being as smart as the two of them are, they knew this would be the outcome, and they went at it. The truth is, Fergus and I have seen very little of our lovely ladies, and they did not see fit to confide in us. I just didn't . . . I had no idea they'd accomplished all of what we just saw. Having said that, I couldn't be more proud of them. Ask yourself, who do you know who could have gotten all of that done in a month? The government would appoint committees, hold meetings to look into things, and there would be more meetings while everyone responsible is vetted, and on and on the list would go. Myra and Annie dived in and made it happen. They made it happen! Someone should give them a medal."

"I second that," Fergus said heartily. "What I wasn't expecting to see was Lizzie Fox and Cosmo Cricket there at the end, handing over that good-sized check from all the casino owners in Las Vegas. They're already on their way to the airport, because Cosmo is in charge of setting up a veterans' clinic in Vegas. It's like he said. If you want something done right, do it yourself, and that's exactly what he's doing, and he has the clout to pull it off, just like Annie and Myra did. Before you know it, every single veteran will be smiling, along with their families. I especially liked the part where Myra said they set up a fund for the families who are in dire straits. Food, clothing, housing, whatever they need, it's theirs for the taking. Our girls did good. They went at it like it was a mission and brought it front and center. There will be no more sweeping things under the rug, and people will be held accountable. Count on it."

"I'll never argue with that," Jack said. "But we really

need to get down to business here. Abner, what do you have for us?"

"There is no master list of employees per se. I'm trying to hack into their CPA's records, but the guy has some pretty sophisticated firewalls. I need to see the roster of employees, because that will give us addresses and Social Security numbers so we can track them. That part won't be a problem. I got into the Sanderses' financial records, and they are robust. But everything is heavily mortgaged. Six months ago, the couple took as much equity as they could out of the clubs and the properties that house the dancers. That tells me they're going to be walking away very soon. Several of the clubs are working at a deficit."

"What's their personal wealth?" Harry asked.

"Fourteen million, give or take. Judging by a quick glance, with their overhead at all the clubs, they could never make that kind of money legitimately. Even if Gabriel is a whiz in the stock market. The couple each take a half million in salary every year. The husband invests it. It's a joint account. I haven't found out yet where that is stashed. So you can probably add another four million to that total I just gave you. My guess is it is probably offshore somewhere. Don't worry. I'll find it, and if I can't find it, my buddy Phil Needlemeyer will find it for sure.

"We don't have anything yet on the background checks for the Sanderses. It's like they were hatched out of an egg twenty-five years ago. That's as far back as I can trace them with their given names. That leads me to believe they changed their names at that point in time. Avery hasn't checked in yet. Maggie didn't say if they were coming back or not. Does anyone know?" Fergus asked.

"Just got a text. They're on the way. Ten minutes out," Jack said.

"I have a text coming in from Bert," Charles said. As he read the short message, he shrugged. "He said he hasn't heard from the Sanderses as yet. My guess is they won't want to appear too eager, and they might even want to negotiate to drive the price up."

"How did Toby's luncheon go? Anything coming in on that?" Harry asked as he popped a handful of seeds into his mouth.

"I just sent off a text to Avery, who should be on top of things. It's possible Toby has been in touch with young Dennis. We should have news on that shortly. By the way, did you boys come to a decision in regard to going to the Supper Club in disguise tomorrow evening to see Toby perform?" Charles asked.

"We did not!" Harry snapped.

Cyrus, not liking the snap to Harry's tone, stopped chewing his bone and let loose with a shrill bark. Translation, "Tone it down."

Jack held up his hand for silence. "I don't think we need to go disguised as women. I don't care what Espinosa says. He cannot transform us to the point where we look like women. Why can't we just go as who we are? A bunch of guys out for dinner and a show. Or we could pretend to be gay, if you think that would work better. It's all a no-brainer."

"We'll have to take a vote on that, Jack. One way or another, you all have to go to the club. All the girls are busy, so you can't go with dates. We'll work on that. We still have some time," Charles said.

Cyrus bolted upright and raced from the room, an indication that Maggie and the gang were here. Snowden, too, as he was the first one to walk into the conference room.

The intrepid reporters wore huge smiles as they took their seats at the conference table.

"Pulitzers all around, baby!" Ted shouted to be heard amid all the congratulatory shouts and pats on the back.

"Enough!" Charles roared. "You can rest on your laurels later. We have a mission to plan and execute. Avery, you have the floor. Wait just a minute. Director Sparrow is sending me a coded text. He had a meeting at the White House, if you recall. It will take just a minute. Fergus, help me out here."

The team sat quietly as they waited to see what earth-shattering news would be forthcoming from the director of the FBI.

"Gentlemen, Maggie. It would seem that the White House wants Director Sparrow and his agents to shut down Annie and Myra's project for the veterans. He said the WH is saying Myra and Annie are giving the administration a bad name. He also said he managed to get hold of Lizzie and Cosmo just as they were ready to board their flight back home. They're going to meet him at his office."

Dennis West stood up, his hand clenched into a tight fist. He shook it fervently. "Then it's *war!*"

Chapter Eight

Pilar Sanders sat in her car, staring out at the blustery day. She'd never liked this time of year for some reason. Cold weather was her enemy. Cold weather dried out her skin, which was far from supple these days. Having to wear layers of clothes just made her look fat and dumpy. Her eyes narrowed as a gold-colored leaf tinged with orange fell on the windshield. It looked dry and brittle, just the way she felt. She flicked on the windshield wipers to chase it away, but it was stubborn and didn't move. She pressed the button that squirted windshield fluid and watched the hated leaf sail off to nowhere. It did not make her feel one bit better. She wished for a moment that she could take wing and fly off like the leaf. It wasn't going to happen. Her wishes never came true, for some strange reason.

Long, bloodred nails tapped the steering wheel. She felt out of sorts, antsy and shaky, knew she was capable of exploding in a sea of venom if she didn't get herself under control. She looked down at her cell phone and sent off a text to her husband to meet her at Supper Club One ASAP. Before she could shove the phone into her designer handbag, which cost more than most people earned in a month, she heard the ping of an incoming text message. She blinked and bit down on her lower lip. Just the sight of his name sent shivers up and down her spine. She did not need this right now. She absolutely did not need this. She tried to frown, but the Botox kept her features frozen in place. She read the message twice and forwarded it to Gabe. She knew that if she didn't respond to this particular text message, there would be hundreds to follow, which would become a blizzard and end up blowing up her phone. No one kept Zuma Delgado waiting. No one. Certainly not the likes of Pilar Sanders.

Zuma's text read **Are we on schedule? Confirm. We would like to double our Christmas order. I haven't seen any advance publicity. Double up and do it now.**

Pilar's heartbeat quickened. *Answer or not?* Gabe would say to play along and tell her to move up their schedule. She closed her eyes in panic. All she could see behind her heavy lids was Zuma Delgado's pockmarked face, his greasy hair, his beady, malevolent eyes, and his yellow teeth before her eyes snapped open. For one wild, greedy moment, she calculated what her cut of *double* would mean. Before she could change her mind, she tapped out two words and sent the text message on its way. **No problem.**

Pilar climbed out of the car. Her heart thumping, she locked it and raced toward the back door of the supper club. She stopped for a minute to look down at the three tabby cats bent on hitting the Dumpster, where the wait-staff threw out the leftover food. She liked cats and had left a standing order with the chefs that they were to feed them every night. As far as she knew, they had obeyed her instructions. The cats looked healthy and well fed. She bent down to pet them, and they purred their thanks. She wondered, and not for the first time, where they slept at night. Maybe she should have one of the staff fashion some sort of shelter for them.

Pilar straightened up and looked around at the empty parking lot. So much to think about. Gabe would know what to do. Right now, she couldn't seem to think on her own. And she was in full panic mode. Which was scaring the hell out of her. Pilar Sanders did not panic. Pilar Sanders always had it all under control. Pilar Sanders never lost control; nor did she ever turn control over to anyone else. Especially the likes of Zuma Delgado. *Bullshit!*

In full panic mode, so light-headed, Pilar ran to the bar for a drink to calm down her nerves. She reached for a bottle of Crown Royal and gulped down the fiery liquid. Her throat burned and her eyes watered as she coughed and sputtered. She took a second hit and had to sit down on one of the bar stools, the bottle still clutched in her hand. She stared at herself in the mirror behind the bar. Who was that person staring back at her?

Pilar was about to take a third hit from the bottle when she looked up to see her husband standing over her. "That's not the answer, Pilar." He pried the liquor bottle from her hands.

"I know. I know. Oh, God, Gabe. What are we going to do? You know how he is. If I didn't respond, he'd just keep texting all day long. I just said 'No problem' to buy some time. We have seven weeks to . . . to . . . Can we get out from under, Gabe? Tell me the truth. Can we?"

"Earlier this morning, I would have said no. But Carlie just told me about the Hong Kong offer. We might be able to squeak by if we play our cards right and get this show on the road. Stat. No screwing around this time. We need to be on the same page, and we need to be united. We're not going to be able to sell the properties. That would be a dead giveaway. When we walk out, we walk out with what we have and leave it all behind. I warned you, Pilar. Why didn't you listen to me?" Gabe said wearily as he took a seat next to his wife. He wished he knew if what he'd said was the truth or not. He was so tired of it all, he almost didn't care. Almost.

"Because I'm greedy, Gabe. I admit it. I never thought . . . I just assumed . . . I'm sorry. I don't know what else to say," Pilar said tearfully. "I guess this is what you meant when you warned me my chickens would come home to roost. I'm scared, Gabe. Really scared."

Gabe nodded as he patted his wife's shoulder. "We'll figure out something. I think we should go home and talk about this. We do not need to make the rounds today. Nothing ever changes. We need to get out in front of all of this and make some really hard decisions. You on board, honey?"

Pilar tried for a smile, but it was sickly at best. When was the last time Gabe had called her honey? She couldn't remember.

Pilar nodded. "Let's stop on the way and buy some flowers and maybe some food from that corner grocery. We need to christen our abode." Her voice was so jittery, Pilar could hardly recognize it as her own.

Gabe nodded, but his expression clearly showed that it was way too late for flowers and cooking, but he was game. Pilar burst into tears again. Gabe was so shocked, he didn't know what to do. The last time he'd seen his wife cry like this, she was ten years old, banging on the rusty trailer door for her mama to give her something to eat. But her mama was busy entertaining a gentleman friend, one of many that fine day. He'd run home to his own mama, and she had followed him back, scooped up Pilar, taken her to their trailer, fed her, and given her a bath. From that day on, as long as they were in Alabama, he had never let Pilar out of his sight.

"I know what you're thinking, Gabe," Pilar whispered. "You're thinking about that day you found me banging on that rusty old trailer door. I can always tell when you're thinking about that. It's going to be okay, Gabe. You just said so, and you never lie to me."

Gabe didn't believe it for a minute, and he knew that Pilar didn't believe her own words, either. The best he could come up with in the way of a response was, "Can you drive?"

Pilar nodded.

"I'll meet you at home, then."

Back at the BOLO Building, Abner's fist shot in the air as he gave a whoop of success. "Cracked it, guys. I can now access all the information for all the dancers! Names, backgrounds, Social Security numbers, home addresses, not the ones where they are temporarily living while they work for the Supper Clubs. Just as a point of interest, the guys go under their legal names. No silly made-up monikers for the ladies to soak up. Give me forty-five minutes, and I'll be able to print it all out for you so you each have a copy."

"Well, that should help speed things up," Fergus said. "Where is young Toby right now? Shouldn't he be here?" The questions were directed at Dennis, who simply shrugged.

"Isn't he with Mia Grande?" Maggie asked. "By the way, how does Toby's boss line things up for the Mr. December gig? Do they advertise, or is that just something they do every year, same old, same old except for the dancer who will be Mr. December?"

Espinosa raised his hand. "They advertise. They make announcements on Facebook. They tweet and do all that Instagram stuff. Word travels. They send out e-blasts to all the colleges in the area. It works for them. They have standing room only. That's all according to the archives I've checked. They have it down to a science. They roll in, do their thing, and roll out as they do their good deeds along the way. Not a hint of anything out of the ordinary. Except maybe one thing.

"While I was checking all their press releases, the candid shots, the plaques given out in thanks, I noticed one guy in a lot of the same pictures. They don't use body-guards, so that's out. The thing is, he shows up in different towns. He's never front and center in any of the crowds, but maybe two rows back. He doesn't look like the rest of the crowd, and that's why I noticed him. He's older, thug-gish looking. Wears some heavy-looking gold chains, has a tattoo on his neck and a big old diamond in his left ear. Like I said, he stood out. The crowd is mostly young women and young, collegiate-looking guys. At awards events, the crowd is a mix of local politicians, town fathers, soccer moms, that kind of crowd. The guy I'm talking about stands out like a bull in a puppy mill."

"Show me," Ted said. Espinosa started flipping through his iPad until he found what he was looking for. Maggie leaned forward to stare at the pictures. Ted shook his head. "I don't think we ever came across him before, at least not that I remember."

"I don't, either, but there's something about him I can't put my finger on right this minute. Ted, do you remember that reporter friend of yours who used to work for the *Miami Herald*? The guy who's in Chicago now? Send him some of these pictures and see if he recognizes him. Miami is full of Cubans, and he looks to me like he might be one of them. Maybe this guy will remember him or something. I hate when this happens. It's going to make me crazy until I figure it out."

While Maggie stewed and fretted, and Ted and Espinosa sent off texts and pictures, Jack looked over at Charles. "Are we on for tonight, or do we give it another day be-fore we hit the Supper Club to see Toby dance? We never did nail that down."

"Tomorrow. Too much is up in the air right now. Fergus and I were just discussing the matter. And, like it or not, you boys will have to go in disguise. Additionally, Avery just informed me he heard from his operatives that Toby's boss is in a bit of a tizzy. The female operative assigned to her has been tailing her all morning. Something must have gone awry, because Ms. Sanders called her husband to meet her at Supper Club One, and they left shortly after he arrived. The operative said it looked like Ms. Sanders was crying. Her husband followed her home, and they are both there as we speak. She said that while Ms. Sanders was sitting in the car, she was either sending or receiving text messages. We won't know what that is all about unless we can get her cell phone or Abner can figure out a way to hack into it. Toby would have to give him her cell-phone number before he can act on it."

"Maybe we could do a pretend mugging when she gets to the club tonight. We've done that a time or two before, and it worked. No reason to think it won't work again if we play our cards right," Dennis said. "We take her money, upload everything on the phone to Abner, then ditch her bag in the parking lot. If the money and credit cards are gone, she'll think it's just a run-of-the-mill snatch and grab. She won't care about the money or cards, but she will care about the phone. She probably won't even report it to the police. What do you think?"

"I think it's doable. It's possible Ms. Sanders has more than one phone that she uses for different things—the guys, the business, her home and husband. This, I'm thinking, would be a sure bet," Snowden said. "I'll set it up. Nice thinking, kid."

Dennis beamed his pleasure at the compliment.

"Do we think she got spooked somehow?" Ted called over his shoulder.

"I think it's a good bet, and if she did, you can bet she picked up some bad vibes from Toby," Charles said. "Where does this leave us? And where is Toby?"

Cyrus was the one who responded to the question by getting up and racing to the alley door.

"There's your answer," Jack said, grinning.

Cyrus led the small parade to the conference room, then took his place under the table, at Jack's feet. He'd done his job and even gotten a treat from the jittery guy he'd just escorted into the conference room.

Toby backed up, bumping into Mia, who stumbled, then caught herself as the gang bombarded them.

"Talk to us."

"What happened?"

"What's going on?"

"Say something."

Toby cleared his throat as he looked around. His gaze settled on Dennis, whom he considered his only friend in the room. "Well, Pilar met Mia. I don't know all that much about women, I admit it, but I thought she looked envious. Pilar, that is. She was pleasant enough, however. The meeting at the Dog and Duck went off as scheduled. Mia's 'friends' were there and were introduced to Pilar. She spent a good bit of time texting at the beginning. She did her best to play the mothering boss, but I thought it fell flat. I think she has trust issues. Where I'm concerned. I have nothing concrete to base that on, just my gut feeling. I did get a sense that something was *off* somehow. Oh, she said she was calling a special meeting this evening, before the first show. And she also told me not to bring Mia. The meeting is just for the dancers.

"She did seem a little excited over that, now that I think about it. Maybe *excited* is the wrong word. Maybe *nervous* would be a better choice. Like I said, the whole thing was just off somehow. She's never done that before. Pilar is very rigid in everything. As long as I've known her, she's never been a spontaneous or serendipitous kind of person. She operates on a schedule and does not deviate from it. If you piss her off, you don't dance that night, and the perks disappear for a week or so. To keep that from happening, everyone toes the line."

An earsplitting whistle shot through the air. Abner was calling for everyone's attention. The room grew silent. Even Cyrus stopped munching on his chew bone to see if his help was required. Satisfied that his help wasn't needed, he went back to his chew bone.

"I have here on my screen, people, the names, addresses, and current information on the last seven Mr. Decembers! Drumroll, please!"

"You want me to pull it out of you, Abner?" Harry growled.

Ah . . . no, Harry. I'm good here. All seven of the dancers have gone on to the male modeling world. All are extremely successful. I'm printing out some of their latest photo shoots. A few are working in Manhattan, some in California. Two of them are currently doing an Armani photo shoot in Hawaii. Nice work if you can get it. They are making bookoo bucks. Actually, all of them are. Three of the seven got married. One guy has a newborn baby. Everything looks legit, from what I can see. I guess being Mr. December paved the way for them in their new careers.

"One other thing. They all have college degrees, so that leads me to believe that Ms. Sanders recruited them all from various colleges. It says a lot that they finished and got their degrees while dancing. If my opinion counts, I'd say all of them are stand-up guys. It's going to take me a little longer to access their financials. I'm not expecting anything other than robust accounts that they earned. Modeling, like dancing, is a hard job, even though we might not think so."

"I guess what you're saying is none of the seven knew or had anything to do with the drug end of things that Ms. Sanders had going on," Charles said.

"That's my opinion, Charles. Once you make Mr. December, there is no place left to go on the Supper Club circuit, so Ms. Sanders cut them loose. She might be the one who had contacts with the various designers and got them their jobs. It makes sense if you think about it. They're all happy, with good jobs, contented in their lives. No blow-back to Sanders in any way. Smart lady, if you ask me," Abner said.

Dennis grinned as he looked over at Toby. "I wonder what designer she had planned for you, Toby. Did you know anything about this?"

"I did not. I don't think any of the others know, either. I told you, after being named Mr. December, the guy was never seen or heard from again."

"But if they're famous models, wouldn't someone have recognized them?" Maggie asked.

The guys hooted. Ted poked Harry and asked him when he looked at a male model last. Harry scowled.

"Guys don't look at catalogs or advertisements," Jack said. "That's a girly thing."

Maggie grimaced, knowing that Jack was right. "Okay, okay. I'll give you that one."

"Now what?" Dennis asked.

"Now we wait for Toby's meeting with Ms. Sanders this evening. After that is when we make a concrete plan. Will someone check with Bert to see if the Sanderses have been in touch?" Charles asked.

"I'll do it," Fergus said.

"Coffee anyone?" Jack asked as he headed out of the room to go to the kitchen, Cyrus following close behind him.

Chapter Nine

Two hours into the meeting in the conference room, Maggie bolted out of her chair, her clenched fists shooting in the air. "I got it! I know where I've seen that guy! Ted, you know, too. Espinosa, help me out here! It wasn't a picture shot with a camera. Think! Remember when we were in Los Angeles two years ago? Maybe two years and a few months. We went out there to do a story on that drug dealer they were making the movie about. We interviewed the star playing the part and had some real deep discussions on where they got all their intel, because it was so real. We logged hours and hours of face time. Remember how the actor, a newbie, thanked us profusely for all the publicity we gave him? Do you remember?" Maggie all but squealed.

Maggie's excitement was contagious. Ted hopped off his seat and started to pace the conference room. "Yeah, yeah. The thing was, no one could find any pictures of the guy, and a cop's informant was the only one who actually ever saw him! Yeah! Yeah! Now I remember. Nice going, Maggie," he said, high-fiving her.

"And all they had to go on was a composite drawing. I have it here somewhere," Espinosa said as he frantically thumbed through his file of pictures. "What's the name? I can't remember the name, but it was catchy as hell. Lots of tats, lots of piercings. Greasy-looking guy, the informant said, and he also said, according to the actor, that the guy smelled bad. *Ripe* was the word he used. I'm remembering, too."

"And to keep the record straight, it wasn't a movie. It was a documentary," Ted said.

"I don't remember anything about that," Jack said.

"Nor do I," Charles said.

"It was a big deal in California, but not so much here on the East Coast. And the guy is still on the loose, as far as I know. I haven't heard anything lately. Nothing has crossed the wires at the paper that I know of," Ted said.

"Contact your friend in Miami right now, the one you said worked at the *LA Times* back when all this was going down. Espinosa, what's the holdup on that artist's sketch?" Maggie barked.

"Okay, okay. I got it! I'm uploading it to all of you now. The guy's name is Zuma Delgado," Espinosa said gleefully.

"Scary-looking dude," Dennis said as he stared down at the artist's sketch. "I bet he looks ten times worse in person. You have to wonder how the Sanderses got involved with someone like that."

Toby shivered as he stared down at the sketch on Dennis's phone. "I never saw him before, and I sure hope I never find myself in his company."

Fergus stepped around the table and said, "Incoming text from Bert. No response yet from the Sanderses. That's it. He didn't write anything else."

"I don't know too much about Gabe Sanders, but I do know that Pilar never does anything unless she checks it out thoroughly. She's probably weighing every possibility with her husband right now. She won't let too much time go by without a response, for fear she might miss out on something. She'll get back to your guy before the end of the day, our time, would be my guess. I say this because if Pilar is spooked, she's going to want to act on the situation. That's probably why she headed home with her husband. She's plotting and scheming right now. I can almost guarantee it," Toby said.

Right then, everyone started talking at once. Ted signaled that he was going someplace a little quieter. He mouthed the words "Miami reporter" to indicate that was who was on the phone with him. Maggie was up and off her chair like she was shot from a cannon, then followed Ted out of the room.

Sensing something that might or might not be to his liking, Cyrus reared up and raced after the two reporters, hoping there was a treat somewhere along the way.

In the kitchen Maggie started to multitask, something she was very good at. She poured herself more coffee and handed out two treats to Cyrus, all the while listening to Ted talking to his colleague in Miami. She liked what she was seeing as far as facial expressions went, because, for the most part, all Ted was contributing to the conversation was a "Yes," a "Don't know," a "Maybe," and a few uh-huhs along the way.

The minute Ted powered down, Maggie was on him like white on rice. "Spit it out!"

Ted walked over to the coffee machine. Before he could reach for a cup, Maggie spun him around.

"I'll pour the coffee. Talk. Do not leave anything out." Equal parts menace and authority rang in Maggie's voice.

"He's flying here later today. I told him he could stay at the *Post*'s apartment. He's willing to share what he has for a three-way byline. I said okay. He said he's been dogging this Zuma guy for almost three years. He called him a snake charmer. Said Miami Vice had a whole task force on his ass, but the guy is slippery. He also said he floats between Miami and Los Angeles, which bears out the Mr.

December deal the Sanderses have going on. He said that was the main reason he took the job at the *Miami Herald* when he left LA. He is determined to get this guy.

"You heard my end of the conversation, so you know I didn't tell him anything I shouldn't have. John Zacharius is his name, but everyone calls him Zack, and he is a top-notch reporter. He's right up there with me and you, Maggie, and you know I don't hand out compliments like that unless they are deserved. Zack will play square with us, so we have to agree to do the same thing. I know how you want to get right up there in everyone's face. That won't work with Zack. We share and share alike. Now's the time to say yay or nay."

"I get it, Ted. You have my word. Share and share alike. Triple byline. In alphabetical order. Robinson, Spritzer, and Zacharius. We're good here, pal. Go on back to the conference room. I'm going to clean this coffeemaker and brew some fresh coffee."

Cyrus looked first at Ted, then Maggie, trying to decide whom he should stay with. His decision was made when Maggie reached over to the treat jar.

As she handed over the treat, Maggie said, "I have a bad feeling about this, Cyrus. It's right between my shoulder blades." Maggie dropped to her haunches to eyeball her four-legged friend. "I hate drug dealers. I don't just hate them. I *really* hate them. It pains me to say this, it truly does, but I think the Vigilantes would be better equipped to handle this guy. They show no mercy. Guys, now, guys are different. Do you agree?"

Cyrus tilted his head to the side and barked twice.

"Hmmm. Guess that means you are undecided. I guess I can understand that, since you belong to Jack. Bear in mind, Cyrus, Jack is married to Nikki, and we both know how that works." Cyrus hung his head. Maggie laughed and handed out another treat. "Go ahead back to the conference room. I'm so glad you can't talk, because I sure wouldn't want you to tell the guys I am fully capable of doing whatever has to be done to that scumbag once we catch him. And we *will* catch him. Trust me on that."

Maggie laughed again when she saw the fur on Cyrus's neck stand straight up. She kept on laughing as she cleaned the giant Bunn coffeemaker. She wiped down all the spilled water and proceeded to refill the machine. Enough caffeine to get all of them through the next few hours.

Maggie's thoughts transferred themselves to Pilar Sanders as she tried to figure out what the woman's next move would be. This was the part of a mission she liked best, settling in to figure out what made the other person tick. *What are you doing right now, Pilar Sanders? Right this very second. Are you plotting and scheming? Of course you are. That's your MO. Well, guess what, Pilar Sanders? I know how to do that, too. Actually, I'm rather good at it. You are toast, lady!*

What Pilar Sanders was doing at that precise moment would have surprised Maggie, had she known. For the first time in too many years to remember, Pilar was attempting to make French toast, using lots of cinnamon so the kitchen would smell, for Gabe's approval. Never mind that Gabe wouldn't eat the mess she was making, because he'd seen the dust in the frying pan his wife was using. He seriously doubted she'd eat the concoction, either. He was in no mood to give her an A for effort. Not even for the colorful blooms sitting on the table in the breakfast nook.

Too much, too little, too late.

"You aren't going to eat this, are you?" Pilar said, pointing to the frying pan. She'd done something wrong; the bottom of the pan looked greasy and dark brown. She swiped at the tears rolling down her cheeks with the sleeve of her designer sweater. The sight of the slimy mucus revolted her. She ripped off the sweater and flung it across the room. Then she took the frying pan, doused it and the contents under cold water, then tossed the lot into the trash bag under the sink.

Gabe blinked, then blinked again. He knew he was supposed to say something. Possibly something comforting, but he just didn't feel like it. Or maybe his wife thought he should take her in his arms and hug her, telling her things would be all right. Well, he absolutely did not feel like doing that, either. Simply because he didn't believe it. He knew they were almost to the end of the road. They weren't there yet. *Yet* was the operative word for the moment. *But only because hope springs eternal*, was his thought.

Gabe gave a moment's thought to going to the bedroom they shared to get her a sweater or robe, but instead he plucked a colorful daisy from the less-than-attractive flower arrangement Pilar had picked up on the way home. He wondered if she would remember how, when they were kids, they used to pluck the tiny petals and say, "He loves me. He loves me not." It always came out that they loved each other.

Pilar stared at the flower. She wasn't thinking about peeling off the petals the way she had when she was a child. She was thinking about the word *double*, which Zuma Delgado had mentioned. *Double. Double* was too much money to just . . . walk away. *Double* was a big score. More than they could ever imagine. *Double* was security. How could she walk away from something like that? She needed to think about that. Really think. She whirled around and mumbled something about a migraine coming on. She ran from the room and locked herself in the bathroom.

Under normal circumstances, and these were far from normal circumstances, Gabe would have gone after his wife and tried to comfort her. Not this time. Instead, he sat down at the table in the breakfast nook and stared at the flowers. With nothing else to do, he pulled out a bright purple Shasta daisy and proceeded to pull off the petals. "She loves me. She loves me not. She loves me. She loves me not," he mumbled over and over. With one last petal to go, Gabe felt his eyes start to burn. "She loves me *not.*"

For the first time in his life, Gabriel Sanders did not know what to do. He did, however, know what he *should* do. He just didn't know if he had the guts to follow through. Then, in the blink of an eye, he thought he had the answer when Pilar's phone, which she had left on the counter, pinged. He reached over to grab it and saw the name of the incoming caller, Bert Navarro. The man in Hong Kong. Well, hellooo!

Gabe cleared his throat, swiped at his burning eyes, and clicked on the phone. "Gabe Sanders," he said by way of identification.

"Bert Navarro, Mr. Sanders. I'm calling you from Babylon Casino in Hong Kong. I was wondering if you and your wife had come to a decision regarding my offer. The reason I'm calling you again is to alert you to the fact that I am going to need your answer ASAP, because of all the planning we have going on for our opening night. I hate to rush you into a decision if you aren't comfortable with my offer. I also need to tell you that the powers that be are trying to solicit the Rockettes, so whoever gets back to us first gets the gig. Are you following me here?"

"I am, Mr. Navarro. My wife and I are very interested. We have one problem, however. All of our past Mr. Decembers have moved on to other things and are not available. Our current Mr. December can be counted on. We have four other equally impressive dancers who will meet your criteria. We planned on a meeting this evening, our time, to see if the boys were agreeable. My wife planned on getting back to you after the meeting. I think I can say with ninety-nine percent confidence that all the boys will jump at the chance. Will that work for you?"

Gabe thought his heart was going to explode right out of his chest when he didn't hear an immediate response. He cleared his throat. He tried to muffle his sigh of relief when he heard Navarro speak.

"I think I can work around that if you can send me some footage of the dancers, names, all the info I requested in my first communication. So then, I'll wait for your call. Can you give me a time?"

Gabe cleared his throat again. "I think we can have an answer for you by nine this evening my time. You're what . . . ? Twelve or so hours ahead of us, right?"

"Correct. I look forward to hearing from you, Mr. Sanders."

Before Gabe could even think about saying good-bye, the connection ended.

Was this the answer? Gabe wished he was clairvoyant. Should he tell Pilar? Such a stupid question. Of course he had to tell Pilar.

Gabe squared his shoulders as he took four deep breaths to calm himself. Something he referred to as 478. *Take four deep breaths. Inhale on the count of seven, and exhale on the count of eight.* Now he was ready to beard the lioness.

Gabe knocked loudly on the bathroom door. He didn't even bother to try to enter, because he knew Pilar would have locked the door. He spoke in his normal tone of voice, certain Pilar could hear him. "The man from Hong Kong called. We talked. I explained the situation. He expects a response from us by nine o'clock this evening. He let me know that the Rockettes are under consideration, and the winner will be the one who gets back to him first. I'm going to give you five minutes to open this door and talk to me, or I am going out. When and if you see me again is uncertain."

Gabe stared at the intricately carved bathroom door for a moment before he shoved his hands in his pockets and walked away. He heard the snick of the bathroom lock, but he didn't turn around; he just kept on walking. His days of groveling were over. Finally.

"Gabe, wait!" Pilar ran down the hallway after her husband. She latched onto his arm and walked barefoot with him into the kitchen.

"Make it quick, Pilar. I'm not in the mood for your bull-shit. My mind is made up. Either we take the offer, which means we sit down right now and iron it out, or I am packing my bags, and I'm outta here." He pointed to her head. "Don't even try telling me that you weren't in that bathroom, trying to figure out a way to play both ends against the middle. I know you. Are we clear on that, Pilar?"

"We're clear, Gabe," Pilar lied. *Double*. How clear was that? So damn clear she couldn't think about anything else. *Double*. Gabe would come around. He always did. *Double*.

She went on. "Tell me everything Mr. Navarro said so I know how to proceed. I think we can count on Toby for this. I don't see a problem with the other four or five lead dancers. We'll need to take two substitutes, just in case. I don't suppose you talked money, did you?"

"No. I guess that's something for tonight's discussion. Whatever it turns out to be, I think we should take it. It's our answer, Pilar. Are we in agreement here?"

Pilar sniffed. "Okay, but that's no way to do business. You never accept the first offer. You negotiate for the best deal. We want paid airfare, paid accommodations, and our food paid for. We want top U.S. dollars for the boys. We can pay a small bonus on top of that out of our own funds to make the deal more enticing to them. If all goes well for the trial month, then we can renegotiate from that point on. If you're worried that Zuma can get to us, forget it. There's no way he's going to go to China to look for us. He'll just latch onto someone else. That's who he is." *Double. Oh, yes, double.*

Gabe listened to his wife. He knew she was right. To a point. He even liked what she was saying, but in his heart of hearts, he didn't believe her. He looked at his wife now, at her clean, shiny face devoid of the thick makeup, the false eyelashes, the ridiculous red lipstick, and thought he could see the old Pilar. The feeling lasted bare seconds. He knew that no matter how much he pretended, no matter how he hoped or, yes, even prayed, Pilar was lost to him.

Chapter Ten

Jack Emery looked over at Harry Wong and gave a slight nod. "I'm going to take Cyrus out. Want to keep me company? I think we can both use a little fresh air." He looked around to see that everyone was busy doing something or other and decided their absence wouldn't be noticed. Except maybe by Dennis, who had the eye of an eagle and the nose of a hound dog on the hunt; but at the moment, Dennis was in what appeared to be a deep, intense conversation with his friend Toby Mason.

Harry unwound his lanky frame, stretched, and rolled his shoulders as he followed Jack out of the conference room. Cyrus was already at the door, waiting. *No surprise there*, Harry thought. Cyrus was right up there with the mystical dog Cooper.

Once outside, Jack leaned up against the building while Harry did some limbering stretches. Jack fired up a cigarette, one of two or three he smoked in a month's time. He didn't really want the cigarette now, but he was feeling charged up and knew that the tobacco would calm him down. He fully expected Harry to swat the cigarette out of his hand, but when the martial-arts expert stared off in the distance, he knew Harry didn't care one way or the other. At least for the moment.

"Cold out here. I always hated the cold. I am never going to like the cold. Makes my skin itch. I'd like to live somewhere where the temperature is a steady seventy degrees every day," Jack said, simply to make conversation.

"Zamboanga," Harry said without missing a beat.

"Well, I don't see that happening any day soon," Jack responded before he blew a perfect smoke ring, which floated upward and then dissipated in the gusty wind.

"Then why bring it up in the first place? We both hate the cold, so what the hell are we doing out here? Cyrus doesn't need us to help him lift his leg. Spit it out, Jack, and get rid of that cigarette before I jam it up your nose."

Ah, now that was the Harry Jack knew and loved. He tossed the offending cigarette on the ground, then ground it to a pulp with the heel of his shoe. He then picked it up and stuck it in his pocket. Jack Emery did not litter. As in ever. He offered up no comment to Harry's threat, but he did spit out what was bothering him. "I hate drug dealers, especially *big*-time drug dealers, because big-time drug dealers belong to cartels, which have no morals, no scruples, and they kill people just for looking at them sideways if they think they are interfering with their drug trade. I hate them as much as I hate the cold, probably more.

"This Zuma guy . . . he was . . . is supposedly Dito Chilo's next in command. But then Espinosa said he's further down the drug ladder, like maybe three or four, so that means there will be a turf war of some kind. If he is the next in command, that will put him right up there at the head of . . . of . . . Chapo's organization, since Chapo was just recaptured and is now sitting in a Mexican prison, hopefully awaiting extradition to the good old U S of A.

"Anyway, neither scenario is good. If it turns out that he is next in command, it makes sense to me that the guy would hightail it to Miami to get away from the DEA and every bounty hunter looking to make a name for himself.

And, of course, to avoid a turf war. He'll need to gather a small army to make all that happen. Again, Miami is the perfect place to do that. What do you think, Harry?" Jack asked as he stomped his feet on the cold concrete.

"I'm not liking what I'm hearing, Jack. So correct me if I'm wrong here. Are you saying that you are or you are not afraid of this guy, and that this mission should be aborted?"

"No, I'm not afraid, Harry, but I have some concerns. You should, too. We don't know enough about Pilar Sanders and her deals with this guy. Toby can't help us, because he doesn't really know anything, either. I'm not liking that we don't have more background. Knowledge is power. You know that. Drug runners and their cohorts do not play by any rules. They make up their own as they go along, with the main one being to kill anyone who stands in their way. Hell, Harry, we don't even know how big this all is. When we first heard about it, it almost sounded routine. Small potatoes. Now I'm thinking we were way off the mark."

"This might surprise you, Jack, but I am in agreement. Bear in mind, those people use guns. We do not! In a fair altercation, we could take them hands down. As good as we both are, neither you nor I am capable of catching a bullet in midair before it hits someone and kills them."

"There is that." Jack sighed. "Any ideas?"

"What's taking Cyrus so long?"

Jack looked at his watch. "He still has a few minutes."

Harry frowned as he stared down at the alley, where Cyrus was sniffing the brick walls. "How does that dog know when fifteen minutes are up?" he asked, his expression as sour as his tone.

Jack shrugged. "When you can tell me how Cooper does what he does, maybe I'll be able to answer that. Until then, let's just pretend both dogs are normal." Jack looked down at his watch again. "Two minutes, Harry."

"So, what's the plan?" Harry asked, his eyes still on

Cyrus, who was now making his way up from the far end of the alley, which was over a block long. He knew in his gut the dog had it timed to the last second.

"The plan is that there is no plan at this immediate time. I'm thinking that after Toby has his meeting with Pilar Sanders this evening, we'll know more. And then we can go full bore. Plus, Ted's colleague will arrive sometime tonight, and he might be able to shed more light on exactly what we're up against. It's sticking in my craw that someone like the Sanders woman can be crucial to a big drug deal. Think about it, Harry. She runs a string of supper clubs that feature male dancers who dance for women and get money stuck in their . . . you know, that thing they wear. How did she get involved in something like this? We need to know the why of it all."

Cyrus nudged Jack's leg and let out a soft woof.

"Right on schedule, bud. C'mon. Let's go inside, where it's warm."

Cyrus woofed again. Harry rolled his eyes as Jack stared into the retina scanner. The moment the huge door clicked shut, Cyrus raced to the kitchen and waited patiently for his treat.

"Cooper never wants treats. He doesn't beg, either. He simply accepts what is. Why do you think that is, Jack?" Harry asked fretfully.

"Like I know, Harry! I don't want to talk about this. We have a mission to think about. That's where all our thoughts should be. As far as the dogs go, they are what they are. We can't change them, and even if we could, I don't think I would want them any different than they are now. We good, Harry?"

"We're good, Jack."

Back in the conference room Charles was speaking. Jack and Harry slipped into their seats, and then Cyrus settled himself at Jack's feet instead of under the table. Jack stroked Cyrus's big head with gentle hands. If Cyrus were a cat, he would be purring in pure contentment.

"I'm sorry, sir, I'm not really understanding what's going on. Is the China offer legitimate, or is it a smoke screen? Is the plan for the Sanderses and the dancers to actually *go* to China? If so, then they're off the hook. Am I reading this right?" Toby asked boldly. "And just for the record, these feet of mine are not leaving U.S. soil. If you tell me that's a game changer, then I am outta here and will take my chances come what may."

"Why don't we just say it's all a work in progress for the moment?" Charles responded.

Toby let out a displeased snort of frustration. "That tells me you don't know the answer to my question. That is not good, from my perspective. What it also doesn't tell me is how I am supposed to act this evening at the meeting. If Pilar asks me to go to China, what do I say?"

Fergus looked offended at the question. "You simply tell her an offer like that out of the blue demands that you have time to think about it, and remind her that you have just fallen in love. Love conquers all, as they say." Fergus smiled.

"Toby, for now we're playing it by ear. We have nothing concrete to go on. We have no proof of anything. Yet. If it's there, trust me, we'll find it. That's when we go into mission mode. You have to trust us. It might seem to you right now like we don't know what we're doing, but I assure you, we do. You are in good hands," Charles said quietly. "Trust is mandatory right now, son."

Toby nodded as he locked his gaze with that of Dennis, who simply nodded.

"I've been scouring the Net for an hour now and can't find any advance notice for the California Mr. December contest," Ted said. "I've gone back four years, and by now, in previous years, there was an enormous number of teasers posted all over the place, especially on the Net. I realize it isn't even Halloween yet, but in previous years, pictures of the contenders are front and center, with new, randomly shot pictures following every week thereafter until the contest in December. Either someone is asleep at the switch or that contest is not going to be happening this year."

All eyes turned to Toby. A deer caught in the headlights, all Toby could do was shrug and flap his hands in the air.

Toby looked up at the clock on the wall, then over at Mia Grande, who was buffing her nails with some kind of long stick. Feeling Toby's gaze, she grinned. It was a winsome grin, as though they shared a really good secret. Right at that moment, Toby didn't know if he wanted to slap her or kiss her. He looked away, hoping he wasn't telegraphing his emotions. Girls were so . . . so . . . unpredictable. And crafty. And sneaky.

Toby cleared his throat. "I have to leave now and keep to my routine. I have an hour at the gym and a mini photo shoot for some random shots to post for the Mr. December contest. No one said it was canceled, so I have to show up. Then it's back home to shower and change and head to the club. Plus, I have to eat out. Any orders or instructions before I leave?"

"Not at the moment," Charles said. "You're free to go, but stay close to Mia. Wait a moment. There's a text coming in from Director Sparrow."

Everyone in the room stopped what they were doing. The room went totally silent as they waited for what Charles would share.

"At the moment, I don't know if this is good or bad, but Director Sparrow's text says he is going to have to sit this mission out because of his orders from the White House. He said Annie and Myra told him in no uncertain terms to make up his mind whose side he's on—theirs, which means the veterans, or the White House and the prez losing face. He goes on to ask if there is a paying job within our group that he can apply for. He also wants to know what kind of health benefits we offer." Charles chuckled as he looked around the room. "Someone tell me how you all would like me to respond."

Abner Tookus stood up and waved his arms about to loosen his shoulder muscles. "That doesn't exactly thrill me, even though it's clear whose side Sparrow is on."

"Our accounts are robust, so I don't see a problem, if Sparrow is serious," Jack said. "That includes health insurance. I seriously doubt it will come to that, but we're on board if it does. We can take a vote. Hands up if you all agree."

Every hand in the room shot in the air.

"There is your answer, Charles," Jack said.

Toby looked at Dennis and shook his head. This was so far over his head, he couldn't think straight. The director of the FBI was asking these people if they had a job for him that provided health insurance if he left his prestigious position as the head of the FBI. *These people.* Those were the key words he had to focus on. But not right now. Right now he had to get the hell out of here before he exploded, thinking about it and dogs that could fold towels. He could think about all of that while he was at the gym. Or not.

"C'mon. I'll walk you out," Dennis said. He waited for Mia to gather up her things, for Cyrus to decide if it was worth his while to trot after the departing guests or not. In the end, Cyrus decided to stay right where he was, at his master's feet.

Harry hated inactivity. With a passion. "I have an idea."

The room turned silent immediately. Harry never volunteered. Never.

"Let's hear it," Maggie said as she gleefully rubbed her hands together.

Harry looked at Abner. "Your friend Philonias Needle-meyer. Is it possible for you to get in touch with him and have him check out Zuma Delgado and the chain of command? Do people like that use banks to launder money? I admit I have no clue how that works. Take away their money and . . ."

"It's war," Ted said. "Some of the biggest drug dealers have a bevy of legitimate businesses they use to launder money. They also have the biggest, the brightest accountants and lawyers out there at their beck and call, people whom they pay *ginormous* amounts of money for their loyalty."

"You work for the CIA, Abner. You guys should know what's going down in Cuba, since the CIA is foreign, whereas the FBI is domestic. Are you hearing anything?" Harry persisted.

"Yes, I do work for the CIA, and I should be there right now, so I'm going to leave and see what I can come up with. I'll get in touch with Phil, and I'll get back to you. But to answer your question, I have not heard anything. Chapo was just arrested, so intel is only now working its way back to us. I should know something later today. See you guys."

"Abner!" Harry called out.

Abner turned. "What?"

"When you talk to your pal, it wouldn't hurt to see what he can come up with in regard to the Sanderses, too." Seeing the expression on Abner's face, Harry turned defensive. "You're the one who said there was nothing that guy can't find out. So here's your chance to prove it."

Abner flipped Harry the bird, to which Harry responded in kind.

"A text is coming in from Bert," Charles said, breaking the lighthearted moment. The room once again went silent.

"The Sanderses are interested. There are some issues. A

few demands. I think it's safe to say they've taken the bait," Charles said, reading the text from his encrypted phone. "So far today, he's gotten two texts from Ms. Sanders. As I said earlier, he had a one-on-one conversation with Mr. Sanders. They are going to get back to him later this evening, after they meet with their dancers. But then I already told you that. Until then, therefore, we're in a holding pattern."

"Then I suggest we brainstorm for a while, then call it a day and meet up first thing in the morning," Jack said.

"Good idea. But Fergus and I want to get back to the farm right away, to see what's going on with our girls and their veterans' health-care efforts. They might require our help. Can I count on the rest of you if that turns out to be the case?" Charles asked.

Cyrus bounded up and ran over to Charles and barked twice.

Charles laughed. "I knew I could count on you, big boy." He fished a treat out of the pocket that he always kept filled for Lady and her pups and, on occasion, Cyrus.

The others settled down to consider alternative possibilities that depended upon what decisions the Sanderses made about China, LA, and the like.

Chapter Eleven

The cold air was refreshing, Toby thought. He hated being cooped up in a room full of people in the middle of the day. Being cooped up onstage in a supper club at night wasn't the same thing. Nights were to be spent indoors; that was the natural order of things to his mind. He took big, gulping breaths as he headed to where Mia's rocking set of wheels waited for them. He looked at her out of the corner of his eye. That was another thing: he hated being driven around by a woman who was his bodyguard, his protector. That damn well was not the order of things. He strode ahead, his long legs putting distance between himself and Mia, knowing she had to run to keep up.

"What's the big hurry?" Mia gasped.

Toby looked over his shoulder. "I live and operate on a schedule. You should try it sometime," he snapped irritably.

"What? What? Is the gym going to close down if you don't get there by a certain time? Will people look at you and wonder why you're late? What?"

Toby slid into the car the moment he heard the remote-controlled ping that unlocked the door. Like he was going to walk around and hold the door for her. She could stand out there till she took root, for all he cared. He tucked his long legs up, then leaned back and closed his eyes. Her comments didn't require a response.

Mia slid behind the wheel. "I'm going to need the address, Toby."

"Of course you do. How stupid of me not to have thought of that. The address is six-twelve Cosgrove. It's between Sycamore and Plantation Road. Just so you know, you cannot go into the gym. It's guys only. I'm going to be there for two and a half hours, so you might want to find something to do."

"Really! Two and a half hours! I thought you said you worked out an hour a day."

"I also do yoga every other day. This is the other day. Then I have to do the tanning bed. Like I said, find something to do while I'm in there, and do not come looking for me like you're my babysitter. I have a reputation to uphold. Then, when I am finished at the gym, I have to check in at the house and hang around like I live there, which I do. Then it's a shower, get dressed, go out to eat, and head to the club for the meeting with Pilar. Maybe you should go to a bookstore and stock up on some reading material to occupy yourself while I'm doing what I need to do to get past this."

"What's suddenly got your panties in a wad, Toby? Everything sounded on target back there at Never Never Land Headquarters, so what's the problem? I thought we were good. Now you're acting . . . like some pansy-ass puke. That attitude does not work for me. And let's get this straight right now. You do not tell me what to do. I tell you what to do, when to do it, and how to do it. I have a job to do, and I'm doing it. Now, you are either part of the problem or part of the solution. Decide now. Are we clear on all of this?"

Toby offered up a cocky salute as he grimaced. "Crystal."

"Good," Mia said cheerfully as she pulled the Ferrari to the curb. "Oh, and, Toby, don't even think about pulling a fast one and scooting out the back door. I have it covered. Break a sweat, cowboy. I'll be right here when you come out all sweaty and cranky and mean looking. At which point I will drive you home, and while you are primping for tonight, I will be getting my car disinfected. No funny stuff, you hear me?"

Toby didn't respond as he climbed out of the car; nor did he look back once he started walking. He kept on walking, wondering how in the hell she knew what he'd been planning. He should have known she'd have someone by the back exit. His shoulders slumped as he headed to the elevator that would take him to the weight room, his nerves twitching and twanging all over the place. He knew he was a hot mess and needed to get to his center core, or he was going to explode.

With that thought in mind, he opted to skip the weights and headed straight to the yoga room. A couple of hours of yoga and he'd be good to go. He would never admit it to anyone, but he loved the deep relaxation of yoga. He always felt renewed after a particularly long session, and he really liked the instructor with the mellow honey voice telling him what to do. So unlike that barracuda with the razor tongue in her fancy set of wheels.

Toby changed out of his daytime garb, pulled on loose-fitting trousers and shirt, grabbed his mat and pillow, and settled in. The instructor smiled at him, even though he was coming in at the end of the class she was conducting.

Two and half hours later, Toby exited the gym, feeling like a million bucks. He felt at peace with himself, renewed in body and spirit, and ready to take on the world and whatever it held in store for him. He spotted Mia and her flashy car immediately. He sauntered over, opened the door, hopped in, buckled up, and said, "Home, James, and don't spare the asphalt." He leaned back, closed his eyes, and, to Mia's chagrin, power napped. The moment the car skidded to a stop in front of the house, Toby's hand was on the door.

"Hold on here, cowboy. Aren't you forgetting something?"

Was he? Ah, yes, the lip-lock. Before he planted his lips on hers, Toby whispered in her ear, "Call me cowboy one more time, and you will regret it." Then he did everything but suck her tonsils out of her throat and between her teeth. Before he climbed out of the racy sports car, he reached up and tilted the Stetson at a rakish angle. "You'll see me when you see me."

He whistled all the way into the house and back to the kitchen, where all he could smell were delicious aromas. "Martha, it's me, Toby," he called out. "I won't be here for dinner this evening. Smells good. Sorry to miss it."

Martha glared. "Again! I'm starting to think you don't like my cooking, young man. Or are you afraid of my cooking? Which is it?"

"Neither, Martha. I just prefer to stare into Mia's incredible eyes across a candlelit table. Did you forget I'm in love?"

Martha shrugged as she went back to chopping vegetables. Toby left as fast as his feet could carry him. Inside his room, with the door locked, he reached into his backpack and withdrew a lukewarm bottle of Coke. He swigged it down in three long gulps before stuffing the empty bottle back into his backpack to dispose of later.

Toby flopped down on his bed and put his hands behind his head as he stared at the ceiling. He tried to define what exactly he was feeling, but the words eluded him. Too bad he didn't know that guy Jack Emery a little better. If he knew him better, he would have called him for advice since he was some kind of love expert. Not that he was in love. At least he didn't think he was, but he was sure having some really strange feelings where Mia Grande was concerned. *Don't go there, Toby*, he warned himself.

Just as he was drifting into sleep, his cell phone pinged.

He fumbled around until he found it, and powered it on. "Dennis, why are you calling me? I was just about to take a nap. I'm beat, physically and mentally."

"I just called to wish you luck with your meeting tonight. Not that you're going to need it. That's what friends do, Toby."

"I know, Dennis. I'm glad you called. Can I ask you something, friend to friend?"

"Sure. It always helps to talk things through with someone."

"It's Mia. I'm . . . I guess what you would call old school. You know, the guy protects the girl, not the other way around. Jesus, Dennis, she packs a gun. She knows martial-arts moves and could probably kill me with her little finger or something like that. I am resenting her and her capabilities. I'm surly, snotty, and obnoxious when I'm with her. You know me. That isn't how or who I am. She is bringing out the absolute worst in me."

"It's her job, Toby. It's what she does. Obviously, she's good at what she does, or Avery Snowden would never have hired her. He works only with the best of the best. I do get what you're saying and where you're coming from, but, pal, you are going to have to get over it."

"That's not the worst of it. She keeps kissing me. I know it's all for show and part of the . . . game, mission, whatever the hell you guys call what is going on. She kisses me the way I used to kiss Carrie. Those kisses meant something. How can she kiss me like that and not mean it? I swear to God, Dennis, when she reminded me I had to kiss her before I got out of the car when she dropped me off, I almost sucked her tonsils out. I was so out of it, I don't know how I made it into the house. What's that mean? Can you ask that guy Jack and send me a text before I see her again and the kissing starts up?"

"Ah . . . sure, yeah, I'll talk to Jack. Look, sorry I interrupted your nap. Send me a text if you have time after the meeting, okay?"

"Yeah, sure," Toby mumbled.

Setting his internal clock for one hour forward, Toby closed his eyes and drifted off to sleep.

Back at the BOLO Building, Dennis let loose with an ear-splitting whistle to gain everyone's attention, not that there were that many members left in attendance.

"What's up, kid?" Jack asked.

"I think we may have a bit of a problem, people. I just got off the phone with Toby. He's not in a real good place right now, but then I assume you all more or less noticed that while he was here. At the moment, he's pretty confused. As he put it, he's old school, where the guy protects the girl and not the other way around. It bothers him that Mia packs some heat. His male pride is wounded. Don't any of you pooh-pooh this away, because Toby is not as tough and gung ho as all of you. This is new to him. He's had a lot on his plate recently—his breakup with his fiancée after moving here, living out of his car, bagging groceries for a living, then hooking up with the Sanderses and becoming a male dancer. That's all playing on him, that plus the danger he's put himself in. But . . . what is really bothering him is . . . um . . . all the kissing that Mia is insisting on." Dennis held up his hands when he saw that Jack and Ted were about to explode with laughter.

He went on. "Don't go there, you guys. Just don't. He's likening the kissing to the way his ex used to kiss him and he kissed her in return. He knows this is all a game, this caper, this mission, but his body is telling him something else. I think he's falling for his protector. Okay, now you can say something. No, no, wait. He specifically asked me to ask you, Jack, since you are an authority on women, what he should do. Okay, now you can talk."

Jack threw his hands into the air. "Where in the hell did he get an idea like that?"

"From me. Sorry, Jack. I just referenced all the times you helped me out when I was . . . whatever I was when I was involved in relationships. Tell me something to tell him, so he doesn't go doing something stupid. Right now, if stupid could fly, he'd be a jet. Take my word for it."

Maggie started to laugh and found that she couldn't stop. The others joined in, to Jack's chagrin. "Yeah, Jack, let's hear your advice." She quickly turned to the others and said, "Maybe we should ask Nikki instead of Jack. Bet she isn't privy to all Jack's secrets." The laughter continued until Cyrus reared up and let loose with a howl of outrage.

"All right, all right, you've had your fun. I think, based on the little I know of your friend Toby, that he is just confused right now. He's not stupid. I do not know this for sure, but I assume that he has not had a . . . ah . . . meaningful relationship since he broke up with his fiancée. If I'm right, then he just might be in a position where he is misinterpreting 'all the kissing,' as he put it. He might want it to be more. I think he's confused right now with Mia being his protector and the romantic emotion he himself is feeling.

"On the one hand, he says she kisses him intensely, which would then make her the romantic aggressor, as well as his protector. Most men would not like that. I wouldn't. Then he says he almost sucked her tonsils out. That's his bid to be the romantic aggressor. But he really wants to be her protector, because, as he put it, he is old school, and men protect women, not the other way around. Does all that make sense?" Jack said anxiously.

Cyrus barked joyfully to show he was on his master's side as the others simply stared at Jack.

Maggie held up her hand. "Have any of you given any

thought to the possibility that Mia just might find Toby to her liking? Aside from the job. Toby is a good-looking guy. He's ripped, and women like that. He has a boyish naïveté to him that women find appealing. At least I do. And the best part of all is that he is what he said he is, old school. He knows how to treat a woman. Just because he prefers to talk about spreadsheets, price-earnings ratios, and marginal tax rates doesn't mean he doesn't have a romantic heart. I'm sure Mia Grande has never met anyone like Toby Mason, and she just might be falling for him. You all need to think about *that*."

"I agree with Maggie," Harry chimed in. "I'm just like Toby."

"Well, damn," was all Jack could think of to say. Ted and Espinosa echoed his sentiments. Maggie giggled, while Harry winced as though he were in acute pain.

"So then, your advice is . . . ," Dennis said as he waited for a response.

Jack sucked in a deep breath. "Listen to your heart and don't do anything stupid is about the best I can come up with," Jack muttered. "And from here on in, Dennis, stop telling people I am an authority on women. I'm not."

"Okay, Jack, but you really did help me all those times. Your advice was spot on each time I was ready to leap into the unknown. I will always owe you for that."

"God, no! You don't owe me anything. Nothing. Do you hear me, Dennis? You don't owe me anything. I was glad to be of whatever help I could. I just listened to you, and you made your own decisions. We're done with this now. Let's close up shop and go out to get something to eat. My treat."

And that was the end of that.

As the group prepared to leave the BOLO Building, the talk centered on the time and Toby's meeting with Pilar Sanders.

"Toby should be arriving just about now," Dennis said as he looked down at the new Apple watch on his wrist, whose workings he had yet to figure out. Why didn't I just get a nice, simple, reliable Timex? he wondered.

Dennis couldn't have been more right. Mia drove around to the back of Supper Club One and parked. She hoped she didn't look as upset as she felt. Toby had hopped into the car, buckled up, and said not a single word on the entire drive to the club.

"Gotcha here right on time, Toby. Ten minutes to spare. Hey, you look good," she said cheerfully as she pointed to his creased khakis, his white button-down shirt, and navy blazer. "And you smell good, too. I'll wait out here in the car till seven thirty, when the other gals get here. We'll go into the club and order dinner. We'll sit in the back, so we can watch the whole room. Is there anything else you think I should know?"

"Nope." Toby unbuckled his seat belt and waited for the words he knew were coming.

"Aren't you forgetting something?"

"Nope. No one is watching. It's dark out here. Try not to get mugged while you play at being Superwoman."

Mia stared after Toby's retreating back. She sniffed, the scent of his aftershave still lingering. She didn't know if she should run after him; the urge, or whatever it was she was suddenly feeling, was so strong. Her eyes started to burn.

Must be the heater in the car, and the filter needs to be changed. Yes, yes, it must be the heater.

Toby fished for his key to unlock the door that said EM-PLOYEES ONLY. Safe inside, he leaned against the door and took several deep breaths. Did he just act stupid? Or did he come across as blasé? He hoped it was the latter. More than likely, though, he'd acted stupid, and hope was just that, hope. He sniffed the air around him, but all he could smell was Mia's scent. She'd smelled like lily of the valley. When he was growing up, his mother had had a flower bed full of the delicate, tiny, bell-like flowers. He used to pick them for her, and she'd gush all over him and tell him how sweet he was for picking her favorite flowers for her. She'd always hug him and kiss him on both cheeks. His eyes burned at the memory.

This was no time to be thinking of flowers or his mother. He had to clear his mind and concentrate on Pilar Sanders. He had to take one more deep breath before he had to beard the lioness.

The moment he had himself under control, Toby saun-tered down the back hallway that led to the second floor and the dressing room for the dancers. When they were off duty, they hung in the break room. Across from the break room was a small office that Pilar used on occasion. That was where Toby headed. He rapped sharply on the door and waited. Instead of calling out for him to enter, Pilar opened the door herself and ushered him toward the one chair in front of a stylish chrome-and-glass desk.

"I'm so glad you could make it, Toby, and you're right on time, too. I asked you here because I have a very stun-ning, lucrative offer to make you. I hope you are as inter-ested in it as I am," Pilar said, getting right down to business.

Toby waited, his stomach churning.

"Where's your ladylove?" Pilar asked as she rifled through papers on the glass-topped desk.

"She's waiting for her friends outside. They're going to have dinner here and watch one show. I'm not sure of their plans after that."

Pilar nodded before she moved all the papers aside. Her hands clasped in front of her, she leaned forward to make eye contact with Toby, whose first thought was, *She's been crying.* How he knew this, he didn't know. He waited pa-tiently.

"In the past few days, I have been in touch with a man in Hong Kong who is in charge of some big hotel casino they are building. The owner also owns the Babylon Casino in Las Vegas. I had to do some research to make sure the man's offer was legitimate. China is far away, as you well know. Anyway, one of the richest women in the world owns the casino in Las Vegas and the one being built in Hong Kong, which is due to open in December. Perhaps you've heard of Countess Anna de Silva. She's the female version of Warren Buffett, Bill Gates, or that Saudi sheik who seems to own everything the other two don't. I'm sure you've heard of her, since she lives only a little ways outside Washington, D.C.

"Anyway, he has made me an offer to take my dancers to Hong Kong for the grand opening. At first they wanted only all the past Mr. Decembers, but I had to tell them that wasn't possible. They are willing to accept all the club's lead dancers, and you are the best of them all. A trip to China, Toby! Is that exciting or what? We haven't finalized the monetary end of things, but it will be substantial. Count on it. Everything paid for, all expenses. Think of the travel, and all free. I am so excited, and so is my husband. Offers like this come along only once in a lifetime. Don't you agree? Of course you do," Pilar babbled.

"Actually, Pilar, I'm not excited. I was looking forward to being Mr. December and the calendar. I told Mia all about it. How am I going to tell her that isn't going to happen? I'll look like a fool. I do not want to look like a fool."

Pilar froze in place. Whatever reaction she'd been expecting, this was not it. "Tell . . . tell her we're revamping the clubs. I need you in Hong Kong, Toby. Gabe thinks we should shut down the Mr. December and the whole California deal and just keep Miami. We discussed having Carlie take over California, but she doesn't have enough experience. She could, however, handle Miami, as it is not that demanding. The pressures for California are so far out of the box, it's almost impossible to contain them."

"What are you saying, Pilar? Either I go to Hong Kong or I'm out of a job, and Mr. December and the calendar are down the drain? Did you forget about my contract?"

"Of course I didn't forget about the contract. We'll honor it. Of course we will. You'll be paid the fee we agreed on, but there won't be a calendar. You can sue me over that if you want. This is a win-win for you, Toby, and the others, as well. The money is all clear money. I'll see to that. A nice nest egg for you and your new girlfriend. A month, Toby, that's all."

She's nervous. She's chewing her bottom lip. I bet if I asked for a raise right now, she'd give it to me. "I see that you're excited, but the offer is not for me. I can't see myself leaving the country. The whole world is in turmoil, as you well know. There are terrorists everywhere you go. People shoot down planes or put bombs on them. Sorry, but I prefer to stay here, safe and sound. Count me out. Besides, I don't want to leave Mia for that long. My heart just wouldn't be in it. As it is, I'm really pissed, and I don't mind telling you how annoyed I am that the Mr. December gig is down the tubes. I was waiting for that strutting power. Hey, listen, it's getting late and I have to change. Thanks for the offer, though."

"Toby, wait! Listen, talk to Mia about it. Maybe she would like to tag along. You said she's rich, so she could pay her own way. She could take a semester off and gain some life experience. It's China, Toby! This offer could put all you dancers and the Supper Club on the map. You'll be able to name your own price. It doesn't get any better than that."

She's desperate. Her voice is cracking. Ha. "I'll mention it to her, but don't be surprised if she says no," Toby called over his shoulder. He stopped in the doorway and turned around. "I'm not getting it. The other lead dancers are just as good as I am. I'm sure they'll jump at the offer. You won't even miss me."

Toby slammed the door shut and sprinted across the short hallway to the break room, then into the dressing room, ripping at his clothes as he went along. Did he pull it off? He wasn't sure. Maybe, maybe not. Pilar Sanders was no fool.

Something was up, and whatever it was, it wasn't good. He could feel it right down to his toes. And then it hit him. He hadn't seen anything on Pilar's desk. No phone, and the iPad she was never without had been nowhere in sight. In her handbag? No. Both were always either in her hand, stuck on like with glue, or in one of her pockets. He couldn't remember seeing a purse, either. Pilar always had a fancy designer purse hanging off her shoulder. That had to mean something, but what? He wished he knew more about women. Mia would probably know, and that guy Jack would know for sure. He had to find a way to send a text to Dennis between sets.

Chapter Twelve

"Tell me again why we're doing this?" Ted Robinson grumbled as he slapped a huge metal magnet on the side of the *Post* van, which effectively transferred ownership from the *Post* to Martucci Heating & Air.

"The Sanders woman has been inside for fifteen minutes. Toby just went in. So what is our game plan here, Maggie?" Espinosa said. "Do we just sit out here or what? Nothing is going on. Pure waste of manpower. We should go inside. Like Ted said, why are we here? And what's our game plan?"

Maggie looked at her colleagues as she waited for Dennis to weigh in. When he just rolled his eyes, she decided to speak. "It's my gut. The hairs on the back of my neck are moving, and my right eye is twitching. Does that tell you anything?" she snapped.

"Yeah, yeah. Settle down, guys. Maggie's woman's intuition is at work. Just remember, she's never wrong," Ted said, a sour note to his tone.

"That is so sweet of you to say that, Ted. But then, it's true, so it hardly counts. You can call it whatever you want, but I *know* something is going to happen right here. I know it. If you all weren't so busy being pissy to me, you might have noticed that rickety pickup truck that pulled alongside Mia Grande's dude magnet car. Ha! I got you all there. None of you saw that, right? Mia is sitting there, and Avery Snowden just pulled in. Shame this parking lot is so lit up." The minute the words were out of Maggie's mouth, six of the overhead halogen lights went out, one by one.

"He shot them out!" Dennis blurted. "Did you see that? Avery must have used a sound suppressor. Wow, it's really dark now. Just those four lights around the door. Well, there were four by the door, but now there is only one," he continued as three more lights blew out. "Obviously, something is going down, and whatever it is, this darkness will mask it perfectly."

"I think we should exit this van, fan out, and be ready for whatever happens," Maggie whispered. "Be very quiet. Avery gets testy when anyone treads on his territory. I don't think he realizes we're here."

"Ah, like what? That guy Snowden can take care of himself. I'm thinking Mia can, too. What do you see us doing?" Dennis asked, his whispery voice sounding jittery.

Maggie made a very unladylike sound deep in her throat. "For investigative reporters and one investigative photographer, you three are sure off your perch tonight. Did you not see those three men over by the Dumpster before the last light was shot out? Harrumph! It must be true that only women are observant. I'm not so sure it was Avery who shot out those lights. Ted, unscrew the overhead light in this van and be quiet when you get out. Remember, now, not a sound."

"Do you think those three men no one can see but you are going to do something to Avery and Mia? Like an ambush?" Dennis asked, his voice now a hissing whisper.

"Avery and Mia were here first. At least Mia was. If the threesome are bad boys, they're here for something else, probably Ms. Sanders or Toby. Right now, I imagine that

Avery and Mia are trying to figure out what's going on just the way we are," Maggie said.

Dennis was already tapping out a text to Avery Snowden, alerting him to a possible ambush. He ended the text with, **We are three car lengths away, one aisle over from where you and Mia are. We are low to the ground. Advise.**

The return text was curt and succinct. **Go home.**

"Like hell!" Maggie snarled under her breath. "Spread out. Oh, oh, hold on. Someone is coming out the door. Look. It's Pilar Sanders!"

The supper club owner was silhouetted in the backlight from inside the club. She stood for a moment, staring out into the darkness, before she turned around and walked back into the building.

"She's probably going for a flashlight," Espinosa said just as the light over the back door to the supper club went dark. "Avery is on the move. He's going for her car. I can see him. Mia is right behind him. I see two sets of legs. What the hell is he doing?"

"My guess would be breaking into her car. You guys really are not observant. When the woman was standing in the doorway, she didn't have anything in her hands, and there was no purse over her shoulder. She probably left them in the car. Avery wants them. I guess he thought this would be a better way than a snatch and grab," Maggie said.

Ted let loose with a ripe expletive. "Then he must be stupid, because the dome light will go on when he opens the door. Which brings me to my next question. How is he going to open the door without the alarm going off? Mercedes-Benz prides itself on its car security."

"I do not know this for a fact, but I would wager that no one at Mercedes-Benz knows Avery Snowden. I also know for a fact that Avery has one of those gizmos that shut down the car, and you just open the door. Just like that. Fergus told me about it once. And I also saw it in a documentary about car thieves. I guess you missed that, Ted," Maggie sniped.

"Where are the badasses?" Dennis whispered.

"I can't see them. They could be anywhere. At least we now know it wasn't Avery who shot out the lights. Okay, Avery is in the car. I heard the door open," Maggie said.

"I didn't hear anything," Ted said.

"You didn't see anything, either, as I recall. I did, so that's all that's necessary," Maggie snapped. "You all need to get with the program here. We're supposed to be a team, so let's start acting like one. Rule number one, be observant!"

"Oh, oh, look toward the door. It's opening. Sanders is on her way out, and she has a flashlight, one of those little pen things," Dennis said.

Maggie looked up and saw Pilar Sanders outlined in the light spilling from inside the supper club. The moment the door closed behind her, the only thing to be seen in the darkness was the small pinpoint of light pointing toward the ground. Maggie turned her head at a familiar sound. "Okay, everyone back up. I just heard the door close. That has to mean Avery got what he came for. Quiet now. Not a sound."

They all heard the shrill squeal at the same time and literally froze in place. Then they heard Pilar Sanders's voice for the first time, and it was reedy, high pitched, and fearful sounding. "I don't carry any money with me. There's nothing of value in my car. Take the damn car. Just leave me alone! Here, take my earrings!"

The voice that responded was a mix of Spanish and English, and it did not sound friendly. All the group could hear was, "No car, no earrings. You take this. Senor Delgado say you no do your advertising. He want to see tomorrow. Much advertising. You *comprende*?"

When Pilar didn't respond to the fearsome-sounding voice quick enough, they heard the sound of a slap, a hard sound, then Pilar's scream. "You *comprende, sí*," said the voice, and this was followed by a grunt of pain from Pilar.

The group heard the sound of serious retching before Pilar managed, "Yes, I *comprende*." Then they heard the sobs.

Avery motioned for everyone to move back as far as they could, which they did, and they waited for Pilar Sanders to start up her car. No one spoke until her headlights vanished from the parking lot.

"What the hell!" Ted said.

"Never mind 'What the hell?' What do you think the four of you are doing? Why are you here?" Avery Snowden stormed.

"We're here because I had a feeling something was going to go down. We didn't know you would be here, Avery. We're reporters, damn good ones, or did you forget that? Therefore, this parking lot is fair game. This is what happens when all parties don't share information," Maggie said testily. "You go your way now, and we'll go our way. But first, what did you get from her car? Don't make me pull it out of you, either." Menace rang in Maggie's words.

"Yeah, don't make her pull it out of you," Dennis said, backing up his colleague.

"Everything I came for. Contents of phone and iPad. It's all here. I'm heading out to the BOLO Building now, and it will be there for you all when you get there first thing in the morning. Go home now, and be damn glad you didn't get your heads blown off. From here on in, you stick to what you do best and leave me to do what I do."

"Fine!" Ted snapped spitefully. "While you're doing that, we'll be talking to the only person who might know this Zuma Delgado person and what's really going on. We'll make sure we keep it all to ourselves. Screw you, Snowden, and the horse you rode in on. All we wanted to do was help." With that off his chest, Ted ushered his colleagues back to the van, where Espinosa took the wheel. "The nerve of that guy! He thinks he's some kind of prima donna."

Ted continued to seethe until a text message came through from his friend Zack, at which point he shoved all thoughts of Avery Snowden to the back of his mind.

Ted fired off a return message. **We'll meet you in twenty minutes. Park in the underground lot at the *Post*. We'll find you. We're in a white van.**

Pilar raced down the road at eighty miles an hour, not caring if a cop or trooper pulled her over. Right now, right this second, she knew she would be dumb enough to try to outrun the officer as she tried to put as much distance between herself and the scary-looking threesome who had attacked her in the parking lot.

She wanted to reach for her cell phone to call her husband, but she needed both hands on the wheel the way she was speeding. Her destination was Supper Club Six, where she was to meet up with Gabe.

Eight minutes later, Pilar roared into the parking lot and skidded to a stop directly in front of the rear entrance. She shifted into PARK, then closed her eyes and leaned back against the headrest. Her heart was still beating so fast that she thought it would leap right out of her chest. She was twitching from head to toe. There was no way her legs would let her move so she could enter the club. Gabe would have to come to her. She pried her hands from the steering wheel and leaned down to pick her purse up off the floor, where she'd left it when she arrived at Supper Club One.

It wasn't where she remembered putting it. And her cell wasn't in the inside pocket, where she usually dropped it, but on the bottom of her bag. Her heart started to thump even harder when she realized her remote had not unlocked the car door. She distinctly remembered not hearing the distinctive chirp, but she'd been in such a panic, she hadn't paid attention at the time. She reached up and turned on the dome light as she pawed through the Chanel handbag. Phone was there; wallet still there. She counted the money. Nothing missing. Credit cards all in their respective slots. And yet she knew someone had been in her car. She quickly typed a text to her husband. She powered down and sat statue still until her husband climbed into the car five minutes later.

Gabe saw it all at a glance, the panic, the tears, the trembling body of his wife as she reached out to him. He leaned over and grabbed her shoulders. "Tell me what happened. Take deep breaths, Pilar. You know what to do. You're *safe*. Do you hear me? You are safe." His voice was soothing, even though he suddenly felt as fearful as his wife looked. "You need to calm down, or I can't help you. Better yet, get out of the car, and I'll drive. I'm taking you home."

"Yes, yes, home. I want to go home, Gabe. Maybe we should take a taxi. They know this car now. We have to get another one. Sell this one. I never really liked it, anyway. Mercedes-Benz cars are overly touted. Tomorrow," Pilar babbled as she climbed out of the car, not knowing if her husband could hear her or not.

"I'm going to park this car, and we'll go home in mine. We can pick this one up tomorrow. Trust me, Pilar, a taxi is not a good idea."

The minute Pilar shut the car door, Gabe stepped on the gas and headed to the west end of the parking lot, where he parked between two dark SUVs and they both got out of the car. "C'mon, honey. My car is the next aisle over. Lean on me. I'll get you home safe and sound."

Once they were inside Gabe's car, Pilar said, "I'm cold, Gabe. Look how I'm shivering. Turn on the heat. Oh,

God! You are not going to believe what happened back at the club. You will not believe it!"

"First, you have to calm down and talk slowly, so I can decide if I want to believe it or not. Take deep breaths and start at the beginning. I suspect this has nothing to do with young Toby, but start there, anyway. Are you listening to me, Pilar?" Gabe demanded as he turned on the turn signal to bypass a Honda Civic that was going too slow for his liking.

"Toby turned down the offer. He's upset about Mr. December. I tried my best to talk him into a month in Hong Kong by saying his new girlfriend could tag along. At her own expense, of course. He said no. Gabe, the kid didn't buy into anything I said. He's trouble. Big trouble. You had to see the way he was staring at me. Spooked me for sure." Pilar kneaded her hands together as she struggled with her breathing while she talked.

Gabe risked a sideways glance at his trembling wife as he momentarily took his eyes off the road. His first and only thought was, *We waited too long. It's happening now.* He knew he was supposed to say something, anything to make his wife feel better. He couldn't think of a thing. "I guess all that means is you did not get in touch with the people in Hong Kong."

Pilar turned to stare at her husband. "Seriously, Gabe, do you think that's where my head was? What I just told you was nothing compared to . . . to . . . what happened next."

"You know what, Pilar? Just relax. We're almost home. We'll talk there."

Pilar clamped her lips shut as she moved over to sit in the corner of her seat, up against the passenger-side door, and hugged herself. She closed her eyes, hoping what she'd just experienced was all a bad dream, and she'd wake up any moment. But it didn't work, and her thoughts turned wild and crazy as she struggled to come to terms with what she knew was going to happen. Someone had been in her car. She was certain of that. Zuma didn't trust her. The big question was why. She was almost positive she hadn't done anything out of the ordinary to raise his suspicions. Toby? The Hong Kong deal? With the way her luck was running, it was probably all of the above. Talk about being between a rock and a hard place.

"We're home," Gabe said as he slowed the car and drove down the ramp to the underground garage. He slid his parking key into the slot, and the bar went up, so slowly he wanted to get out and push it upward himself. The minute the bar was over the hood of the car, he stepped on the gas and barreled down the concourse to the ramp that would take him and his car to the second-floor parking level. He swerved in, tires screeching on the cement. He equated the sound to a jet crashing through the sound barrier. He knew it wasn't even close to that actual sound, but in his state of mind, that was exactly what it seemed like. He turned off the engine and turned to look at his wife.

"Can you make it to the elevator, or do I have to carry you?" His voice wasn't kind; nor was it unkind. It was simply flat. Pilar recognized it for what it was: no more games, no more excuses. "Fish or cut bait" was Gabe's favorite expression when things got to this point. And he was at that point right now.

"I can make it. I'm okay now, Gabe. Thanks. I was really rattled there for a while, but I'm steady now, and my head is clear. Right now, I think I'm more angry than anything else."

Then she was out of the car and racing across the parking garage to the elevator. Gabe had to run to catch up with her. Neither said a word until they were inside the condo with the doors locked behind them. Pilar headed straight for the kitchen, where she opened the cabinet for a bottle of whiskey. She splashed a glass half full, gulped it down, and looked at Gabe.

"Do you want a drink?" she asked.

"No. And you don't need any more, either. You need a clear head right now. We both do."

Pilar nodded. Her throat burned from the fiery liquid. She was no drinker, was almost what some people called a teetotaler. She looked at the flower arrangement on the table in the breakfast nook. This morning the flowers were vibrant and perky. Now they looked wilted and half dead. "You see, Gabe, the flowers are dying. That's why I don't like them. They die. They don't last. Everything dies."

"Nothing lasts forever, Pilar. You know that," Gabe said quietly. "Now would be a good time to finish your story."

"It is a story, isn't it? Our lives are a story. Maybe I should write a book when we retire. We might even make some money off it. Okay, these . . . three . . . goons—I don't know what else to call them—accosted me in the parking lot. All the lights were out. That should have warned me, but for some reason, it didn't. When I was ready to leave the first time, only the overhead lights above the doorway were on, and the lot was dark, so I went back inside for a flashlight. All I could find was a little penlight one of the kitchen staff gave me off his own key ring.

"They were on me before I had a clue anything was wrong. They were Zuma Delgado's people. They slapped me, and then one of them punched me in the stomach so hard that I threw up right there in the parking lot. They said Zuma wants to see me tomorrow, so that must mean he's here. Right here in D.C. They said there was no advertising. Zuma wants to see heavy advertising. That's it in a nutshell. They just melted into the darkness then, like they were never there, but their smell stayed behind. It made me gag. I admit it. I panicked. I didn't know what to do.

"Then I realized someone had been in my car. Nothing was taken, but my cell phone was at the bottom of my purse. Not in the pocket where I always keep it. My wallet and its contents were intact. The iPad was also out of place. The big thing is that when I pressed the remote to open the door, it didn't chirp. At the time, I was so rattled that I wasn't paying attention. I don't think it was Delgado's people who were in my car. I think it was someone else. I caught a whiff of a scent I have smelled before. Like aftershave. Subtle. I smelled it when I bent over the seat to gather up my stuff from the floor. At the time, it barely registered, but I remember it now. The guy, or whoever it was, must have bent over, and his face brushed across the seat. Faint scent, and an expensive one, but it was there."

"And this means what?" Gabe asked irritably. "Now you're saying there are two forces who are against us. Is that what you're saying?"

"Can you think of a better explanation? I told you that Toby is involved in all of this somehow, someway. And he is refusing to go to Hong Kong. That tells me a lot. What time is it, Gabe? We have to call Mr. Navarro or, at the very least, send him a text. I think you should do that since you spoke to him this morning."

"And tell him what?"

"Tell him we need more time. At least another couple of days. We need to fall back and regroup. Stall. Whatever you think will work, so we don't lose out on the deal."

Gabe dropped his head in his hands. He wished he was a kid again, so he could run and hide and cry his eyes out. Instead, he shook his head to clear his thoughts and stood up. "No. I'm done. If you're too blind to see what's going on, then there is nothing I can do to help you. I told you hundreds of times, and the last time was this morning, to be precise, that I have no intention of going to prison. Not even for you, Pilar. I'm going to get my passport out of the safe, along with some cash, and I'm going to do what we both said we were going to do when the time was right. This is *my* right time. You do what you want. I'm done. We worked this all out a thousand different times. Half is yours, and it's all set up. My half is mine to do with what I want."

"What! You're leaving me holding the bag! Oh, no. It doesn't work that way! We're partners."

"Tell that to your lawyer if you end up behind bars. I am leaving right now, and I am not coming back. Do what you want."

Pilar continued to screech at the top of her lungs as she pummeled Gabe's back. She followed him toward the safe built into the wall just off the living room. She tried to prevent him from opening the safe, but he shrugged her aside. He gathered up a small-caliber pistol that he had a license for, and a manila envelope with his name on it.

A similar envelope, bearing Pilar's name, along with a second small-caliber pistol, and a stack of mortgage papers remained inside the safe. He closed the door to the safe, spun the dial, and replaced the picture on the wall that covered the safe.

"You can't leave me like this! We're married! You said, 'Till death do us part.' You swore to me you meant it. I would never leave you. Never!" Pilar screamed.

Gabe felt his insides start to crumble. He closed his eyes for a moment as he willed himself to turn a deaf ear. "I'm going, Pilar. You have about ten minutes to decide if you're coming with me or not. That's how long it will take me to get to the garage level. I won't wait."

"What about your . . . your *stuff*?"

"Where I'm going, I won't need that *stuff*, as you put it."

Dumbfounded and frozen to the floor, Pilar watched her

husband walk out the door and out of her life. Ten minutes. All she had to do was open the safe, take her envelope and the gun, and she could make it to the garage in the allotted time if she wanted to. Her eyes glazed over. How could she do that?

Pilar Sanders realized she couldn't do that. It simply was not who she was.

Chapter Thirteen

"Hey, guys, listen to this," Dennis said, then read an e-mail from Toby. "That guy Snowden just showed up in the break room and told me he was assigning me a new babysitter. She's supposed to arrive when we do the first show. He sent Mia to follow Pilar Sanders to wherever she's going. What's going on? And don't tell me nothing, either."

"He sounds worried. I'm starting to think your friend is a bit of a prairie flower. In other words, a *wuss*," Maggie said tartly.

"No, he's not, and I resent your saying that, Maggie. Toby's just . . . What he is . . . is he's different. He'll come through. He isn't used to this sort of life, so cut him some slack. He'll be okay. So what do you want me to tell him?"

"The truth. Lay it out for him. He is, after all, the client," Ted said. "Tell him, if he can, to check in between sets. Tell him that as we get more info, we'll keep him in the loop."

Dennis did as instructed. "He said okay. He was ready to go onstage. Each show lasts forty minutes. We're good here."

Ted turned on his blinker and entered the *Post*'s parking garage. He headed toward a vintage, shiny, black Thunderbird, which was Zack's trademark. He tapped his horn and swerved into a parking space two car lengths down from the Thunderbird. "That's Zack's car. He refurbished it. Took him years. Okay, everyone out."

Espinosa was first to exit, then Maggie and finally Dennis. Ted grabbed his backpack and slung it over his shoulder. He loped his way over to where a short, chubby, bald man wearing bright red sneakers and a matching ball cap was getting out of the car. They clapped each other on the back and did a manly hug before introductions were made.

"I'm hungry," the human soccer ball said.

"What else is new? You're always hungry. But we are, too, so let's head to the cafeteria. We can have some privacy and eat at the same time," Ted said, leading the way across the parking garage to the elevator that would take them to the cafeteria.

The group made small talk, mostly about the blustery weather here in the District, as opposed to Miami's sunshine, and about having the right clothing.

Pleasing, pleasant aromas even at this time of night assailed the reporters as they walked down the line, picking and choosing a little of this, a lot of that, and finally huge slices of cherry pie with whipped cream on top.

Settled at one of the long cafeteria tables, Zack spoke first. "Even though it's not polite, I can talk and eat at the same time. Let's get to it, so I can catch a few z's. I'm about dead on my feet."

"Yeah, yeah, we eat and talk, too. Time is money. I'll bring you up to date on what we have, what we think, and what we actually know. It's the knowing part that has us stumped." Maggie quickly brought the round little reporter up to speed. They all watched as he shoveled food into his mouth, nodding from time to time at Maggie's information.

Zack popped a garlic twist into his mouth and savored

it for a moment, before he said, "You guys don't know the half of it. Listen up. Here goes. I've been on this guy for so long, it seems like forever. He's third in line to take over Guzmán's spot in California. That's Dito Chilo, who is now in prison, as you well know. I just happened to be in the same bodega as Zuma when the news that his boss had been captured came across. The owners had this small TV on the counter. I couldn't believe it.

"You should have seen the shock on Delgado's face. He was out of there so fast, his feet left skid marks. I'm pretty fast myself, so I was on him like white on rice. He didn't catch me, because he only had eyes for his phone. The two guys ahead of him to take over from Guzmán are serious badasses. He's no fool. He had his car loaded down with his cohorts in thirty minutes, and five minutes later, he was on I-Ninety-Five, headed this way. I didn't have time to get anything, so I'm here with just the clothes on my back and my backpack. We were more than halfway here when you called." Zack stopped talking long enough to drain his coffee cup.

Dennis sniffed at what he was hearing. "That car you drive is pretty distinctive, especially those wheels. Do you expect us to believe he didn't spot you? Where is he now?"

Zack attacked the rest of the food on his plate. "Right now I do not have a clue. I stayed with them while they checked into some sleazebag motel on the highway. I slipped the night clerk twenty bucks to tell me what room they were in and how long they were staying. I promised him a Benjamin, possibly two, if he would keep me apprised of their comings and goings. I'm not ashamed to admit that I have a pretty liberal expense account. At least you guys know where they are, so it's win-win. Excuse me. I need some more coffee." Zack left the table to get another cup of coffee.

The little group looked at each other. Dennis rolled his

eyes. "I'm not buying that those guys didn't pick up on a shiny, black, vintage Thunderbird. Those dudes live for cars and jewelry."

"I heard that," Zack said, sitting down at the table. "Here's the thing, kid. No one pays any attention to a little fat guy like me. I'm bald, I wear glasses, I'm round, and I do not look like I pose a threat of any kind. I look like this because I *want* to look like this. I have more bylines right now than you will have in your entire life. I got it going on."

"Yeah, but do you have a Pulitzer?" Dennis asked, tongue in cheek.

"Three, to be precise," Zack said as he forked half the slice of cherry pie that was on his plate into his mouth. "You have to get up real early to get ahead of me, kid."

"I'll remember that," Dennis said, his cheeks pink at the put-down.

"Okay. I think I'm done. What's our game plan here? I need to warn all of you about something. Zuma and his thugs carry some serious firepower. They like guns. I want to say one more thing here before we call it a night. In order for Zuma to step into the number one slot, he's got to pull off a big score. I mean *big*. I'm sure he's thinking that the Sanders woman is his answer. That has to be it, because there is no other reason for him to be here in the nation's capital that makes any kind of sense. Y'all chew on that, show me the way to my bed for the night, and tell me where to meet up with you in the morning, at which point we'll start to make things happen. Or not."

Back in the underground garage the group split up, with Ted offering to take Zack to the *Post*'s apartment. The plan was to meet up at Betty Lou's Café in the morning for breakfast.

Maggie, Espinosa, and Dennis trooped up the ramp and

walked around to the front of the building, where they hailed separate cabs to take each of them home.

"See you guys in the morning," Maggie said, climbing into the first cab. She leaned back, closed her eyes, and tried to come to terms with what was going on. She felt antsy, like she was missing something. She sighed. She hated when this happened, but, as always, she knew that whatever it was that she was either missing or not missing would reveal itself eventually. It was the word *eventually* that made her crazy.

Mia Grande was careful to stay two car lengths behind Pilar Sanders. She'd switched cars with Snowden since Pilar had seen the racy Ferrari and would recognize it in an instant. The pearl-white Stetson had stayed behind in the car. She was now wearing an Atlanta Braves baseball cap, her hair tucked up tight underneath. She clenched her teeth at the way the owner of the Supper Clubs was weaving in and out of traffic. She was hard-pressed to keep up with Pilar's erratic driving, but with skillful defensive driving, she was able to stay with the woman right up to the moment when she pulled into the parking lot of one of the Supper Clubs. *Now what?* she wondered.

Was Pilar going to get out of the car and go inside, or was she just going to sit in the parking lot? Mia was too far away to see what she was doing, even though the lot had at least a dozen weak, yellowish, overhead lights. Frustrated, she realized there was nothing she could do but wait it out. She hated this part of surveillance.

Ten minutes crawled by before the back door of the club opened to reveal a man standing silhouetted in the light from inside. A light tap of Pilar's horn told him where to go. He ran and climbed into the car. A few minutes later, both car doors opened, and the man and Pilar changed cars, with the man driving. Mia assumed the man was Pilar's husband, although she'd never seen him. Common sense said Pilar would run to him in her emotional state. They were probably going home. She shifted from PARK to DRIVE and waited until the car was at the exit before she drove off, careful to stay close but not too close.

Mia then did something Avery Snowden had warned her never to do. She sent a text while driving. Immediately after she hit SEND, a call came through. She listened as her boss berated her, then told her there was a small remote in the glove box that would allow her to trick the security gate at the complex where Pilar and Gabe Sanders lived. He then sent a text saying, **Do that again and you'll be on the unemployment line.**

Properly chastised, Mia kept her eyes on the road and the car she was following. She tried not to think about Snowden's comment. She was jolted from her thoughts when she saw the Sanderses' car's blinker start to flash. She slowed to a crawl to allow the car in front of her to speed past the Sanderses' car, then slowed even more as she let the Sanderses' car move forward behind the other car. A car cut in front of her, blew its horn, then sped past her, by which time the Sanderses' car had turned off the street. If nothing else, it gave Mia a few seconds' reprieve before she swiped Avery's remote to raise the black-and-white-striped bar blocking the entrance to the Sanderses' complex. She crawled forward, keeping her eyes on the Sanderses' car's red taillights. She parked in the first empty slot she saw, though she knew full well it belonged to one of the tenants. She cut her headlights, turned off the engine, and slowly eased her way out of the car. She could hear the sound of the other car's engine clearly. Three aisles over, four cars down. She quickly moved through the two aisles, crouching low. Her gut instinct told her the couple were totally unaware they were being followed. She felt safe.

Mia could see them now. They were talking, but the

words were indistinct. She inched closer and was able to see the man holding Pilar Sanders up. In the end, he simply picked her up and strode toward the elevator. The woman was crying. It didn't sound to Mia like the man was consoling her, just the opposite. She caught a glimpse of his face, and he looked . . . damn angry. *Hmmmm.*

Mia made her way back to her car and called Avery Snowden to report in. She ended with, "What do you want me to do?"

"We haven't been on this case long enough to have viable patterns when it comes to these two. What we do know from Toby is they never miss a night with the clubs. One or the other visits each one. Usually, they split it, with each one covering half. The evening is still young, so my thinking would be that the husband brought the wife home because she was traumatized, and he will be going back out. Follow him if he does. Give it an hour, worst case ninety minutes. If there's no movement, call me, and we'll decide what to do at that point.

"Oh, one other thing. It might be a good idea to leave the garage and find a parking spot on the street, in case he does leave. This time, he might be more aware if he sees a car following him out of the garage. Carnegie is a one-way street, so you're good in that respect. Double-park if you have to. Does that work for you?"

"It works for me, Mr. Snowden."

"Call me if anything happens. Call me even if nothing happens. We need to be on top of this all the way. Something here is not sitting right. According to Toby, that woman is rock hard, and it's the husband who is the pussycat."

"You're wondering if it's all an act, right? I wondered the same thing. I guess she was too unsteady to walk, because the husband carried her to the elevator. He did not look happy, I can tell you that. I got one real good quick look at him. Let's see how this all plays out and go from there." Mia blinked, then blinked again when there was no response other than the signal that the connection had ended.

Mia got out of the car and walked around to where Gabe Sanders had parked his car—a champagne Lexus sedan. She memorized the license-plate number and looked in all the windows, but there was nothing to see other than that Gabe Sanders kept a tidy car. There wasn't so much as a gum wrapper to be seen.

She walked back to her car, jotted down the number of the license plate in a little notebook she kept in her ruck-sack. Then she turned on the engine and backed out of the parking space she had borrowed, relieved that the tenant hadn't come to claim it. She headed up the ramp and out to the street. She hated the idea that she was going to have to drive around the block and back to get a parking spot, if one was available, but she did it, anyway, and was rewarded when a young bearded guy pulled his Jeep Cherokee out onto the road. She expertly backed in and settled down to wait. Her side-view mirror gave her a full view of the garage exit. She knew she could end up sitting here for a very long time.

Stakeouts were one of the few things she didn't like about the business she was in. But even with that, she couldn't imagine doing anything else with her life at this point in time.

Mia tried to clear her mind, to shelve Snowden's rebuke, a rebuke she deserved, but it still smarted. She turned her thoughts to Toby and found herself smiling. She liked the guy. Really liked him. "I won't let anything happen to you, I promise," she whispered to herself. The smile turned into a grin as she tried to picture Toby on the stage, gyrating in front of a bunch of lusting women trying to stuff bills into his G-string. The grin turned to outright laughter when she realized that tomorrow night she would be doing the same exact thing and probably enjoying every minute of it.

From that point on, Mia let her thoughts drift every which way as she waited for some sign of activity at the garage across the street. Twice she saw cars leave, but neither one belonged to the Sanderses. An hour into the stakeout, she debated all of a minute whether she should get out to stretch her legs. She decided against doing so almost immediately. Instead, she rolled down her window and the one on the passenger side. Cold, fresh air blew into the car. She inhaled deeply just as she saw a set of headlights at the top of the ramp. Bingo!

Mia had the engine turned on and the car in DRIVE in a nanosecond. She pulled out into traffic one car behind the Sanderses' car. She couldn't be sure, but she thought there was only one person in the car. The car in front of her was a VW Jetta and low to the ground, allowing her a full view of the Sanderses' car, but with the high headrests, she still couldn't tell for sure if another person was in the car. She thought not. She fished around on the passenger seat for her phone and hit the number one, which would automatically dial Avery Snowden.

"He's on the move. I'm a car length behind. I can't tell if there is anyone else in the car or not. Call me crazy, but I think this guy is headed to the airport."

"Where are you exactly?" Snowden asked.

Mia told him.

"Okay. I'm headed your way. Right now, I'm closer to the airport than you are, so I'll get there first. Watch for me. I'll take over, and you go home and get some rest. We'll talk in the morning."

"He's on his cell phone. I think he got a call, or he made one. My gut is telling me that once he identified the caller, he just tossed the phone on the seat. I'm thinking this guy is *upset*. Who is watching Ms. Sanders?"

"Consuela. Go home now, Mia," Snowden said, using her operative name to keep in character. Mia heard the rebuke that was still in his voice.

"I'm on my way. Good night, Mr. Snowden." There was no response, and she hadn't really expected one. Mia wished she could run and hide somewhere. There was nothing worse in her mind than to disappoint your boss, the man who signed your paycheck.

Avery Snowden grinned in the darkness. He knew the hard-ass reputation he had among his operatives.

When you broke the rules, you endangered your fellow operatives. All he allowed was one screwup, and after that, you were toast. Mia was one of his best, if not *the best*. He would hate to lose her, but he would cut her loose in a nanosecond if she failed to follow orders a second time. He sighed as he wondered what it would be like to retire to some private island where it was sunny all day, balmy at night, and a hundred people were waiting to shower you with whatever your heart desired. He let loose with a belly laugh that literally shook the car he was driving. He'd last in that kind of environment twenty-four hours. If that.

Retirement thoughts stayed with him as he finally picked up and followed Gabe Sanders. Mia was right; her instincts were spot on. Sanders was indeed headed for the airport. Retirement was for people who wanted to sit on their asses and eat themselves into oblivion while watching game shows on a giant television screen. He'd read that somewhere on the Internet. Well, that wasn't going to happen to him. His DNA wouldn't allow it.

Snowden slowed to follow Sanders to the long-term parking lot. Three cars were behind him. That was good. There would be a parade of travelers into the terminal, and he wouldn't look out of place. Luck was on his side, so much so that he was able to park two cars away from

Sanders. He had enough time to exit his car and walk around the two cars parked next to Sanders, allowing him to look into the car. The first thing he saw was the cell phone Mia said he'd tossed on the passenger seat. No one these days left their cell phone unattended. Parking lots, even those as well lit as this one was, were a haven for carjackers. His gut told him Sanders had left the phone behind on purpose. Why? Because once he got inside the airport, he'd buy a burner, charge it probably in the first-class lounge, and be good to go in thirty minutes.

Sanders leaving the cell phone behind told Snowden that the tiff, or whatever it was that he'd had with his wife, was dead serious. So serious it looked like it was a parting of the ways.

Surprisingly, the airport was crowded at this time of the evening, so it allowed Snowden to follow Sanders easily. He felt like patting himself on the back when the man entered a store and immediately headed to the back, where he picked up a burner phone for eighty-nine dollars. He headed straight to the cashier, where Snowden himself was in line with a copy of *Field & Stream* and a pack of cherry-flavored Life Savers in his hand. He paid for his purchases and walked out to the concourse, where he stood next to a plate-glass display case to fiddle with the wrapper on the Life Savers. He again felt like patting himself on the back when he followed Sanders to the private Delta lounge. He took a moment to wonder if Sanders had a destination in mind, since he hadn't bothered even to look at the wall-mounted arrivals and departures boards. He told himself Sanders would probably take whatever flight was leaving when he was ready, no matter where it was going.

He waited.

Forty-one minutes later, Sanders walked out of the lounge and headed straight for the Delta ticket counter. By quickening his stride, Snowden was able to jockey into position right behind him, close enough to hear that he was booking a flight to Atlanta and paying cash. He also heard the words "You're lucky, sir. This is the last available seat on tonight's flight."

Hearing that, Snowden spun on his heel and raced out of the airport. In the long-term parking lot, he sent off a text to Abner Tookus, asking him to hack into Delta's flight manifest to see where Sanders's ultimate destination was. Certainly not Atlanta. That was too close to home. His next text was to Tom Fazio, a retired Navy SEAL on his payroll who lived in Dunwoody, Georgia.

Be at the airport when he deplanes. Follow him. I don't care where he goes. Stay with him, and whatever you do, don't lose him. I'm going to upload a picture when I go off, so be aware. Also, be aware that once he deplanes, he might try to alter his appearance in small ways, just enough to confuse anyone he thinks might be watching and, of course, the cameras. He was carrying a small carry-on bag, so it is a distinct possibility. Check back with me as often as necessary.

Snowden fumbled around inside his backpack and withdrew a small remote, similar to the one Mia had taken from the glove box. He looked around, sauntered over to the champagne-colored Lexus, and pressed numbers until he heard a soft chirp. He opened the door, slid into the driver's seat, and immediately reached for the cell phone on the passenger seat. He deftly palmed it and exited as fast as he'd entered. He didn't lock the car, simply because he couldn't. The gizmo in his hand allowed only for breaking and entering, not for securing the safety of the vehicle.

Back in the racy Ferrari, Snowden powered up Sanders's phone. He scrolled through the texts first. *Whoa!* Sixteen from the little woman. Nine phone messages. The first ones were of the "poor me" variety and went from there to "How could you do this to me?" to "If I knew what a disloyal rat you were going to turn out to be, I never would have married you" to the final one, which pretty much said it all: "Go ahead, you chickenshit. Run like the rat you are. I don't need you. I never needed you. So there, Gabe Sanders! Oh, and one other thing. I never loved you. I just married you to get out of that stinking trailer in Alabama."

"Ouch!" Snowden said to the empty car. "That had to sting a bit. No wonder the guy left the phone on the seat."

Snowden pocketed the cell phone, slipped the Ferrari into gear, and drove out of the parking lot. His destination was the BOLO Building in Georgetown, so he could set everything up for the boys in the morning. He corrected that thought. The boys and one girl: Maggie Spritzer.

Chapter Fourteen

Pilar sat at the round table in the breakfast nook, her hands folded in front of her, her eyes on the wilted flowers in the center. She remembered how she used to sit like this when she was a little girl in school. She worked her fingers the way she had back then, kneading them, twisting them one way, then the other, cracking her knuckles simply to hear a sound in the quiet kitchen. A small sigh escaped her lips when she saw that the bloodred polish on her thumbnail was chipped. She wondered how and when that had happened. Then she looked down at her feet and noticed she was barefoot. She frowned as she struggled with her memory. What happened to her shoes? Did she lose them? Obviously, she had, since she wasn't wearing them. She made a mental note to file a complaint with her insurance company, since she'd paid twelve hundred dollars for the designer stilettos. Way too much money to throw away. She hated insurance companies for the way they bilked people. Finally, she would get something back on all those outrageous premiums she paid out year after year. She loved those shoes.

Pilar looked around, her eyes half glazed, her stomach in knots. Her gaze finally settled on the digital clock on the range. She grimaced. Gabe should be back by now. That was the precise moment when she realized Gabe *wasn't* coming back. Ever. She had just refused to believe it at first, so she had sat here and waited. And waited. And then waited some more.

She'd sent texts. She'd called. Not one had been answered. She vaguely remembered crying, pleading, then, to her horror, begging. When that didn't work, and there was no response, she'd gotten downright ugly, saying things she didn't mean. Nothing had worked. Gabe was gone, and she knew it. She had had her chance, and she'd blown it. Now she was alone, with the devil's own disciples hot on her trail.

Her eyes wandered to the digital clock again. So much time had gone by. It was almost midnight. The witching hour. What did that mean? Was something supposed to happen at the witching hour? Ha! It had already happened. Her husband was gone. He'd left her. Coward that he was. She'd called him that, too. And his response had been that he'd rather be a coward than a fool who was going to go to prison for the rest of his life. He'd stalked off, saying he was a smart coward. It was true, she supposed. The thought left her numb.

Pilar's chipped thumbnail drew her attention again. She wondered if she would be able to get an emergency appointment at the Nail Emporium in the morning. Maybe if she came up with some outrageous story, like she was going to a luncheon at the White House, they would take her in. What was one more lie on her chart of life?

Pilar had to literally pull her hands apart, because they were clenched so tight. Her knuckles ached. She had to do something before the witching hour struck. All manner of crazy thoughts swirled and raced through her brain. Maybe she should hide in the shower. Maybe she should crawl into bed, on Gabe's side, and pull the covers up and over her head. Or, maybe, she should just lie down and die right now. Or . . . She brightened momentarily at the thought of opening the safe, taking her envelope, and walking out of this place the way Gabe had.

But the greedy core of her being nixed that thought immediately. How could she leave the shelves of Chanel handbags behind? The rows and rows of Louboutin and Jimmy Choo shoes? No way could she do that. Nor could she leave all the Armani and Chanel suits, plus accessories, behind. She'd need a truck to take all her belongings. Only an idiot would leave everything behind. What, she wondered, was the difference between an idiot and a fool? She rather thought an idiot could be forgiven, but a fool deserved no mercy. A fool was stupid. An idiot was just plain dumb.

The phone on the table chirped that a call was coming in. Pilar grabbed it so fast it slid from her hand onto the table. At last Gabe was getting back to her. She cursed when she saw the name Bert Navarro. The man from Hong Kong. She'd totally forgotten about him. This was simply no time to make any kind of decision concerning Hong Kong. Morning would be soon enough. If the offer fell through, then it fell through and was not meant to be.

Pilar made her way to the bedroom and sat down on the edge of the king-size bed and howled her misery. When she couldn't cry any more, she got up and trudged into the bathroom, where she avoided looking into the mirror. She washed her face and brushed her teeth before she changed into her favorite granny flannel nightgown. Maybe she would sleep, and maybe she wouldn't. Either way, she'd get up early and make a plan.

And maybe when she woke up, Gabe would have had second thoughts about his departure and returned. *And cows leap over the moon*, was Pilar's last conscious thought before falling asleep, into dreams of moving to a palatial mansion somewhere and having a conveyor belt installed that would hold her many purses and beloved shoes. She'd read in one of the tabloids that the only person who had one was Candy Spelling in Hollywood. She remembered how envious she'd been when she read that article. If it was good enough for Spelling, then it was certainly good enough for her.

Pilar Sanders woke slowly. She was cold, and she was shivering, even wearing the flannel nightgown that Gabe always made fun of. She'd forgotten to turn on her bed warmer before she went to sleep, and she'd also kicked the covers off during her fitful sleep. She reached out, tapped the button that would turn on the heated mattress pad, something Gabe hated but he tolerated because the warmer had dual controls. He must have told her a thousand times if she'd put more meat on her bones, she wouldn't need a bed warmer or a granny flannel nightgown. As with most of his advice, she'd ignored it.

There was no reason, no hurry to get out of bed, so she curled into a ball and let her thoughts take her all over the place. Tentatively, she reached out to touch Gabe's pillow. A sob caught in her throat. A quick glance at the bedside clock on Gabe's side of the bed said it was a minute after seven o'clock. More proof that her husband wasn't coming back.

In all the years they'd been together, they had never spent a night apart. She thought about crying but decided not to because her eyes would get all puffy and red, and she'd have to use up an hour with a cucumber poultice to take away the swelling, and she wasn't in the mood. Crying definitely was not an option.

She wondered where Gabe was. How far he'd managed to travel in his hasty effort to get away from her and the situation they were in. If he'd made good connections and flown through the night, he was probably in the Caribbean by now. He'd lie low for a few days or maybe just one day before he headed to what was to be *their* final destination. Now, though, she had to wonder if that was where Gabe would really go. Maybe he'd changed course, gone somewhere different, so she couldn't find him. That would be so like Gabe. The final insult.

Pilar was warm now in her cocoon. So warm that she started to doze off. She snapped back to reality when she realized she had to get in touch with Bert Navarro. She might as well get up and start the day. Once she was showered and dressed, with a cup of coffee in hand, she could decide on what kinds of decisions had to be made now that she was going solo.

But the warmth of the cocoon sucked her closer to sleep. Pilar was drifting off to dreamland when she heard the doorbell chime. "Gabe!" He was home; he must have forgotten his key. Joy of joy, her husband was home. She bounded out of bed and ran to the front door, her arms outstretched to welcome her husband home. "Gabe!" she shouted as she threw open the door. Her eyes popped at the sight of the man standing in the middle of her doorway. She grew light-headed and had to reach for the door frame to hold herself upright. The man's name hissed through her teeth. "Mr. Delgado."

"Invite me in, Senora Sanders, or your neighbors might talk about your early morning visitor." The words were spoken softly but were full of menace. There was nothing for Pilar to do but step aside. "Coffee would be nice," Delgado said.

Gabe, Gabe, where are you? I really need you. I know he's not going to do anything to me right now. He needs me. How did he find me? Oh, God, what am I going to do?

Pilar walked out to the kitchen like a programmed robot. Her movements were jerky, awkward, uncontrolled. A voice inside her head warned her to listen and to keep quiet. She wished again for her husband's presence.

"Where is your husband, Senora Sanders?"

"He goes out early to get coffee and bagels and meets up with a few friends to catch up on things. He does it every day. He'll be back in about an hour," she lied. "Why?"

"I think it's time I met your partner, but I don't have that much extra time this morning, so meeting him will have to wait. You will give him my regards, of course."

"Of course," Pilar mumbled. Now that the coffeepot was filled, she didn't know what to do, so she just stood by the sink, her hands clasped in front of her. She gave no thought to her bed hair, her granny flannel nightgown, or her bare feet. All she wanted was for this man to get out of her kitchen. How did he find me? she thought.

"Sit down, Senora Sanders. You look so tense. Please, relax. I'm here to talk business, nothing more. Two business associates having an early morning cup of coffee. Isn't that how they do it here in the nation's capital? I myself prefer something a little more private due to the . . . delicate nature of our business, so that's why I came to your home. I also want to personally apologize for my colleagues' behavior last night. I'm told they frightened you. That was not my intention at all. They were simply told to give you a message. Good help is so hard to find these days, don't you agree?"

Pilar's head bobbed up and down. "Then why did they break into my car?" she asked in a squeaky whisper.

"I beg your pardon."

"Your people were the only ones there after they threatened me. They didn't take anything, but they went through my things. Somehow they managed to break into my car, and that could not have been easy."

Zuma Delgado punched in a set of numbers on his phone and rattled off a string of high-pitched, frantic-sounding Spanish. He listened intently, then rattled off another string of Spanish before hanging up. "My people did not break into your car. Trust me when I tell you this. They did tell me that they saw other activity in the parking lot, but it was so dark they couldn't tell who it was. And yes, my people are the ones who shot out the lights. It was necessary. They think several men and one woman were there, but that is pure conjecture on their part. They were going by the sounds of footfalls. I repeat, my men would *never* dare disobey my orders, much less lie to me. I want you to believe me."

For some ungodly reason, Pilar believed him implicitly. "Then someone besides you and your people is watching me," she said, a little more bravely this time. "For a long time now, I've felt like someone has been following me or watching me." She opted to keep her suspicions about Toby to herself for the time being.

"You should have apprised me of that immediately, but I'll deal with that later. For now, I see that the coffee is ready, so let's drink it and get down to business so I can make you a very wealthy woman."

Pilar liked the sound of that. Maybe the mansion and the conveyor belt would pop up in her future and not just in her dreams. Just the thought scared her to death.

Avery Snowden's phone rang just as he finished brushing his teeth. He clicked it on and heard Consuela's voice wishing him a good morning.

"Anything to report?"

"That's why I'm calling. A man resembling the picture of Zuma Delgado you showed all of us just showed up. A cleaned-up version. Casual attire, fresh haircut, clean shaven. Driving a Hertz rental car. When he saw that he couldn't get into the parking garage, he found a spot on the street easily enough, what with most of the people heading off to work. He walked right by me. It's him. He walked around to the front of the building. I could not follow him. It would have been too obvious. He hasn't returned, so I have to assume he gained admittance somehow and is right now visiting Ms. Sanders. What do you want me to do?"

"For starters, move out of the parking space you're in

and park someplace else. Get in the backseat, and don't let him see you when he comes out. I'll be there as soon as I can. If he leaves before I get there, follow him, text me, and I'll catch up and take over."

Avery was dressed and out of his apartment in less than fifteen minutes and driving to Pilar Sanders's condo building. He broke his own rules, sending text message after text message as he drove. First to Charles, to meet at the BOLO Building. He explained that he'd been there the night before and what had gone down. His next text was to Mia, followed by one to Consuela, who said Delgado was still in the condo. Mia was running in Rock Creek Park with Toby.

Avery slowed, turned on his blinker, and rounded the corner. He saw Consuela's parked car immediately. He expertly slid into a space two cars behind her just as his phone pinged that a text was coming in. Tom Fazio. He cursed when he read the message:

I lost him, Avery.

What happened? he typed back. Avery clenched his teeth so tight, he thought his jaw would crack.

We're here in the Bahamas, as I told you late last night. He checked into Emerald Bay and said he would be there for three days. He paid in cash. I took a room and paid the desk clerk to alert me if he left. Unfortunately, when the clerk took his break a few hours later, Sanders walked out, and he didn't see him. How he figured it out was when he went outside to smoke a cigarette around three this morning and saw that Sanders's car was missing. The place isn't that crowded right now, so the missing car was easy to spot. And because he wanted the second hundred I promised him, the guy went up to his room and checked it out. Nothing was touched or used. He's gone. He had only a small duffel—you know the

kind—shaving gear and a change of underwear fit in. I can attest to that myself.

What's your best guess? Off the island or he just relocated to another hotel, perhaps one that is less well known?

I think he's gone, as in gone. The clerk told me one of the other employees recognized Sanders. The reason he remembered him was that he was such a good tipper. He said he's been here many times, but always with his wife. The guy I talked to has only been at Emerald Bay for sixteen months. You aren't going to like this, but here goes. If the guy is right, then Sanders has his own plane, which he keeps hangared on the island. He's a pilot. I can't confirm any of this yet, but I'm on it, unless you have something else in mind. I'm also thinking a lot of preplanning went into this.

Do what you have to do, Tom.

Do I have your permission to lay out some serious cash?

Whatever it takes.

Well, for starters, I know this retired navy pilot who runs his own small airport in St. Louis. If anyone can dig up info on the guy's plane and the guy himself, it's Mike Bernstein. I might have to buy a plane. You okay with that?

You gonna just look at it or fly it?

You're a funny guy. Of course I can fly it. I spent a whole year with Bernstein before I decided I liked water better than flying through the air.

Go for it. Don't forget to check in.

Always, big guy. Always.

Avery sat for a moment after he powered down, wondering what Charles and the gang would think when a bill

came in for an airplane. He allowed a small gurgle of laughter to escape his lips. Charles would roll his eyes. Jack
would shrug, and the kid with the huge fortune would say,
"Whatever."

Avery sent off a text telling Consuela she could leave,
and he'd take over.

Through the rearview mirror, Avery could see Consuela
exit the backseat of her nondescript car, then text as she
walked around to the driver's side and climbed in.

The text was short and simple. **He's been in there one
hour and twelve minutes. His car is the beige Taurus. I have
the license-plate number. Call me if you need me.**

Avery looked around at all the black cars parked on the
street. Other than one white Range Rover, the Taurus was
easy to spot. It was four cars up, and it looked from where
the subject was parked that he was boxed in pretty good.
It would take him a good while to maneuver his way out,
which would give Snowden time to gun the engine and
pull out at almost the same moment Delgado did.

He settled down to wait, wishing he'd known this was
the way it was going to go down. Had he known, he would
have planted some listening devices inside the condo.

Avery leaned back, the picture of an aggravated husband waiting for his wife, who was taking way too long to
return to the car. His eyes never left the side-view mirror as
he waited.

One hour and thirty minutes and counting.

Chapter Fifteen

Jack Emery looked around the crowded conference room and wondered how things had gotten to where they were in such a short time. It looked to him as if everyone in the world had suddenly descended on the BOLO Building. If the occupants weren't talking, they were shouting, surly expressions on their faces. Cell phones were ringing right and left as the fax machine did double duty, spitting out sheet after sheet of paper.

As the chief greeter, Cyrus looked exhausted from running back and forth to the security door to usher in the different members who arrived within minutes of one another. He was now under the conference table, with a pile of chew bones for his efforts.

Jack felt a headache coming on. He whistled sharply, a high-pitched, keening sound that rewarded him with instant silence. "What the hell has gotten into you people? You all sound like a bunch of squabbling ten-year-olds. Everybody sit down, and let's call this meeting to order."

"I'll tell you what the hell is going on here, Jack. We are like a bunch of chickens running around, chasing our tail feathers in the process. Read my lips. We do not have a plan. This is what happens when everyone goes off in a different direction. It's obvious to me that a lot went down last night after we broke up and went home. We need to be brought up to date. Everyone is here. Let's just go around the table and have everyone provide whatever it is they have in the way of information. Then we can form a plan," Maggie said, a deep scowl on her face.

"Now, why didn't I think of that?" Charles said, tongue in cheek. "Avery, it's nice to see you so early in the morning. I got your text last evening and came in extra early to download everything on the flash drive that you left. Which, by the way, is pretty much nothing. Avery, you have the floor."

Snowden leaned forward as he quickly and concisely explained what had happened in the supper-club parking lot and how he'd had Mia tail Pilar and her husband back to their condo before he ended up following Gabe Sanders to the airport, where Sanders booked a flight to Atlanta.

He immediately followed up with the morning's events before anyone could start hammering him with questions. He ended up with, "Mia is now shadowing Zuma Delgado. I met her at a gas station, where we switched up vehicles. Toby is driving the Ferrari, and he followed me in this morning. Mia should be checking in shortly. Another operative, Hana, is on stakeout at Pilar Sanders's condo building. Since she hasn't checked in yet, I have to assume that Sanders is still inside. Doing what, aside from hitting the panic button, I have no clue.

"A friend who is a retired Navy SEAL and who I use from time to time on operations followed Gabe Sanders from Atlanta to the Bahamas. I'm sad to say he lost him. Sanders checked into the Emerald Bay and paid for three nights in cash. Thinking the guy was in for the night, my guy, Tom Fazio, hit the sheets for a few hours' sleep, but not before he greased the night guy's palm. When he went down to the lobby early, before the sun was even up, the night clerk told him that Sanders had left sometime during the night. He thinks it was probably around three in the morning, because that's when the clerk went outside to smoke a cigarette and saw that Sanders's rental car was gone.

"This guy has been on staff for only about sixteen months or so. When the day staff came on, they exchanged words, like what went on during the night hours, what the day staff should be aware of, that kind of thing. One of the day guys knows Sanders. Said he has been there quite a few times but always with his wife. Seems the Sanders guy is a good tipper, and that's why he remembers him. Plus, are you all ready for this? He owns a private plane, which he keeps hangared there at a private airport.

"Tom headed to the airport and found the rental car, but the plane was already gone. I hesitate to say the work crew are stupid people, but they are. Either that, or Sanders paid them to be stupid. No one knows anything. There's only one young kid there during the night, and he hasn't shaved yet. He didn't even know that Sanders's plane was missing until Tom pointed it out. Plus, all his files from the office are gone, so I have to assume Sanders took them with him.

"The kid had one thing going for him—he's good with numbers, and he knew the tail numbers of every plane hangared there. So that was all Tom had to go on. He contacted a navy pilot friend named Mike Bernstein, who owns a private airport in St. Louis, to see if he could track the plane down somehow. Tom is also a pilot. When he retired, he thought about going into business with Bernstein but decided he liked the water better than the air. I gave him the okay to buy a plane and go after the guy. The bill will show up on your statement soon. It's probably there by now. It was an executive decision, people," Snowden said tightly as he saw the expression on Jack's face. "Look at it this way. Annie can add it to her fleet. She's got a Gulfstream, a Little Bird, a Learjet, and now she will have a private two-seater. Tom said it was a steal at two hundred grand."

"I'm sure she'll be happy to hear that," Charles said, his face expressionless.

"Wait. There's more. Just as I arrived here, I got a text from Tom. The kid who is so good with numbers said the tail numbers on the Sanders plane are 216379Z. He said Bernstein couldn't track it, because Sanders didn't file a flight plan. But he did track a private plane with the tail number 246879Z. Tom said he thinks Sanders changed the numbers before he took off. He changed the one to a four and the three to an eight. Clever bastard. Looks like he's headed for Tahiti. Tom is on his way. I don't know exactly how he knows this, but if Tom said the guy is going to Tahiti, then that's where he's going."

"You have to admit that's pretty damn clever," Ted Robinson said. "I'm impressed. My guess would be this was part of a plan should things ever get dicey and they had to take it on the lam. What is not computing is why the wife stayed behind. Is she stupid, or is she fearless? Which is it?"

"Probably a little of both. So what does all that mean?" Dennis said.

"I think it means that Mr. and Ms. Sanders have parted ways. Either he left her holding the bag or she wouldn't go with him. I guess he's the smarter of the two. He's out from under whatever is going to go down. I don't think there's a thing we can do to him legally. We have no proof of anything. At least we know where he is, and Tom will sit on him until such time as we need him. Or not," Snowden said.

Abner raised his hand. "Their brokerage account just took a big hit! It's been cut in half. Guess the husband took his share. Looks like he wired his share to the Antilles. Having said that, Ms. Sanders will not be living in a tent anytime soon. The account is very robust. All the properties are mortgaged to the hilt. They took all the equity out of them about six months ago. Eighteen days ago, they took out the equity on the condo they live in. What that says to me is that the Sanderses planned to just walk away with the clothes on their backs and head to Tahiti. I think Ted is spot on. This was the plan. They could live like royalty until they die on the kind of money they had socked away."

"What made them split up?" Harry asked.

"My guess would be cold feet on the husband's part," Fergus said. "He figures he's out from under whatever it is that's going to happen, whatever had Delgado show up in the District, when he is strictly LA and Miami."

"He took his share and ran. I'll bet it has something to do with the Mr. December coming up. The one the wife was calling off, according to Toby. I think they both got spooked, the husband more than the wife. She elected to stay, for whatever reason. And the fact that Delgado showed up at the condo this morning can't be a coincidence," Jack said. "Maybe she had no other choice, or she was plain old gut scared."

"Can Mr. Sanders fly a small plane all the way to the South Pacific?" Dennis asked, his eyes wide as he tried to keep up with the steady flow of information emanating from those who had it.

"Of course he can. He just has to stop to refuel. Then again, maybe not. He might land somewhere, ditch the plane, and fly commercial. He's on the run, so there are no rules. When people do what these two were doing, there is no doubt in my mind they went all the way and got new identities. That is not hard to do on the black market if you have the money to pay for it," Jack Sparrow, who had managed to make it to the early morning meeting, the White House be damned, said thoughtfully.

"I've seen way too many cases like this to even try to figure it out. The guy has a plan, obviously one he thinks is foolproof. And it might well be. So far, he has pulled it off, so what does that tell you?" Sparrow asked.

"It might tell me my guy is screwed if he can't keep up with Sanders," Snowden said irritably.

"I don't think so. Sanders doesn't know he has a tail. The farther away he gets, the less vigilant he'll be. He might actually be feeling pretty good about now. There is every possibility he might stay a day or so at one of his stops before heading to his final destination. To unwind, so to speak. That's when your guy will catch up, and remember, he now has the new tail numbers to go by," Sparrow said.

"I agree with you, Director," Maggie said. "Now that we have Mr. Sanders nailed down, let's move on to Ms. Sanders."

"Bert just sent a text saying Ms. Sanders called him a short while ago and thanked him for his offer, but at this time she had to decline. Time-wise, the call was made right after Delgado left her apartment. We need to scratch that whole deal," Charles said.

Toby Mason raised his hand, holding his cell phone in the air. "I just got not one but two texts from Pilar Sanders. She said the Mr. December contest is back on but will be held in Miami. She said she turned down the China offer. She wants to talk to me before our first performance tonight. The second text said I should be on my toes tonight because there will be some special people in the audience, watching the performance, people who could really help all the dancers' careers, especially mine, since I will be Mr. December."

"I would assume the special people will be Delgado and his muscle," Maggie opined. "That means for sure you guys have to be there at a ringside table."

Espinosa grinned. "I have everything ready for the transformation. It's going to take every bit of the rest of the day
for me to turn you guys into ladies. I pulled out Alexis's
red bag of tricks before I left home this morning. The special latex is softening up as we speak. I'm excited. I told you
all before that Alexis practices on me, so I know exactly
what to do and how to do it. I even have your outfits all
picked out. Alexis really has good taste. We are going to
shine tonight, boys!"

Harry bolted out of his chair like he was fired from a
cannon. "You need to get unexcited right now. You are
not practicing on me for anything!" he bellowed.

The room went silent. Harry never, as in never, raised
his voice. He threatened only when he was prepared to follow through on the threat. And right now, he was so agi-
tated, his eyes were virtually round.

To everyone's surprise, Espinosa stood up to the number
one martial-arts expert in the world and said, "You need
to get over yourself, Harry. We're a team. As a team, we
work together, and tonight we have to work together. We
are operating under cover this evening, and as such, we
have to act and look the part. You are part of this team.
So, as part of the team, you are going to be transformed
just like the rest of us. So calm down and do not make me
go to a higher authority."

Everyone in the room knew who the higher authority
was—Yoko. They all waited to see Harry's reaction to Espinosa's threat.

To Jack, it seemed like all the oxygen in the room had
been sucked out. He felt the need for a breath of cold,
fresh air. Jack nudged Cyrus with his foot. A second later,
he was up and headed toward the kitchen and the door
that would take him and Cyrus out to the alley. Once outside, he leaned against the building, struggling to take
deep breaths. "Damn! And damn again!"

Cyrus whined at his feet, not understanding what was distressing his master.

"That was a first, Cyrus. Espinosa standing up to Harry. It wasn't just that he threatened Harry, which he did, but he also threatened with the big gun, meaning Yoko. Harry is totally fearless. We both know he can incapacitate a person with a Q-tip. The only person walking this earth whom Harry fears is Yoko. And I am not even sure it's fear, more like he doesn't ever want to disappoint his lotus flower. He's on board, so that's all that matters. I have to tell you, big guy, I was a little worried there for a few minutes. Harry can be a wild card sometimes."

Jack leaned down and scratched Cyrus in his sweet spot. "You don't really give a good rat's ass about this, do you? See, I was worried that you might decide to take matters into your own paws and go and bite his ass. Goddamn, now that's one hell of a scary thought. The only thing missing right now is Cooper."

Cyrus rubbed his snout up and down Jack's leg in a show of love.

"I know you live for the day you get to bite someone's ass. It's gonna happen, but I don't want it to be Harry's ass you bite. We're good on that, right?"

Cyrus barked once. He pushed his snout harder against Jack's leg. Time to go back inside.

"What would I do without you?" Jack said as he waited for the hydraulics to lock into place. Cyrus headed to the counter, where the treat bowl was. Jack fished out two. "That's your limit for the day. You hear me?" Cyrus wagged his tail. Translation: Understood. Sort of. Kind of.

"Can we get on with this meeting? I have to go to the White House again," Jack Sparrow said through clenched teeth. "POTUS is not letting up. He wants me to have no more contact with Annie and her project. I have to make a decision. It's no secret that POTUS and I do not see eye to eye on most things. I run a tight operation. I cleaned up the Bureau, and I'm proud of what we've accomplished, but I cannot stand by and let our veterans get hung out to dry due to incompetence at the VA and this administration's unwillingness to tackle the problem head-on.

"I wasn't kidding when I asked if there was a paying job with benefits in this organization. I'm prepared to tender my resignation today. And my top aides will walk away with me. Annie called me last night and offered me a job setting up additional clinics. She said I could hire as many people as I want, and the health benefits are sterling. She also said the public has been sending in donations to help. She told me to do whatever it takes to make it all work. I want to do that. Having said that, I don't want to leave you guys in the lurch. I can't guarantee who will replace me. With me gone, the FBI won't have your backs. Help me out here, boys, and Maggie."

Maggie was the first to speak. "That's a no-brainer, Director. You go with the veterans and Annie. We'll muddle through. We have the *Post* to watch our backs, and Abner at the CIA to do the same. We're good, so I think you should do what feels right. Let's take a vote. Raise your hand if you agree with me." Every hand shot into the air, even Toby Mason's.

Sparrow reached inside his jacket and withdrew a crisp white envelope. "My resignation. I came prepared, hoping you guys would see it my way. I'll be in touch."

A lot of handshaking and backslapping went down before the soon-to-be ex-director headed to the exit. Mindful that there were no more treats forthcoming for the day, Cyrus stayed under the table.

"I saw that coming," Ted said.

The others nodded.

"I see it as a good thing," Charles said. "Myra and Annie were discussing the proposal with Fergus and me last night. Annie put it this way. 'Setting up the clinics is the most rewarding thing Myra and I have ever done.' End of quote. And who can argue with logic like that? And they plan to keep on doing it. The *Post*, thanks to Maggie and the gang, is covering it all full bore. Director Sparrow assured me that he has contacts and sources he will put at our disposal if and when they are needed. I see this as a win-win for all concerned."

"I need to leave, too," Avery said. "I have a lot of irons in the fire that need tending."

"So where does all this leave us? What's our plan of attack? Shouldn't we be alerting the police, someone in authority, about Delgado's appearance?" Abner asked, his fingers at rest over the laptop keyboard.

"He hasn't done anything wrong that we can prove. He has every bit as much right to visit the nation's capital as any other tourist, and that's exactly what he would say if the police paid him a visit. You can't accuse unless you have proof. He went to visit Pilar Sanders. So what? He can say he was visiting a friend, and if she backs up his story, you have nothing. People from out of town visit other people all the time," Charles said.

"What about Pilar Sanders herself? How about one of us trying to talk to her? Like maybe tonight at the supper club or maybe even this afternoon, if she stays in. I'll gladly volunteer for the job," Maggie said. "If I tell her we know all about her husband and what he's doing, she might break down, and then we would really have something to go on."

"Won't work," Harry said. "We need to catch them in the act. We all need to wonder how he's going to get his product from California to Miami. Plus, that's a good six weeks away. It's not even the end of October, even though it feels like the middle of January."

"I have two of my people standing by, ready to spring into action the minute the Sanders woman leaves her condo. They'll plant bugs in every room. We already have a GPS tracker on her car. I can have a bug installed under her dashboard in ten minutes, so if she talks or makes calls on her cell while in the car, we can pick it up in an instant. Get in touch if you need me," Snowden said from his position in the open doorway.

Once again, mindful that his treat intake was all used up, Cyrus barked his good-bye but didn't bother escorting Snowden to the door.

"Any other loose ends before we head out with Espinosa?" Jack asked.

"What do you want us to do in regard to Zack, my colleague, who got into town last night?" Ted asked.

"I'd say give him free rein to do whatever he thinks he can do. He knows where Delgado is. Just hope he doesn't get in Snowden's way or interfere with his operatives. Avery can get a little pissy when you step on his turf," Jack said as he gathered up his files and papers to stuff into his briefcase.

"Do we want him to show up tonight at the supper club?" Dennis asked.

"Why not? Another set of eyes certainly can't hurt," Jack said.

"What about me?" Abner asked as he, too, closed his computer and stuffed it into his rucksack. "Do you want me at the supper club tonight as I am, a guy? Or do you want me to continue to track the finances for more hidden monies? I have a text from Philonias, asking me to call him. I told him to try to track Delgado and the drug monies. He'll find out who the money managers are one way or the other. Finding laundered money is the guy's specialty. I'm thinking we're going to want to confiscate those funds to pay off that plane Snowden's friend bought, with maybe a little bit left over."

That brought a laugh from everyone in the room.

"Meet us at the supper club around seven thirty. We have a reserved table, thanks to Toby. Mia will be front and center, but on her own. We'll all be there, so don't act surprised. Just find us and join us for dinner. Snowden's people will be watching Pilar and Delgado and his people," Jack said. "And, Ted, I don't think I'd tip off your colleague Zack just yet. If he shows up, it's just one more set of eyes. Let's just hope none of us give off bad vibes and spook them."

Espinosa led the parade out to the exit door. He called over his shoulder to Jack and Harry, who would be the last to leave after they locked things down tight. "You all know where Alexis and I live. Let's not dawdle, boys. This is not a Mickey Mouse operation I'm going to be conducting, but works of art on all of you."

Jack thought Harry paled under his tawny skin at Espinosa's words, and grinned.

"What about me? Where do you want me to go?" Toby asked.

"How about you and I go out to lunch?" Maggie said. "Then you can go back to your house and take a nap while I check in at the paper to make sure I still have a job."

"Works for me," Jack said as he turned off the kitchen light.

"Ah, Jack," Harry whispered in his ear. "Do you really think I'll turn out looking . . . you know . . . okay?"

Jack had to struggle not to laugh out loud. Somehow, he managed to lock his eyes on Harry and, with a straight face, said, "I think you will end up looking gorgeous. Take that to the bank."

Cyrus barked.

"See? Even Cyrus agrees."

The color came back into Harry's face, and he actually grinned. "Espinosa is going to take pictures, isn't he?"

This time Jack did laugh out loud. "Count on it!"

Chapter Sixteen

Pilar Sanders sat in the breakfast nook, her eyes on the wilted flowers. She felt like she was carved in stone and cemented to the tile floor. She heard Zuma Delgado say, "Don't get up. I can find my way out." She nodded, because she couldn't have moved if she wanted to. She blinked when she noticed him appear back in the doorway. "Make sure your husband is at the club this evening, Senora Sanders. There are some things I want to discuss with him."

This time, Pilar didn't acknowledge the words in any way. *Just go. Just get out of my house. Go outside and get yourself killed in traffic. Just get out of my house, and don't ever come back.*

Pilar had no idea how long she sat at the table. She'd heard the door close. Thank God it was self-locking and Delgado couldn't get back in. *Oh, Gabe, you were so right. Why didn't I listen to you? Where are you? Please call me. Please.*

She thought her prayers were answered a moment later, when her cell phone chirped. She looked down to see who the caller was—Carlie Fisher, her business manager. Her disappointment was so raw, she started to cry. She needed to get it through her head that Gabe was not coming back. Wings sprouted on her feet at the realization. She ran to the wall safe and removed the picture that covered it. What was the combination? She couldn't remember. Gabe was always the one who opened the safe. He'd said he wrote it down somewhere, but where? Damn it. Where was it? Then she remembered he'd used a permanent marker and scribbled the numbers on the ice machine in the refrigerator, saying, "See? It looks like a serial number."

Pilar ran back to the kitchen and opened the freezer of the Sub-Zero machine, and there it was, just like Gabe had said: eighty-six, forty-four, nineteen. Four right, three left, and two right, and the door should open. She ran back to the safe, but it took her three tries before the mechanism clicked and the heavy door unlocked. She stared into the depths, at the packet that had her name on it. She bit down on her lower lip. *Take it out. And do what? Leave it in. And then what happens?* If she took it out, got dressed like she did every day, and carried an extra-big purse so the packet wouldn't be visible, she could head to the airport and take the next flight that she could get a seat on.

But what if she was followed? What if she was stopped, and they, whoever they were, took the packet? What if they killed her? Gabe would never know. They'd throw her body in the Potomac, and when they found her, no one would be able to recognize her bloated body. She'd never been fingerprinted, so unless they knew which dentist she went to, she'd go down as a Jane Doe. She shuddered at the thought. More tears flooded her eyes. She gritted her teeth as her arm shot forward, only to be withdrawn a moment later. Who was she kidding? She stared at the inside of the safe for a full minute before she slammed the heavy door shut. She replaced the painting, careful to make sure it was straight and not listing to the side, because the frame was so heavy. She walked into the bedroom.

No way out. Good-bye, conveyor belt. Good-bye, Gabe. Hello, federal prison!

Like hell! There was a solution to everything. You simply had to search for it. Well, she was good at that. One way or another, she'd find a way out of the mess she had gotten herself into. If Lady Luck was on her side, she just might be able to find a way to join her husband. But right now, she needed to get grounded, to focus, to make a plan. And she needed to toughen up. From this point on, she needed to stop showing fear where Delgado was concerned. She needed to stand up to him, to make her own threats. He needed her. More than she needed him.

One of Gabe's favorite sayings was, "You can't fix stupid." "Well, we'll just see about that!" Pilar shouted to the empty bedroom.

Thirty minutes later, Pilar was back in the kitchen. It struck her as funny that in the past few days she'd spent more time in the kitchen than she had in all the years she'd lived in this condo. The first thing she did was toss out the wilted flowers, vase and all. Then she made fresh coffee. The next thing she did was to open her laptop to her business program. She sent off a detailed e-mail to Carlie Fisher, outlining everything she needed done by the close of business today. She then e-mailed all the vendors she'd dealt with over the years in Los Angeles, explaining that due to circumstances beyond her control, she would not be holding the Mr. December contest in LA this year but in Miami instead.

Next, she connected with the vendors in Miami, from whom she received a robust response. She received the same sort of response from the pageant officials in the Florida city when she explained she was moving this year's Mr. December contest to their city and asked for special consideration due to short notice. Then she went out on a limb and promised sold-out performances, with a bonus payment if that didn't happen.

Right now, right this second, she would and could lie

through her teeth, do or say anything, to try to get out from under. What did she care what happened? If she played her cards right, she wouldn't be anywhere near Miami and the planned contest for opening night. If she managed to play her cards the way she hoped to, she'd be halfway around the world, and Delgado and his people would be in prison.

She thought about the downside. No conveyor belt, no big cash win. She could live with that. She had no other options if she wanted to get out from under. The only thing that bothered her was leaving all her bags, shoes, and designer outfits behind. Then again, maybe not. With a few cards left in the deck to play, she might be able to unload it all on one of those secondhand shops. She'd looked into it once. She could get fifty cents on the dollar, which was better than nothing, if she just walked out and left it all behind. With six weeks to go to the pageant, she could take all her jewelry to one of the best jewelers and see what they'd give her. A tidy sum, to be sure. Gabe would be so proud of her for finally coming to her senses. If he ever found out.

Feeling better by the moment, Pilar sent off a text to Toby Mason, explaining once again that the China deal was off, that important people would be watching the performance tonight, and that he needed to be in top form.

Get a haircut, she texted. **Get highlights. Use extra bronzing lotion. I'll meet with you to discuss Mr. December in Miami.**

Pilar then scrolled through the directory on her phone for the top jewelers and started calling to see who expressed the most interest and was willing to come to the apartment to view the pieces she was willing to sell. She finally found a jeweler in Georgetown, who said he would be happy to meet with her at one o'clock. Pilar agreed to the time and went on to the consignment shops that handled movie-star apparel turned in by politicians' wives and other high-income Washingtonians. Even Jackie Kennedy had used their services back in the day. They had pamphlets that said the former first lady would wear something once, then turn it in for 80 percent of what she'd paid for it so she would not be photographed wearing the same thing twice. It took only an hour's worth of calls before she found the person she wanted, who promised to come by to view the items at four o'clock.

Satisfied that she was now on a roll, Pilar emptied her coffee cup and prepared a fresh pot. She felt calm now, despite her caffeine intake. She felt like she was truly ready to take on Zuma Delgado. If Gabe were here, what would he do? He'd smoke a cigarette. Pilar was up and rummaging in the kitchen drawers, where he always kept a spare pack in case he had a craving. She finally found the ugly things in the back of the utility drawer. She wasn't a smoker, but she had smoked once in a while with Gabe when they were celebrating something or other. She fired up a cigarette, propped her feet up on Gabe's chair, and puffed away as she sipped at her coffee. She let her mind roam. Did she forget anything? Something small she'd overlooked? She couldn't think of a thing.

One hundred pounds of pure uncut cocaine with a street value of five million dollars. Cut the cocaine, and the value jumped to ten million dollars, depending on the purity of the cocaine. With five shows, that meant Delgado would be raking in fifty million dollars, possibly more for the gig in Miami. And for her help, Delgado had promised her ten million dollars. She'd almost choked when she'd heard the numbers he rattled off so nonchalantly. Ten million dollars, and all she had to do was wrap ten packages with huge red bows. The ten wrapped packages would then be used as the prizes at the end of each show. When the winning contestant was handed one of the gift-wrapped packages, which he, in turn, handed off to Pilar, to be replaced with a similar package that held a thousand-dollar laptop computer and a plaque. Easy-peasy.

Gabe was so right; you can't fix stupid.

Pilar finished her cigarette and lit up a second one. She thought maybe she should eat something, but there was nothing in the apartment to eat. She debated calling one of the restaurants nearby to order a salad and sandwich. If she didn't eat something now, it would be late tonight before she would be able to sit down to a meal. Gabe's words rang in her ears. If you don't eat breakfast, then you must eat lunch, and you must consume at least two bottles of water a day. That was fine and well and good when Gabe was around to make sure it happened, but now that she was on her own, it didn't seem all that easy.

Good Lord, when had she turned into such a slug? Before she could dwell on her own question, she flicked on her phone for the app that would take her to Boxcar Betty's, where she ordered a ham and cheese on rye with two pickles and a side order of potato salad. She was given the amount, plus delivery, plus tip. She shrugged. Twenty-five dollars was a bit much, she thought. Obviously, Gabe hadn't thought so. She shrugged. When in Rome . . .

The rest of the morning was spent on the phone with Carlie Fisher as they fine-tuned the Miami schedule. The first radio ads would start tomorrow morning and run all day, on and off. The first TV commercial in both English and Spanish would air in Miami tonight, at nine o'clock. That should satisfy Delgado that she was on his side. *Just go through the motions, just bide your time, keep the sleazebag happy, and you might, just might, walk away from this in one piece.* How she had thought otherwise still baffled her. All it took was sitting across from him, staring into his cold, dead-looking eyes. She had to get away as soon as possible.

For one wild, crazy moment, Pilar gave some thought to

going to the feds and confessing and asking for immunity. She negated that thought as soon as it entered her head. If she did that, she was on their radar screen forever.

In a rare moment of honesty, Pilar admitted to herself that she was to blame for her current situation, because of her greed. She'd gotten her and Gabe into this, and now it was up to her to get herself out of the mess she'd created. In another rare moment of honesty, she was glad that Gabe had gotten away. He'd just done what she asked because he loved her heart and soul, and she'd taken advantage of his love. There was no way she could blame him for her current circumstances. Her eyes burned with guilt. *Wherever you are, Gabe, I hope that you're safe and happy and that you don't forget me. Please, don't ever forget me.*

Whatever was going to happen going forward would be what it would be. Pilar sighed as she settled down to wait for her lunch to be delivered. She had ninety minutes to eat and get ready for the day and for the jewelry man to arrive. It would take her only five minutes to get her jewelry ready, since she kept it all in one place. Inside a box of maxi pads that had been opened, then sealed at the bottom. She kept the box in the master-bath linen closet. Gabe had said she was crazy, but she had ignored him. Going in and out of the safe twice a day was a pain in the neck. She'd won her argument by saying, "Who would steal a box of sanitary napkins, since most burglaries are committed by men?" She'd finally worn him down, and he'd never said another word about her makeshift *jewelry safe.*

Pilar's food arrived. She handed over the twenty-five dollars and sat down to eat. She wolfed it all down within ten minutes. She'd never eaten so fast in her whole life, but suddenly she was starved, because she hadn't eaten in over twenty-four hours.

Her stomach full, she cleared the table. She decided to

finish the coffee and have another one of Gabe's cigarettes. In some cockamamy way, smoking her husband's cigarettes made her feel closer to him.

The one last cigarette turned into three more before the jeweler arrived right on time. Pilar had transferred the sparkling gems to a velvet-lined jewelry box Gabe had given her years ago but in which she kept only her high-end costume jewelry.

The jeweler, a fussy little man named Madison Miller, checked each piece of jewelry with a jeweler's glass, scribbled notes, and thumbed through a catalog he'd brought with him. Pilar thought about smoking another cigarette to while away the time while the jeweler decided what to pay her, but decided against it.

"If you don't mind my asking, Ms. Sanders, why are you selling all these lovely pieces of jewelry?"

Pilar knew the question would come up and had the lie all ready. "My husband is being transferred to Paris. I don't want the hassle of trying to take the jewels with me. I can always buy more. I find, though, the older I get, the less I care about such things. I suppose you find that hard to believe or understand."

"Not at all. I see it all the time. I can give you two-point-four million dollars for the lot. I truly do not think you could get more anyplace else, but you are welcome to try. That is my offer."

Pilar didn't see any point to haggling. "I think that's fair. Are you prepared to take the jewelry now?"

"Yes, and I came with a check. You might want to call your insurance company when I leave to cancel your insurance policy."

Pilar almost laughed. She had never insured her jewelry, to Gabe's chagrin. She simply did not believe in insurance. "Yes, of course. I have it on my list of things to do."

Her jewelry in the fussy little man's briefcase, the check

on the table, Pilar walked him to the door, where they shook hands.

"Enjoy your time abroad, Ms. Sanders."

"I will, and thank you."

Back in the kitchen, Pilar looked at the check and didn't feel a thing. It could have been for ten dollars, and she would have felt the same way. She didn't even care that she had just sold off her beautiful jewelry, all gifts from Gabe. She had kept a diamond cuff bracelet that Gabe had given her for their twentieth anniversary and a diamond choker he'd given her on their twenty-fifth anniversary because she planned on wearing both when she left here for good, along with her five-carat diamond earrings and, of course, her diamond wedding band and engagement ring. If anyone questioned the value, she'd just shrug and say it was high-end costume jewelry.

Pilar sat back down at the table. She missed the ratty flowers. How was that possible? she wondered. She sighed as she filled out a deposit ticket and placed the check in an envelope that went into a FedEx envelope, which she would drop in the box in the lobby when she left for the evening, for delivery to her brokerage account. She took a moment to wonder if she was being too quick. Maybe the people from the consignment shop would pay her today. No, they wouldn't pay until they could cart out her belongings. Tomorrow, probably, but today they would settle on a price.

What to do with the remaining hours until they arrived? She could cry, she could think about Gabe, she could feel sorry for herself, or she could do something constructive. She eyed the nearly half-empty package of cigarettes on the table; then her gaze went to the coffeepot. *Why the hell not? Smoke and drink coffee. It could be worse.* She could be smoking pot and drinking booze. She realized that before she left for the evening, she would have to take another shower and wash her hair again so she didn't smell like a chimney stack. She crossed her fingers that she wouldn't get addicted to cigarettes.

TV! That was what she could do; she could watch the news. She couldn't remember the last time she'd done that. *Game shows? Soap operas? The shoppers' channel? Hard news on the cable channel? Cartoons?*

In the end Pilar sat back in the chair, propped up her feet on Gabe's chair, and stared off into space as she puffed on what was left of his cigarettes and swilled more coffee.

Chapter Seventeen

While Pilar Sanders schemed and plotted, Jack Emery and the gang said good-bye to Maggie and Toby, then piled into the *Post* van and headed for Connecticut Avenue, where Joseph Espinosa and Alexis Thorne lived. Ted, who was driving the van, took the corner literally on two wheels as he headed down the long driveway that led to Alexis's studio at the back end of the property, where their transformation was to take place.

The mood was sullen, cranky, just downright short of hostile, with only Espinosa being upbeat and cheerful.

"I didn't know you guys had a studio," Jack said tightly as he eyed Harry out of the corner of his eye. "Did you guys buy this property together, or does it belong to Alexis? You never said. What I mean is, you guys aren't married but are commingling."

"I didn't know I was supposed to report in to you, Jack. But no offense taken," Espinosa said. "Yes, we bought it together. We did all the legal work to protect ourselves in case our relationship goes south. You know, like Bert and Kathryn's. With our romantic track record of on again, off again, it seemed like the wise thing to do. At least for the time being. It may change in time, and then again, it may not. We live in what we call the big house, and it's a work in progress. What that means is we work on it weekends, painting, repairing, laying carpet, stripping wallpaper, that kind of thing. I take classes at night at Home Depot and Lowe's so I don't screw up."

He went on. "Originally, we were going to rent out the studio to help with the mortgage payment, but Alexis wanted a studio. She likes to volunteer for several little theater groups, and this was perfect for all of that. As I told you, she practices on me, and I've paid close attention. I can transform anyone into someone so they are totally unrecognizable. Okay, everyone out!"

Harry rolled his eyes for Jack's benefit.

Dennis hopped out and looked around. "I like this. I can see why Alexis would want this place as a studio. Who did the pumpkins and straw? Good eye. It looks . . . you know, down home, homey. Halloweenish."

Espinosa flushed. "I did it as a surprise for Alexis last weekend. She loved it. Okay, come on in. I'll turn up the heat and put the coffee on."

"How big is this studio?" Fergus asked.

"A little shy of three thousand square feet. It doesn't look that big from the front, because it goes all the way to the back end of the property. It's really nice here in the spring and summer, with the big trees. Make yourself at home, guys, while I get things set up. Coffee first. Since we missed lunch, we can order in. There are magnets for local eateries with phone numbers on them on the mini-fridge. Take your pick."

The boys did exactly that as Espinosa banged around in the tiny kitchen. They marveled at the plaques attached to each door.

"Wig room. Wow! Look at all those wigs," Dennis said as he pointed to shelves that lined three walls of the room, which was full of every imaginable kind of wig, with the third wall totally mirrored and with a long counter running underneath it. Three beautician's chairs faced the mirrors. All manner of combs and brushes were lined up on the counter.

The next room was the makeup room, where the gang stood staring at the array of pots, jars, and bottles of *stuff* that women needed to be beautiful. There were sponges and cleansing pots, all with delicate little signs attached. One wall held different-colored nail polishes with matching lipsticks. Underneath those shelves were perfumes and lotions, along with bronzing tubes of all sizes and shapes. The third shelf was dedicated to eye treatments. Boxes and boxes of false eyelashes were stacked one on top of the other. The last section of the wall was dedicated to a Peg-Board, where jewelry winked and sparkled under the bright lights. The room literally glittered. The men looked around, marveling at the shiny labels and, in some cases, instructions covered in plastic and attached to a colorful string.

"There's more product here than in a department store," Charles said as he tried to take it all in. He eyed the three beautician's chairs as he tried to calculate the cost just as Espinosa entered the room.

"What do you think?" their host asked, pride ringing in his voice.

"I think it's safe to say we're all very impressed. It must have cost a fortune to outfit all of this," Jack said, waving his arms around.

Espinosa burst out laughing. "Remember that bonus the firm paid out from the class-action suit we kind of helped the girls with several years ago? Alexis used every cent of it to set this up. Each time she gets a bonus, she adds to the studio. You haven't even seen the wardrobe room. That alone takes up the whole back end of the studio," Espinosa said, much like a new father extolling his firstborn's attributes. "By the way, what did you all decide for lunch? The coffee is ready. Who wants to go first?" Espinosa asked, rubbing his hands gleefully as he eyed the unwilling volunteers.

"We didn't. What will it be, folks?" Charles asked.

A heated discussion followed, with the end result being Chinese. Dennis ordered online. They then followed his lead and headed to the kitchen for coffee.

"So who is going first?" Espinosa asked again.

Charles waved his arms about. "Since Fergus and I are just here for moral support, take your pick." He took a sip of the scalding brew in his cup and winced.

"Where did you get an idea like that, Charles? You and Fergus are not sitting this one out. You are going to be transformed just like the rest of us. This is a team effort and project," Espinosa said. "Since you guys are so fearless . . . not, let's go with Dennis as the first transformee. Now, there is something you all need to know. This works in stages. First, the latex on each of you, and then we go to the next step. Total makeup time is a little over three hours. It's like an assembly line, and you cannot hurry the process. I'll also be working on myself in between. We are going to be taking it right down to the wire. Let's go to the studio, Dennis."

Dennis hopped to it, grinning from ear to ear.

"Who do you want to look like, kid?" Espinosa asked.

"Jennifer Aniston," Dennis shot back smartly. "I saw a wig back there that I absolutely fell in love with." He clapped Espinosa on the back to show he was going with the flow by being a good sport and enjoying every minute of it.

"Good choice, kid, really good choice. When I'm done with you, Aniston's husband will think he married twins if he gets a gander at you and my handiwork."

Back in the kitchen, the gang sputtered and mumbled to themselves at what they had agreed to do.

"Okay, okay," Jack said after whistling sharply for their

attention. "We agreed to do this, so let's stop complaining. Shame on you, Charles, for thinking you and Fergus could skip out on us. We're supposed to be a working team, so either join up or go back to the farm. What's it going to be, Charles?"

"Of course, you're right. I don't know what I was thinking. My apologies, mates. I'm with the team one hundred percent, and I think I speak for Fergus, as well."

Fergus nodded.

"I wonder how Maggie is doing," Ted muttered to no one in particular. "Is anyone but me surprised that she isn't here to oversee us?"

"I, for one, am not the least bit surprised. We all know Maggie marches to her own drummer," Abner said. "I overheard her talking earlier to either Annie or Myra. I'm not sure which one, since I heard only Maggie's end of the conversation. She's supposed to meet up with them after she tucks Toby in for the afternoon. I can't be sure, but I think I heard her say something about Jack Sparrow joining them."

"That's interesting. I wonder why she didn't share that with us. By the way, has your guy Zack checked in yet today? We need to know what he's up to. I'd hate to be blindsided this evening, when we're at the Supper Club," Jack said.

"I'm texting him now, but that doesn't mean he's going to get back to us right away. He's probably tailing Delgado or his goons somewhere. Anything from Avery on the Sanders woman?" Ted said.

"The Sanders woman is still in her condo. Avery has his people spread all over. Oh, I spoke too soon. I have an incoming text from him. Oh, dear, this is not good. Oh my! This is definitely not good," Charles said.

"For God's sake, what is he saying?" Jack said, exploding.

Charles looked up from the text he was reading and

looked at the gang. "Avery isn't sure, because he said Tom Fazio isn't sure, but they think Gabriel Sanders's plane went down over the Pacific. Right now, Mr. Fazio is in Bora-Bora. Search parties are active."

"How does he know this? It's not like he was tailing the guy in a car. How do you tail an airplane?" Harry asked.

" 'A distress call,' is all Avery is saying. Mayday call. Perhaps Mr. Fazio heard it himself. He said he would get back to me. He did ask what we want Mr. Fazio to do. Stay or return."

"I'm not buying that," Jack said, his eyes narrowed to slits. "This is just too damn convenient, to my way of thinking. If the guy had a plan, he could have planned for this, had a built-in extraction. All he had to do was call ahead to an accomplice. I bet if we wanted to spend the time and effort backtracking this guy, we'd find out he took classes in jumping out of airplanes. I'm not saying I'm right, but give some thought to the possibility that I'm on the money.

"Think about it. Obviously, Tahiti was Sanders's final destination. Or he wants anyone who gets suspicious to think that. His plane goes down just as he's about to reach his final destination. Nah, it's way too pat. We don't know for sure if he has false identities, but I think it's a good bet he does. A good scenario is that his accomplice takes him to one of the islands, like Taha'a, Huahine, or Mo'orea, where he lies low until he thinks it's safe to surface. I read somewhere in his dossier that Gabriel Sanders speaks fluent French, because he had a French mother and learned the language from the time he was a baby. He can blend right in. And the reason I know about the islands around Tahiti is that Nikki and I celebrated our tenth wedding anniversary there. Just for the record, it's beautiful, peaceful, and the people are just plain nice.

"The guy really did think this through, and if I'm right,

he covered all his bases to be sure. Since he has no idea we're onto him, he probably thinks he's safe. At least for now. For all we know, this might *not* be the end of his journey. Without expert surveillance around the clock, I don't see how Avery's man can nail him. And with a new identity, plus a totally new look, I'd say it's almost impossible, especially if he's lying low in some little village, soaking up coconut milk and lazing around on the beach. His skin will be bronzed, his hair bleached, and he will either shed weight or put on more to further disguise himself. In short, gentlemen, it's a crapshoot. Either we call Avery's man back or put him on twenty-four-hour surveillance, which means he will have to hire locals, and we all know how that works out in the end."

Ted had been busy typing away on his iPad. "Tahiti has a population of only one hundred twenty-seven thousand people. It's in the Society Islands. Roughly eighty-three percent of the population is Polynesian. Beautiful place. Modern. Lots of artisans there selling shells, flower leis, and shell necklaces. Hell, the guy could pose as one of those vendors, as tourists abound in that neck of the woods. He could stay anonymous forever. Personally, I can't think of a better place to go undercover and hide out for the rest of your life. And he obviously has the money to do it."

"I think we should let this all sit for a bit and not rush into any kind of decision where Mr. Sanders is concerned. For all we know, he could be a thousand miles away from Tahiti, and we'd never know it, and the plane crash is just another ploy or delaying tactic. Knowing what we now know, we should also give some credence to the possibility that Mr. Sanders is on his way back here, and his little excursion was a dry run for when he and the missus decide to make it final. Meaning, of course, after one more payoff with the Mr. December contest," Charles said.

"All valid points, Charles, and we should consider all of them." Whatever Jack was going to say next was cut short when Espinosa called out.

"You're up, Jack!"

Startled, Jack stood up and headed to what Espinosa called the "setting room." Harry tried his best not to laugh.

"You just wait until it's your turn!" Jack sniped.

"Hold on, everyone. Maggie is sending me a text. Well, damn! You guys are not going to believe this," Ted said. "Well, yeah, you are, because Director Sparrow gave us fair warning. He just got handed his walking papers by the president because he wouldn't stand down. Sparrow had his resignation in his pocket when the president delivered the coup de grace, along with those of his six top lieutenants. He and the former upper echelon of the FBI are, as we speak, on their way to meet with Annie, Myra, and Maggie."

Ted went on. "I guess he knew it was going to go down that way, so he had his guys pack up his office. He no longer works at the J. Edgar Hoover Building. He is a free agent. *Was* a free agent. Annie and Myra snapped him up. Annie wants to run a special edition, so Maggie is in charge of that. And the rest of us are missing it so we can get duded up for an all-guy dance routine. What's wrong with this picture?"

"What's wrong with it is you're jealous," Harry said, laughing.

"Damn straight I am. Somehow, Maggie will find a way to turn this into a Pulitzer for herself."

"I thought you loved Maggie," Abner said. "How can you be jealous of someone you love?"

"It's easy when it comes to a coveted Pulitzer. I do love Maggie, but I also love Pulitzers. It's different. You can't possibly understand unless you have printer's ink running in your veins. Crap!" Ted bellowed so loud, he could be heard all over the studio.

Maggie Spritzer was thinking the same thing as she climbed out of the cab she'd kept after dropping Toby off at his "frat house" residence. She looked up at the huge building that Annie and Myra had purchased for the veterans. Coming around the corner was ex-Director Sparrow and six tall, buff-looking men who you just knew were in law enforcement. Maggie thought they all looked happy, because they were smiling. Introductions were made.

"That was quick, Mr. Sparrow. How did POTUS take it?"

"I hate to say this about the leader of the free world, but the man is an imbecile. He's so worried about his reputation, he can't think straight. Or act straight, either. His chief of staff tried to rein him in, but Mr. President kicked him out of the office, but not before I handed over my resignation before he could fire me. He thought he had me by the short hairs—oops, sorry about that, Maggie—when he said that I was not to step foot inside the Hoover Building again and that my belongings would be boxed up and sent to my home. I told him not to worry, that my things were already out of the office. And then I handed him the six other resignations I was carrying with me. The guy loves to talk, as everyone in the country knows, but that time he was totally speechless, so I just left. I have no idea what kind of spin the White House is going to spin in regard to seven sudden resignations out of the blue, then all seven of us going on Annie's payroll."

Maggie's face darkened. "Whatever it is, I will outspin them. You can take that to the bank. Annie wants me to get a special edition ready for the morning. Big, bold banner headline, head shots of all seven of you *defectors*. That's *above* the fold. Smaller pictures of Annie and Myra, along with what you will be doing for other centers that are in the process of being set up. Under the fold, pictures of the doctors at this facility, crowd shots of the vets being treated. Special stories on the vets, their families, even their service dogs. Inside, on page three, will be you guys and your service records and a few quotes, so we need to get this show on the road, guys. Please tell me, Mr. Sparrow, that you don't have any regrets."

"Only one, and that is that the guy who will probably replace me is going to be a real thorn in your side. He's going to start digging and won't come up for air until he finds something to latch onto. I'm feeling kind of like I'm letting you all swing in the wind by leaving."

Maggie laughed. "If you were a betting man, Mr. Sparrow, who would you put your money on? The new director or Annie and Myra?" She laughed again at the expression on Sparrow's face.

"Hustle, boys. Annie and Myra do not like to be kept waiting, and I have a special edition to get out." With a wide flourish, Jack Sparrow opened the door, gave a sweeping bow, and waited for Maggie to sail through the door like she was the queen of something or other.

"Welcome to our new world, boys!" Jack Sparrow said as the huge plate-glass door closed behind him.

Chapter Eighteen

Alexis Thorne's studio was alive with chatter as the boys waited their turn to go to the "setting room," with Dennis in the next room, waiting for his latex to settle, and Jack getting his first taste of how he was going to look as a female. To say Jack was surly was an understatement. Cyrus, not understanding what was going on, whined and whimpered and refused Jack's offered treats.

"Do you really have to sing while you're doing this, Espinosa? I think that's what is upsetting Cyrus," Jack growled.

"I do my best work when I'm singing. Alexis hums, so live with it, okay? Just sit there and be quiet, or this is going to turn out to be a mess."

"Then sing in English. Cyrus doesn't understand Spanish."

"You want a big, old honking nose, keep it up, Jack," Espinosa said ominously.

Jack recognized the threat and clamped his lips shut. He closed his eyes and let his thoughts go to Pilar Sanders and the night that loomed ahead for all of them. He wished he was a seer so he could see into the future. He asked himself again, for the one hundredth time, why someone like Pilar Sanders would get involved in drug running.

* * *

Across town, Pilar Sanders was asking herself the very same thing. Tears dripped down her cheeks as she stared at the check the consignment shop had left for her. The snobbish lady had looked down on her as her helpers carried the last of her treasured designer outfits, handbags, and shoes out the door. She had taken a big hit money-wise but hadn't argued over the amount with the woman. She had voiced her reaction to the amount by saying it was a tenth of what she'd paid for what she was parting with. The snobbish woman had smirked, knowing she was making the deal of a lifetime, as she calculated the amount she could mark up the merchandise.

"I know," was all she had said. Pilar had wanted to slap her, but she'd used every ounce of willpower remaining to keep her hands at her sides. She'd cried when she closed the door and locked it behind the woman.

In the kitchen, Pilar filled out a bank deposit slip for the second check. She winced at the mere one hundred eighty thousand dollars she had received for her last transaction. While she wasn't happy with the amount, she was smart enough to know it was better than walking away and leaving everything behind. Her plan was to drop the deposit in the FedEx envelope, with the four million dollars for her brokerage account, in the box in the lobby and the money bag with the smaller check in the night deposit on her way to the supper club. That was when the thought finally hit her that her car wasn't in the garage. She would have to take a taxi. She hated the smelly, dirty vehicles and the drivers who didn't speak English. She supposed she could call a car service, but it was late, and she needed to be on time. A taxi was her best bet. She'd just have to live with the possibility that someone she knew would see her in one of those hateful yellow monstrosities.

Pilar finished what she was doing. She looked over at the counter to see her one and only Chanel bag. She'd paid forty-three hundred dollars for it, and she was really going to have to crunch the money bag into it. It wouldn't work, and she knew it. A dressy handbag with the signature gold braided chain was what she was looking at. A little more than a flat envelope in size. No room for anything.

She felt a groan escape her lips. What had she been thinking when she parted with all her handbags? She should have at least kept one of the quilted totes so she could carry things like the manila envelope in the safe. A second groan of dismay escaped her lips. She'd have to use one of her cloth beach bags when she walked away for the last time. How tacky was that?

Pilar eyed the digital clock on the range. She had less than an hour to get dressed, call for a taxi, stop in the lobby, and head to the club, with one stop at the bank to make the night deposit. Tomorrow, the moment the checks cleared, she would instruct the bank and her brokerage firm to wire the new deposits to the Antilles, where Gabe's favorite offshore bank was located.

God, Gabe, where are you? What are you doing right now? Are you thinking of me? Do you have any idea of the bind I'm in here? If ever there was a time for you to be at my side, this is it.

Pilar looked around, half expecting a lightning bolt to strike the tile floor. When nothing happened, she swiped at her tear-filled eyes and shuffled off to her bedroom to get ready for what she knew was going to be one of the worst nights of her life.

Back across town, with a little more than ninety minutes to go, Espinosa quickened his pace as he worked on transforming the boys, with Charles and Fergus the last to head for the "setting room." He'd saved them for last because, to his mind's eye, they would be the easiest to transform.

"I'm not looking forward to this evening, Charles. Are you?" Fergus asked.

"Not by a long shot, mate. Not by a long shot. I'm thinking we're either too early on this deal or we're too late. It's six weeks till the Mr. December contest or pageant or whatever we're calling it. Six weeks is a long time to sit around twiddling our thumbs, don't you agree? So much can go wrong in that amount of time." Charles looked down at an incoming text. Avery Snowden.

"Anything interesting?" Fergus queried.

"Yes and no. The Sanders woman is still inside. Avery can't get in to set up his listening devices until she leaves. His operative says there is a lot of traffic in and out of the building, but she has no way of knowing where anyone is going. Some use the garage, and some park on the street and walk around to the entrance. Deliveries are made up front, she thinks. She saw three women with two SUVs loading up what she thought were tons of shoe boxes and other boxes with designer labels. A refrigerator was delivered, but the truck was too big to go under the overhang leading into the garage, so they had to dolly the appliance to the front entrance. Lots of people walking dogs are using the front entrance. That's it—"

"I just thought of something, Charles," Fergus said, interrupting whatever he was about to say next. "Avery's person is watching the wrong entrance. The husband drove her home last night. When he left, he took the car. She hasn't left the building since. She is either going to call a car service or take a taxi, which means she'll be leaving by the front door, not the garage. You see it that way, don't you? You need to tell Avery to reposition his operative right away."

"Good catch, Ferg. I totally missed that, and obviously, Avery did, too." Charles quickly sent off a text to the old spy. "Sometimes, Ferg, I think we're getting too old for all of this. We should have caught that early on. And another thing . . . I much prefer the old way of disguise—different hairstyle, sunglasses, ball cap or fishing hat, reversible jackets. And, of course, colored contact lenses. All of this," Charles said, waving his arms about, "puts air in my knickers."

"If you recall, Alexis said that works only in the movies. *Old* movies. What they were using back in the day, as she put it, couldn't hold up under klieg lights. The stuff would start to melt. She also said that masks, even when they were applied by an expert, could not beat biometric tools that can measure retinal pigmentation, which cannot be changed. That's why she's outside the box with whatever it is she's doing now. Joseph seems to have a good handle on it all. I guess we have to look at it as progress in that field. Everything else changes with time, so it's natural to assume that inroads would be made in that profession also. At least Alexis stays up on it all."

"I guess," Charles grumbled. "That doesn't mean I have to like it."

"Okay, you two are up. You won't take long, since I'm just doing a patch job on both of you. Because of your age. No one will be looking at you two, so do not take that the wrong way. You are to be chaperones to the young crowd. The wigs and accessories will suffice," Espinosa called out cheerily.

Charles looked at Fergus. Fergus looked at Charles.

"I think we're trying to decide if we should be insulted or not at your implication," Charles said tightly.

"Can you decide that later? We're pressed for time, and you still have to get your toenails and nails polished. It has to dry, or it smudges. Women are very sensitive to their nails and toes. And I told you to pick out your earrings. Did you do that? No, you didn't, because I do not see any earrings. Why are you doing this? Even Harry didn't give me this much trouble," Espinosa said tartly.

"What trouble?" Fergus huffed. *Toenail polish! Dear God!*

"Never mind. Come on and don't dillydally."

"Yes, Ferg, do not dillydally," Charles sniped as he trailed behind Espinosa, Fergus dragging his feet behind him. All three men pretended they didn't hear the squabble going on in the makeup room as Espinosa pushed them forward.

"You do mine, and I'll do yours," Jack said.

"I am not painting your goddamn toenails, Jack Emery. Get that through your head. And just for the record, you have ugly feet," Harry snarled.

"You're just mad because I picked the Cherry Berry polish, and you had to settle for that sick-looking Purple Passion. Admit it, Harry!"

"Eat me, Jack!" Harry bellowed.

"You have to be really careful that you don't smear your toes. If you do, you need a Q-tip dipped in this stuff," Ted said, motioning to a bottle of nail polish remover. "It smells like turpentine. I picked Crimson Fire. And the lipstick is a perfect match. See!" Ted said, then puckered up for everyone to see his luscious lips. "I used a darker shade for the outline. Espinosa said it will last longer."

Harry banged his head on the wall. No one paid any attention.

"I never had hairless legs before," Abner said, stretching out his legs. "I think I kind of like it. They feel like silk. I think Isabelle is going to like how they feel. And before you can ask, I picked Suicide Red for my polish. Whatcha think, guys? And the lipstick is too perfect. So creamy. I already licked it off twice. I am so glad I blew off the CIA today to participate in this . . . ah . . . event. Yes, sirree, this lipstick is as sweet as honey," he trilled.

Harry banged his head on the wall again.

It was Dennis's turn to chirp up. "I think I got the best color of all. Red Ruby Blood. Abner is right. The lipstick is to die for. I'm going with the gladiator sandals. What are you guys wearing?"

Harry put his fist through the wall when Jack handed him a pair of vibrant purple slingback flats.

"You have to match your outfit to the sandals, Harry. Since you are being so damn ornery, I'll pick out something for you. Listen, you need to get cracking and get those toes and nails done. Dennis, help him," Jack said.

"Touch my feet, and they'll be picking up your remains in Canada."

"Can't. I have to pick out my outfit and wig. Abner, you're done. Help Harry."

"Can't," Abner said as he literally flew out of the room.

Jack looked at Ted, who simply shook his head.

"Okay, Harry. That leaves me. You want it the hard way or the easy way?" Jack asked.

Harry smiled. "Have at it, buddy. It will give me great pleasure to see you painting my toes and fingers."

"You crafty son of a bitch!" Jack roared. "That was your game plan all along, wasn't it?"

"Be careful now. I don't want to see any smears and smudges. I think I can put on my own lipstick. Of course I'll want to test it out to see if it's really kiss proof, like the label said. I'll try it out on you, you crafty son of a bitch!"

Jack eyeballed Harry for a good long minute before he doubled over laughing. Harry joined in. Cyrus leaned forward to lick at Harry's lips. He laughed harder.

"Keep laughing, and I *will* smear this shit. Damn, Harry, I can't believe we're doing this."

"I have an idea. When we're done tonight, let's figure out whose idea this was and kill the son of a bitch!" Harry said.

"Works for me. I gotta say," Jack said, leaning back to view his handiwork, "this color looks good on you."

"Ya think, Jack? You're not teasing me now, are you?"

"Never!" Jack guffawed. "Ya know, I think you are going to pull this off. We all are. I gotta say, Espinosa knows his business. We need to ease up on him, so he doesn't get a complex. He's just doing what he has to do to get this show on the road. Let's pick out our outfits. I have no clue what a woman would wear to something like what we are going to. Do any of you?"

"Semi-dressy would be my guess. These things are usually a girl's night out, meaning they get together after work, meet up, and have dinner and see the show, so I think it's a good bet that they're in semi-business attire, which can be fashioned up or down with jewelry or a scarf, something like that," Dennis said.

The others stopped to look at the young reporter.

"And you know this, how?" Abner asked.

"Espinosa told me. I don't know anything about women. Is he right, Jack? You're supposed to know everything there is to know about women."

"Yeah, yeah, he's right. I remember Nikki saying something like that when we would meet up for dinner after work, and I would say she looked different from when she left to go to work in the morning. C'mon. Let's get to it."

The treasure trove that was the wardrobe room proved to be a mini-nightmare.

"What size are we in women's clothes?" Ted grumbled. "Are we going long to our ankles, short to our bony knees, or baggy?" He looked helplessly at Jack, who just shrugged. "Are you sure we have to match the outfit to the sandals?"

"Yes!" Dennis shouted as he pawed through the racks. He yanked out a turquoise-blue mandarin sheath and tossed it to Harry.

Harry shot the young reporter a killer look. "It's ripped. Look!"

"It's not ripped. That's a slit up the leg. Good thing you Chinese guys are hairless," Dennis shot back.

"I'm not wearing this," Harry said, exploding.

"Then find your own damn dress, Harry."

"Yeah, Harry, find your own damn dress." Jack cackled as he pulled out a lemon-yellow high-necked dress with long sleeves that came with a short jacket. "What's this puckered stuff on the front?"

"It's smocking or ruching," Ted said. "Maggie has a dress like that."

"I do not believe this," Harry said over and over as he fingered the silky material. "These false eyelashes are killing me. They itch, and I can hardly see."

A ripe discussion followed on the length and the curl of their lashes. It was followed by considerable cursing, mostly from Harry.

Cyrus pawed the carpet and howled.

Ten minutes later, everyone had an outfit in hand.

"Next is jewelry and perfume. Let's go, boys," Jack said, leading the way to the room that held all they needed. "Take your pick, boys. Studs, dangling, hoops. The object is to sparkle. There are fifty-three bottles of perfume here, so unless you all want to sample the lot, I suggest we pick one, and we all get to smell alike. What's it gonna be?"

"Let's go with this one called Wild Ginger," Ted said, and before anyone could yea or nay it, he was spraying the air. Cyrus ran to the door, barking like he had been mortally wounded.

"That's going to give me a headache," Harry said.

"Get over yourself, Harry. Perfume fades in time," Jack said. "By the time we get to the club, you'll hardly be able to smell it. Nikki told me that, so it must be true. Get your earrings, so we can dude up. It's almost time to leave."

They did a snatch and grab before they beelined out of

the room to the dressing room, where they stripped down to their Jockeys and one set of boxers. No one looked at anyone else as they pulled on their outfits. When they were finished, they looked around at each other just as Espinosa said, "Say cheese, girls! You all look lovely." He opened a closet door to reveal a full-length mirror. No one oohed or aahed. But Cyrus did bark. Loudly.

Charles and Fergus appeared out of nowhere, dressed in their new finery. Cyrus was so upset, he ran and hid, barking the whole time.

"We brought these wraps, stoles, or extralong scarves, whatever you want to call them. It's crisp outside, and unless you want to wear bulky coats, I suggest you all wrap your shoulders under these. They're neutral in color, so they'll match your . . . ah . . . outfits," Charles said. "In case you wonder how I know this, I pay attention when Myra gets dressed for the evening. You know, house to car, car to wherever, and no coat necessary. That kind of thing. We should be on our way. In my opinion, no one would ever guess you are men under all that . . . stuff."

"You two don't look so bad, either," Ted said as he whipped his wrap around his shoulders with a wild flourish. "I do like these little sparkly things on the fringe."

"Yeah, yeah, a little pizzazz," Dennis said as he fingered the sparkling little circlets sewn onto the fringe. "I think we're as ready as can be. Are we coming back here later?"

"Yeah. We're not taking Cyrus with us, so of course, we're coming back," Jack said.

The gang headed for the door as Cyrus cowered in the tiny kitchen area. He whined.

"Look, pal, this is a onetime thing. Don't sweat it, okay? We'll be back before you know it. In the meantime, watch over my gear and don't bite anyone's ass while I'm gone. We good, Cyrus?"

Cyrus barked twice, but he didn't move.

The gang trooped outside. The side of the *Post*'s van now bore huge decals saying it belonged to the Lynsdale Dance Academy. Espinosa, dressed in a bright red two-piece pantsuit, climbed behind the wheel. "Listen up, everybody. When we get to the club, remember to keep your legs together, like girls do. And no scratching, either. Women do not scratch, because they do not itch like guys do. Remember that. Think female every minute you're inside."

"Why don't you just give us a handbook?" Harry snarled as he fidgeted with his shoulder wrap.

"Are we having fun yet? You having fun, Abner?" Dennis asked.

"For sure. I really like this lipstick. I think it must have some kind of narcotic in it, because my lips are numb. I'm going to get a case of it for Isabelle."

"Shut up!" Harry bellowed.

The rest of the ride to Supper Club One was made in silence. The time was 7:02 p.m. when Espinosa parked in the lot, which was almost full.

Charles squirmed in his seat as he struggled to turn around to face the others. "See if any texts came in before we go inside. No business and no phone usage while we're inside. Is that understood?"

"Maggie said she's going to make the deadline for the special edition," Ted said.

"Mr. Sparrow said he and his men made the right choice, and he can't wait for the special edition in the morning," Fergus said.

"Avery said his operative moved in the nick of time and was able to follow Ms. Sanders to the bank, then here to the club. I don't think this will come as a surprise, but she said she was not the only one following Ms. Sanders. A swarthy-looking man in an Avis rental was right behind the taxi. She said he's here in the parking lot, and she gave me his license plate. She herself is parked in row G, and she's the fourth car in. The tail is parked in row J and is five cars in. He is still in his car, and she is in hers," Charles said.

"No updates on Mr. Sanders and his perils at sea?" Espinosa asked.

"No, nothing. Perhaps later. Be mindful of the time difference," Charles said.

Ted looked over at Dennis. "Anything from Toby?"

"Only that he's here, and so is Mia. He's probably, as we speak, in discussions with Ms. Sanders."

"If that's it, then perhaps it's time to head indoors to our dinner. Toby did reserve a table for us, didn't he?" Jack said.

"Yes. He said he wasn't sure if Mia would be joining us, as if we're friends of hers, or if she was going to sit alone. I guess we'll find out when we get inside."

"Let's do it, boys!" Ted said. He was the first one out of the van. The others, holding up their dresses and trying to hold on to their wraps and purses, were a sight to behold.

"I think we should all say a prayer that we're happy we are not wearing high-heeled shoes," Jack said, tongue in cheek, as he looked at Harry, who gave him the evil eye. "Oh no!" Jack said, his eyes wide with horror.

"What?" everyone shouted as they stopped in their tracks at Jack's tone.

"What! What! That's what," Jack said, pointing to Harry. "Oh my God! Now what?"

The others gasped in horror.

"Harry, your eyelash is coming off," Dennis cried dramatically.

"Relax, people. Stand still, Harry. I'll have it fixed in a second." Espinosa spit on his finger, dabbed the false eyelash, and held it in place for the count of ten. "See? All fixed!" Espinosa gurgled happily. "Remember now, we're just a bunch of girls out for an evening of fun with our dowager aunts. Meaning Charles and Fergus. By the way, who has the money?"

"What money?" Abner asked.

"The money for us to slip into the guys' G-strings," Jack said.

"I have it," Charles said. "Three one-hundred-dollar bills and five ten-dollar bills for a stellar performance. I'll divvy it up over dinner. I also have the cover charge, which I think is over the top, but I will pay for all of us."

The boys tripped around the walkway that led to the main entrance. They laughed and giggled and poked at one another as they followed Charles and Fergus. As Charles paid the cover charge and gave the name of Ruby Rose for the reservation, the hostess looked up and said, "Nice perfume. What's the name of it?"

Before anyone could blink or say the wrong thing, Dennis trilled, "It's called Wild Ginger, but it has a hint of jasmine in it." The hostess winked at him as she smiled.

"Follow me," said the hostess, whose nameplate said her name was Margie. "We have a full house tonight, with three specially reserved tables. Normally, we do not take reservations, but when it's Ms. Sanders who requests them, then, of course, we have to do what she says. Here you go, ladies. Enjoy your dinner and the show. You are perfectly ringside. It doesn't get any better than that." She smiled again, showing a mouth full of beautiful pearl-white teeth. She winked again at Dennis, who was making a mental note to come back sometime soon looking like himself to see if he could chat her up.

"Forget it, kid. I think she's a lesbian. Toby said all the hostesses are," Jack said.

"I knew that!" Dennis said defensively. It really was true. Jack knew everything there was to know about women, even if his knowledge was secondhand. He knew how to put it all together so it made sense. *How could I be so stupid?*

A waiter dressed in a bow tie and a pair of skintight shorts appeared at their table. "Can I take you lovely ladies' drink orders? Just as a reminder, the cover charge does not include alcohol."

"Bourbon on the rocks, all around," Charles said.

When the drinks came, Charles once again gave their order. "Filets all around, all medium rare, ranch dressing, and the twice-baked potatoes. Go!"

Everyone started to talk at once.

"I don't like bourbon, and I like my steak rare."

"We aren't here to eat and drink, but to observe. When everything is the same, it counts down on the time. Let's make a toast to a successful evening." The boys clinked their glasses, but only Fergus and Charles drank.

"Nice place," Abner said.

"Cloth tablecloths and napkins," Ted said. "Maggie always said that is a sign of a good restaurant. This place is five star as far as the food goes."

"Look around, boys, but do it casually. Tell me if you see anything that doesn't quite seem to fit in," Charles said. "Try not to be obvious. A trip to the ladies' room might be required at some point."

"I see Mia. She's with some other young women, a table for four," Dennis said under his breath.

"I see Ms. Sanders at a table with five . . . ah . . . dark-skinned–looking men," Ted said. "My cell is vibrating, Charles. I think it might be Zack. Should I take it or not?"

"I say take the text. Just don't be obvious," Jack said, countermanding Charles's orders. "I'd say Ms. Sanders looks a tad uncomfortable, and the men look stone-faced and just as uncomfortable," Jack said.

"Now what?" Espinosa asked.

"Now we wait," Charles responded. He lowered his voice and asked Ted what the text said.

Ted dropped his voice to match Charles's and said, "He said he tailed the men all day. They bought cheap clothes at Target. They ate at a fast-food joint. They started out as six, three to a car, but along the way another six men met up with them at one of the fast-food places. He followed Zuma after that. The guy kept going from fast-food joint to coffeehouse, and back and forth, and he was on his cell the whole time. He's here, inside this restaurant, right now, and so is Zack. He doesn't know we're, uh . . . who we are, so if we want to talk, we'll have to find him."

Charles simply nodded, because their food arrived just then.

Waiting was the name of the game.

Chapter Nineteen

Thirty minutes into the meal, which no one was eating, Jack dropped his napkin on the floor so he would have an opportunity to look around the room while he retrieved the bright pink piece of cloth. He watched as Pilar Sanders shook off Zuma Delgado's hand to get up from the table. A trip to the ladies' room? One of the swarthy-looking men also got up to follow her. Jack watched as Sanders sucked in a deep breath as she shoved the man back down onto his seat. When it looked like there might be some fireworks, two well-muscled waiters stepped in with a tray of drinks. Jack wasn't an expert at reading lips, but he was close. He'd bet even money the waiters were telling the entire table to remain seated, or they would be escorted outside. They then pointed to four Godzilla look-alikes at the entrance. Men whose bodies were as big as tree trunks. Zuma Delgado nodded at his men, as if to say, "Stand down."

Dennis was up and literally running after Pilar Sanders before anyone at the table knew what was going on. Mia was close behind.

"This can't be good," Abner said out of the corner of his mouth. "You don't think those guys are going to rumble, do you?"

"No. I think, and I could be wrong, but I think they're here to cover their investment, to make sure the Sanders woman toes the line and nothing goes wrong. Just her expression alone tells me she does not want to be here. For all we know, she could be their prisoner. They're more or less operating on the fly. Los Angeles is where they're comfortable. Now that things are heating up for them, and Miami is new turf, they're naturally a little nervous. Plus, there's the fact that they are sitting in the nation's capital. My money says they're all illegals. They need to stay under the radar in case Sanders decides she wants out. I'm thinking she does, but she's between a rock and a hard place right now," Jack said.

"Ten minutes to showtime," Ted said, looking at a sparkly watch on his wrist.

"I wonder what's going on in the restroom," Espinosa said as he fiddled with a curly ruffle on his pink blouse, which matched to perfection the color on his artificial nails.

"Mia's in there, so nothing will happen. Young Dennis is safe," Charles said quietly as he picked at the twice-baked potato on his plate.

Charles was right; there was nothing happening in the ladies' room. Dennis was in a stall, with his ear pressed against the door, but he could see through the side where the door didn't fit flush with the frame. He sighed with relief when he saw Mia enter and head toward the row of sinks.

"Ms. Sanders! What a surprise! My friends and I just had a lovely dinner. The food was absolutely scrumptious," she trilled. She continued to babble as she washed her hands, then leaned closer to the mirror to observe her flawless complexion.

"Oh, Mia! I forgot that tonight was the night you were coming to the club. I'm sure you and your friends will have an enjoyable time. Toby is an excellent performer." Pilar

Sanders eyed the one-hundred-forty-dollar tube of lipstick Mia was applying. But her eyes were really on Mia's sixty-five-hundred-dollar Chanel purse. The same exact purse as the one that she'd sold off with the other purses this very afternoon. Jealousy rivered through her veins.

"This is just the best lipstick." Mia giggled. "Stays on all day, and it's true, it is kiss proof. Toby is the proof. Is something wrong, Ms. Sanders?"

"Wrong?" Pilar frowned. "Why do you ask?"

Mia dropped the lipstick back into her purse. She shrugged. "I don't know. You look sad or scared. Maybe nervous. Are you worried that the boys won't perform well? I guess I would, too, if I were in charge. Toby told me you told him that important people would be in the audience tonight, and you wanted them all to be at their best."

Pilar nodded. "I'm like a mother hen sometimes. And, yes, I do worry about my boys. I guess I'm not very good at covering my emotions. Really, I'm fine."

"Are the important people who are here for the performance the ones at your table? Will Toby and the others be able to see them from the stage?"

Too many questions. This girl is too sharp. Pilar looked at her watch instead of replying. "Three minutes till the lights go down. You need to hurry, dear, so you don't trip and fall over the steps. Everyone needs to be seated when the bell chimes the three-minute warning, and it's going to chime any second now."

Inside the stall, Dennis flushed, then opened the door. Neither woman looked at him as he headed for the sink to wash his hands. He did it lickety-split and was right on Mia's heels as they headed toward their respective tables.

Dennis slid onto his seat and started to mumble. "For all of you who have ever wondered what a ladies' room looks like, it's pretty and smells like powder, perfume, and hair spray, and it is *clean*. Mia really didn't get anything out of her, and she tried. The girl is a real pro. Sanders is jittery and nervous. Her table companions are the important people she told Toby would be watching him and the other dancers. By the way, that chime you heard was the three-minute warning to the start of the show. No one can move around once the lights go down."

The words were no sooner out of Dennis's mouth than the room went totally dark. Three minutes later, the stage came to life, with the blinding white klieg lights overhead. The primitive sound of drums could be heard as a hush came over the room. The sound built to a breathtaking crescendo just as the curtains parted. The room turned silent; then a siren, along with pulsing music, erupted as five bronzed and oiled cops hit the stage. The sound of the music increased until it was deafening to the ear, and women screaming as the dancers jumped and thrust and pivoted added only more volume. When the cops' hats flew into the audience, Charles caught the first one. Mia caught another and waved it in the air. She hopped up on a chair and yelled at the top of her lungs, "More! More!"

"Yeah, yeah," the women shouted as they, too, climbed on their chairs.

Jack looked around. "When in Rome, *girls* . . ."

Dennis didn't need to be told twice. He was already on his chair, twirling a dinner napkin in the air. Harry followed suit, not realizing his eyelash had come loose again. Jack reached over and plucked it off and mouthed the words, "Rip the other one off." Harry obliged as he hooted and hollered with the rest of the women.

It was Mia who noticed the "deer in the headlights" look on Toby's face as he stared down at the tables below the stage. His step faltered. Mia strained to see what he was seeing and decided the woman in Toby's line of sight was his ex-fiancée. *Damn.*

Then, in an unprecedented move, Mia hopped off her chair and made her way to where Carrie was ogling Toby. She grabbed her by the arm and pushed her up onto the stage, jumping up as well. "This guy is mine. You got that!" Mia said as she pointed to Toby, who was too befuddled to do anything but continue to dance.

"Toby! It is you! I had no idea. Wow. You are something else. Who is this person?" Carrie said, trying to shake off Mia's viselike grip.

"Like I said, bitch, he's mine. All mine." Mia rubbed her hand up and down Toby's oiled chest as she licked at her bloodred lips.

It was all Toby needed. His day had finally arrived. He winked at Mia to let her know he could handle it from here on in.

And then it was the dance of unrequited love and revenge, with the other dancers taking a backseat to what was going on right in front of them.

Toby reared back, planted his feet firmly on the stage floor, and let out a roar of pure animal lust before lunging forward until he was body to body with his ex-fiancée. The room went deathly silent as the drums beat a steady, sensual throb. He moved like a cat, a big, sexy male panther, as he stalked his prey, his pelvis jutting forward, his muscles moving to the beat of the music.

Dennis squirmed in his seat. "Holy shit!"

"I second that," Ted hissed.

"Oh, that guy *is good*," Abner said, breathing hard.

"Damn good," Jack said.

"I say we give him all the money Charles is holding," Harry said. He followed that up with, "If I ever find out Yoko comes to a place like this, I'll strangle her."

"You really need to get over yourself, Harry. The girls used to come to one of these clubs every Friday night for their weekly girls' night out. It's just fun for them," Jack said.

"Look! Look! Something is going on between those two, and the audience senses it." The tempo of the drums increased to bear out what Charles was saying.

Everyone in the room watched what was playing out on the stage, not realizing they were holding their breath for what was to come.

Dennis knew what his friend was doing: he was getting his pound of flesh for all the hurt Carrie had inflicted on him. He saw Toby smile; then he grinned. He saw the sparkle in his buddy's eyes as he let his bronzed, sleek muscles go to work. He felt his jaw drop when Toby grabbed Carrie's shoulders and pushed her down to her knees. She looked up at him, awestruck, as he danced inches away, did a whirligig, then a pelvic thrust.

"How's this for *earthy*?" he bellowed before he danced away to join his fellow dancers. At that moment in time, Toby felt more powerful than he'd ever felt in his life. His gaze sought out Mia, and he flung off a sharp salute. She giggled as she watched Carrie's friends help her off the stage.

"Nice going, buddy. Bet you feel like a million bucks right now," Dennis whispered to himself.

The women in the audience roared, whistled, clapped their hands, and stomped their feet as they called out for more, more, more, waving dollar bills in the air. Mia's fist shot in the air, the signal to Toby that he'd pulled it off.

"Is that guy something or what?" Dennis squealed in excitement for his friend.

Jack's eyes were on Pilar and her guests as the house-lights came up, and the dancers hopped off the stage to mingle and accept the bills that were finding their way to their G-strings.

It looked to Jack like Zuma Delgado was saying, "What the hell was *that*?"

Pilar Sanders was laughing. "That, Mr. Delgado, was perfection." She got up and walked over to Toby, who was standing at Mia's table, and put her arms around him. "That was an A plus, kiddo. Your best performance yet. You made me proud tonight. I'm just sorry Gabe wasn't here to see it."

Toby laughed as he bent down to kiss Mia. The clinch was long and sweet. When he finally broke away, he led her over to Carrie. "I'd like to introduce you to my fiancée. Mia Grande. Carrie and I were once engaged." He turned and said, "Come backstage with me, honey."

Mia patted Carrie on the shoulder. "Like I said, he's all mine. Every last inch of him, and don't you ever forget it." What totally stunned Mia was the realization that she meant every word she'd just said aloud. God help her. She had just fallen in love with Toby Mason.

"Now what?" Harry asked.

"Now we sit here and pretend to drink until the next show. Or if Sanders and her guests leave, then we can leave, too. This is how they make their money. On the drinks between shows. Toby told me they base their profits on each customer's ordering three to four drinks. Doesn't matter if it's soda or plain water. The price is the same," Dennis said. "On a really good night, some of these guys can make as much as a thousand dollars, and it's clear money. No one but Toby claims it all on his taxes. He's honest that way. Pilar told him he had to stop doing that because he was a threat to all the others, who might get audited. He said he told her okay, but he claims it, anyway. That's just the kind of guy he is."

With the houselights up, the patrons were walking about, taking bathroom breaks, and chatting each other up. A young woman approached their table with a napkin and pen in hand. She homed in on Harry and said, "I know you. You're Lisa Ling. I love your show. Can I have your autograph?"

Harry's jaw dropped as he fiddled with one of his earrings. Jack kicked him under the table. "Shhh. Don't tell anyone," Harry whispered as he scribbled the name Lisa Ling on the paper napkin.

"Ooh, this is just so wonderful. I won't tell anyone till after you leave," she gushed and then walked away from the table.

"I should have videoed that," Espinosa grumbled.

"Oh, look. Mia is coming back to the table. Good, good. She's coming to our table," Ted said.

Mia sat down, her face flushed. "I don't have anything to report other than Ms. Sanders said she was proud of Toby's performance. No one said anything about my performance. I didn't know what Toby would do when he spotted his ex. I just reacted. He's just so sweet, you want to knock yourself out to protect him. Don't look now, but the Sanders party is about to leave. What's the game plan now?"

"The game plan is we get out of these ridiculous clothes, and the sooner, the better," Harry said through clenched teeth.

"If the Sanders party is leaving, then there's no reason to stay behind. Did Toby share with you what she said to him at the meeting earlier?" Charles asked.

"He said she seemed *brittle*. Like a gentle breeze would snap her in two," Mia replied. "That was the word he used. He also said she looked like she had been crying and had extra makeup on to cover up the ravages. I can attest to that since I saw her in the bright light of the restroom. Her eyes were red and bloodshot. Mr. Snowden has someone outside waiting to follow all of them. That's all I know, other than I am to stay here until Toby gets off work and take him home. I better get back to my table so you all can do whatever you have to do."

The gang made a pretense of gathering up their shoulder wraps and purses. They waited for Charles to tally up the bill; then they all left.

The night had turned chilly, and there was a harvest moon. The wind was brisk as they chatted quietly among themselves as they headed for the van. This time Ted climbed behind the wheel, and Espinosa rode shotgun.

"I don't see Sanders or her guests. They sure did leave in a hurry. Charles, check with Avery to see who is tailing them and where they're going. It might help us decide what our next move is going to be," Jack said.

Charles obliged. Then he waited for a return text. When it finally came through, he looked at the others and said, "This is interesting. He thinks they're headed to the Sanders condo, but he isn't sure. Delgado is in Ms. Sanders's car with her. The others are behind them in three tail cars. What's interesting is the discussion Ms. Sanders had in the parking lot with Delgado when they left the club. He said it started out calm enough but then turned ugly. Sanders stood up to him. He wanted to know where the husband was, and Pilar told him the truth.

"I guess originally she must have lied to him and said he wasn't around, or something to that effect. He threatened her for lying to him. She got in his face and told him not to threaten her again, because he needed her. Then he got verbally rough and told her he no longer trusted her and was leaving a man to guard her. As in live in her apartment with her. She belched fire, but Delgado would not budge. That's it. And, by the way, Avery's operative was successful in planting the listening devices in the Sanders condo, so that's a good thing, and it will give us a leg up as to what is going on."

"I just had Espinosa send a text to Zack," Ted said.

Espinosa rattled off the incoming text. "He's in the parade following the Delgado team. He said there is a real turf war going on in Los Angeles with Dito Chilo's incarceration. Everyone is jockeying for position to take over the drug cartel. Seems that the guy Delgado has to ace out is some vermin named Diego Sanchez. A real badass dude, according to Zack. He wants to meet up for breakfast in the morning. He plans to work through the night. I'm not sure what that means, so I'm going to okay it. Denny's at nine o'clock."

"Okay, folks. We're here. Time to shed all these lovely outfits and pray to God we never have to see them again," Ted said as he slipped the van into PARK and cut the engine. They could hear Cyrus's sharp barks as he waited to welcome them home.

"Getting nippy out here. Temperature is dropping," Abner said. "Listen, guys, since I took off today, I need to head out to Langley and put in some time. Otherwise, I might lose my job, and the CIA needs me. You need me. I need me." He was ripping at the wig and the false eyelashes as he tripped along behind Jack and Dennis.

"Listen up, all of you. Go ahead home. I'll put everything back, since I know where it belongs. Alexis is really fussy about stuff being misplaced. I'm already home, so it's no problem," Espinosa said.

Thirty minutes later, everyone but Espinosa piled back into the van. This time, Dennis drove.

"Where to?" he asked.

"Since all our cars are at the BOLO Building, I guess that's our destination," Jack said. "My skin is itching from that damn latex," he grumbled.

"Use that lavender lotion Espinosa gave you," Charles said. "It works wonders."

Cyrus barked. No one knew or cared why. They were tired and just wanted to go home.

"I don't ever want to be a female again," Ted said. "I prefer to admire them from afar and not wonder or worry about why they are what they are and do what they do and wear what they wear and smell like they do. You with me, guys?"

Every hand in the van went straight up in the air. Cyrus barked three times.

"Tomorrow is another day," Jack said wearily. "I think Cyrus and I will crash at the BOLO. You guys are welcome to stay. We have plenty of cots."

"No takers, Jack," Charles said. "We'll be in touch in the morning."

Chapter Twenty

Halloween came and went, with barely anyone noticing. Maggie never ended up having her Halloween party, as she was too busy with the investigation. What the boys did notice was that nothing constructive was going on that would help their mission. The days crawled by, each one as stressful as the day before. By the end of the third week of November, Jack called a special early morning meeting. Everyone, even Maggie, showed up.

"Coffee and bagels and fresh fruit," Jack said, pointing to the sideboard in the conference room. "We're here today to make some hard decisions. We are fast approaching the time when Pilar Sanders and the dancers head off for Miami. As it stands now, and for the first time since we started doing what we're doing, I am disappointed in all of us."

Jack's statement brought a chorus of groans and sharp words.

"Back that up, Counselor," Snowden snapped. "It's no one's fault that we have nothing to go on. We did not overlook one single detail. All things considered, we're right where we should be at this point in time. Yes, our other missions lasted only days or, at the most, a week, from start to finish. Each mission is different. You work with what you have. And you're right about at least one thing—we don't have much. We have the Sanders condo bugged and under surveillance. We know Sanders has one of Delgado's guards living in the condo with her, even if it is under duress, as we suspect, so it stands to reason she is not going to make any cell-phone calls that would incriminate her in any way.

"I think we can safely assume that Delgado does not trust her and she doesn't trust him. We have been privy to the calls she has made to her business manager, to take-out restaurants, dry cleaners, and so on. We've even heard sharp words exchanged between her and her guard, who, by the way, does not speak any English. None of this has helped us. Her routine is the same. She shops during the day, she banks, she lunches by herself, and she goes back to the condo and has lengthy conversations with Carlie Fisher, her business manager. The pageant is on schedule. There is nothing else to report on her.

"I have over a dozen of my operatives tailing Delgado and his people. All they do is ride around, stop at fast-food places, meet up with people who look just like themselves, where they talk for five minutes, then disappear. His people are very careful not to stand out in any way or go places where they might cause suspicion. We do know they use burner phones, because we've seen them pitch them in the Potomac. We've also seen them buy new ones at different drugstores, usually two at a time. We tried Dumpster diving for their throwaway trash to check for DNA. We got two hits. Lowlifes imported from California. They're getting their ducks in a row. In a week they'll all be headed for Miami. We know this because Sanders assigned Carlie Fisher to make the arrangements for the van she herself will be driving to Miami. The dancers are going to be flying down as a group. Reservations have been made at a ritzy hotel. First class all the way.

"All the venues have been confirmed. All their publicity is in place. It's just waiting it out. The plan is for them to leave here December fifth. The two big events will be held on the ninth and tenth of December. Charles and Fergus also made our reservations, and we will be at the same hotel. So, in that sense we're talking two weeks till this closes out. What I meant earlier was we have a little more than a week to get ready to travel. We're using Annie's plane as our mode of transportation. That's my report."

"What has Delgado been doing?" Ted asked.

"He pretty much hangs out at that fleabag motel where they're all staying. There's a roach-infested little coffee shop in the lobby, and he sits in there for hours with his laptop, which, by the way, looks to be state of the art, and when he isn't working on the computer, he's talking on his cell. He's been our biggest problem as far as surveillance goes. We have to change operatives two, sometimes three times a day so he doesn't get suspicious. Let me tell you, that guy has eyes in back of his head."

"What about Tom Fazio? What's going on in Tahiti?" Dennis asked.

"Absolutely nothing. The search parties located the plane but said there was no sign of a body. Tom is convinced Sanders had help once the plane went down, and at this point in time, he could be anywhere in the world or right there under Tom's nose, in disguise. He's perfectly willing to stay on. It's costing us, just so you know. He's been flying back and forth around the islands, showing the guy's picture and asking questions. It's all been a dry well so far. If I have a vote on this, I say let him stay until December, when this gig goes down. He might appear around that time or make some kind of move in regard to his wife."

The boys and Maggie all agreed.

"I guess that covers it then, except for Ted's colleague Zack," Snowden said, relieved to be out from under the accusing stares everyone had directed at him throughout his disquisition on the current state of their mission and the reasons for it.

"Zack was called back to Miami yesterday. He's on his way, as we speak. He called me as he was leaving, saying he'd be our eyes until we got there. He seems to think the action is going to start there momentarily. He's a loner, but he is also a team player, if that makes sense. Too many people here tailing each other. He said it was getting harder and harder to tell the good guys from the bad guys. That's it in a nutshell, guys, Maggie."

Harry threw his hands in the air. "That leaves us exactly where we were when we got here this morning. This is a total waste of time."

Hearing Harry's words, Cyrus bolted to his feet. It was time to leave, he had decided. He nudged Jack's leg to show he was ready.

"Not yet, soon."

Cyrus settled himself at Jack's feet as he looked around to see what the delay was.

"I see no reason to meet every day unless there's an emergency. We can all be in contact via our cell phones, and Avery will forward all reports, and that goes for the rest of you. Does anyone have a problem with that?" Charles queried.

No one did, not even Cyrus, who barked twice to show he was in complete agreement.

Ten minutes later it was just Jack, Harry, and Cyrus left in the building. They quickly cleaned up, turned off the lights, and headed for the exit.

"I don't know about you, Harry, but I'm not liking any of this. You getting any bad vibes?" Jack said.

"Yes and no. I understand what Charles is saying. Past missions, we went full bore, barely able to catch our breath. This one . . . we can take a five-hour nap in the middle of the day and not miss a thing. We're just not used to being this inactive. Too much time for the bad guys to perfect their deal and not enough time for us to figure it out. I think that guy Zack nailed it when he said there are too many players in this game."

The heavy security door closed behind them with a sharp hiss. Cyrus took off in a dead run, barking at the top of his lungs. He was back within minutes, panting and nudging Jack's leg.

"I still say we should have snatched the Sanders woman and sweated her," Jack said. "We know that once we have her, we're not going to let her go. Even though we have nothing on her, better safe than sorry. Toby's info has been spot on from the very beginning. What reason is there to think that's going to change?"

"It is what it is, buddy," Harry said, straddling his Ducati. "You know where to find me if you need me," he called over his shoulder just as he was about to pull away.

Cyrus barked as he raced to Jack's car, then waited patiently for him to open the passenger-side door. He hopped in and buckled up.

"I guess we should head on home, with a pit stop for a couple of burgers. You good with that, pal?" This time, Cyrus didn't bother to bark. He simply pawed Jack's arm to show he was okay with the burger deal.

Jack let his thoughts take him to Pilar Sanders and how no one but him wanted to do a snatch and grab. His gut instinct was telling him that if they didn't do something soon, the mission was going to go south in a big way. The thought made him cringe. He wondered where she was right now and what she was doing.

What Pilar Sanders was doing was trying to shake her tail, a man named Santos. She had hated him the moment she set eyes on him. He smelled like garlic and onions and hair tonic. Her entire condo smelled like him, and no amount of air fresheners could fight the smell. She was now in Neiman Marcus, in the lingerie department. She'd been certain he wouldn't follow her or, at the very least, wait by the elevator. But he did. He was right behind her as she walked from rack to rack. Her arms full of nothing she had any intention of buying, she headed for the dressing room. She stiff-armed him at the entrance to indicate he could not follow her. She pointed to the sign. He shook his head, his expression belligerent.

Pilar raised her voice loud enough for the floor manager to intervene. "This man will not leave me alone. You need to call store security and get him away from me."

Santos started to protest in Spanish just as two sharply dressed men approached.

"Get this creep away from me. He's been following me all over the store. Check your security cameras, and you'll see I'm right. And I think he's carrying a gun!" Pilar told them.

Seeing that any resistance on his part was going to start a scene, which would probably result in his arrest, Santos waved his hands and turned around, but not before he fixed his beady eyes on her. If looks could kill . . .

The minute the two security men and Santos set foot in the elevator, Pilar dropped the lingerie she was carrying and raced for the EXIT sign and the steps beyond. She literally ran down the steps to an outside door and around the block, where she hailed a cab to take her home. She had to get her manila envelope and its contents out of the safe and secured somewhere in her bedroom before he returned. Time was moving too fast, and it scared her. She'd tried to find a way during the past two weeks to retrieve the envelope, but the safe was built into the wall just off the living room, where Santos sat every hour of every day. She knew there was going to be hell to pay once Santos called Zuma Delgado, but she could not bring herself to care. The manila envelope was all she had left. It was her only security. *Damn it, Gabe. Where are you?*

Pilar climbed from the cab when it reached her building. She tossed a twenty-dollar bill at the driver, thinking it was the best twenty dollars she'd ever spent, and hit the ground running. She was glad she'd worn low-heeled boots, because it made for easier running. She hit the lobby, sprinted across to the bank of elevators, where one stood invitingly open. She stepped in, hit the button, and muttered, "Hurry, hurry, hurry."

By the time the elevator stopped at her floor, Pilar was breathing hard. It took her three tries before she was able finally to open the door. Inside, she set the dead bolt and ran to the wall safe. Her hands were shaking so badly, it took her four times to spin the numbers until the safe hiccuped and she could swing the door open. She clutched the envelope like it was her lifeline, which, in a very real sense, it was. She slammed the safe door shut, spun the dial, then replaced the picture, careful to make sure it was hanging perfectly straight.

Still breathing hard, she ran to her room, her eyes going everywhere. She needed someplace safe, but where? Where? Every thought that entered her mind was negated. No place was safe. Maybe, maybe not. There was one place that *might* be safe. Just one. She opened the door to Gabe's closet and looked around. Neat as a pin. Just like Gabe himself. She looked at his golf bag, which hung from a special heavy-duty hook on the wall. She couldn't reach it. She needed a chair. She ran back to the study and dragged the desk chair back to the closet. She started to gasp for breath. For one wild moment, she thought she was going to black out. She leaned against the wall, trying to force a calmness she hungered for. Five minutes turned into ten minutes before she felt like she could climb on the chair.

She yanked at the clubs and then stuffed the envelope down, but not down so far that she wouldn't be able to reach for it if she was in a hurry to retrieve it.

Pilar was back to breathing hard when she hopped off the chair. She sat down and dropped her head between her knees. She wished she could pray, but she no longer remembered the childhood prayers she'd been taught. She started to cry then, when she remembered how Gabe had always said God didn't make deals. Especially for people like her and him. She remembered being surprised that he had included himself. And yet she knew Gabe prayed. Daily.

I am so sorry, Gabe. I am so sorry, so very sorry. I wish I could unring the bell. Wherever you are, I hope you know this.

Her breathing almost back to normal, Pilar realized she had another problem. If she took the chair back to the study, she would have to drag it back out when she went to retrieve the manila envelope. Better to leave it here, push it in the corner, pile stuff on it, and beady-eyed Santos might not even notice. It was the only solution she could think of. Minutes later, she was satisfied with the way Gabe's closet looked. She walked out, closing the door behind her. That wasn't strange; she'd closed it after he left. Nothing out of the ordinary.

She was in the kitchen, watching the coffee drip into the pot, when her doorbell chimed to life. She felt her heart skip a beat as she headed for the door. She opened it wide and stood staring at Zuma Delgado and Santos. She stepped back for them to enter, then walked back to the kitchen.

"Pull a stunt like that again, Senora Sanders, and you're dead meat."

"And why is that, Mr. Delgado? The baboon doesn't speak English, and I don't speak Spanish. I tried telling him men are not allowed in women's dressing rooms. Even a lowlife like him should know that. He kicked up a fuss, and security took over. I came home. That's the beginning and the end of it. Oh, one more thing. Stop threatening me. Now if there's nothing else, I'd like to drink my coffee in peace and quiet. Tell the baboon to go watch cartoons."

"I do not care for your tone or your attitude, Senora Sanders."

"And I do not give a good rat's ass whether you like it or not. I'd say this is a stalemate. Get out of my house. It's bad enough the baboon over there is stinking it up. I don't need that cheap cologne you're wearing to add to the smell."

Pilar turned her back to pour her coffee, certain Delgado was either going to shoot her or knock her out cold. All she heard was rapid-fire Spanish from both men, then "Adios, Senora Sanders. I will see you this evening at the club."

Pilar whirled around and almost blacked out when she saw that her kitchen was empty. She sat down, because she knew her wobbly legs wouldn't hold her up a moment longer. She gulped the hot coffee, not caring that she was searing her throat. She closed her eyes so she wouldn't cry. If only she could turn back the clock. If only. If only.

Jenny Wentworth, one of Avery Snowden's best operatives, sat two tables away from Zuma Delgado. Spanish was Jenny's native tongue, so she could understand everything he was saying on the phone. She had been sitting here for well over an hour and had never once raised her head from the book she was studying. She was posing as a university student doing research and living on the cheap, hence her stay at the fleabag motel. A sloppy-looking egg salad sandwich and a cup of putrid coffee were in front of her. From time to time, she would scribble something in a small notebook. She could feel Delgado's eyes on her every so often. His voice had a tone that carried, even though he was speaking in Spanish and thought no one could hear or understand. She knew he had discounted her immediately due to her Waspy look and pale blond hair. So many stupid people in the world. She slipped her hand into her pocket, fingered the cell phone, and pressed the number three for her replacement.

Jenny scribbled a note to herself that was meaningless. She had to get out of here and report to Avery what she'd just heard. All these past days of sitting here, trying not to eat the tasteless food and to stay alert, were taking a toll on her. She couldn't wait to get outside in the fresh air, so she could take a deep breath. Hopefully, this would be her last stakeout of the scuzzy Delgado. She didn't make a move, though, until fifteen minutes later, when a tall, lanky, jeans-clad street guy walked in and headed to the counter. Her replacement. She was out of the door in a flash and headed to a white Volkswagen Beetle with peeling rusty paint. She chugged out of the small parking lot, smoke belching from the tailpipe, and headed to the nearest garage, where she settled down to call her boss and report on the day's activities

"He's heading out tonight, Mr. Snowden, as soon as it gets dark. He's leaving only someone named Santos and Juan Carlos behind. He got a call from someone, but I could hear only his end of the conversation. He's going to be staying at a place in Miami Beach called the Pink Pelican. It's in a seedy part of town, where no one pays attention to anyone else and the cops don't go, just SWAT teams. He repeated that, so I'm sure I got it right. If I heard right, and I'm sure I did, I know how he's going to get the drugs delivered to him. They're going to be delivered to the kitchen of the Pink Pelican, packed in crates of lettuce and boxes of jarred salsa.

"He's nervous about being here. He thinks people are

onto him and his gang. He is also worried about the Sanders woman. He said she's forgetting her place, and she has gotten too lippy to suit him. He told whomever he was talking to on the other end that he was uploading a picture of Gabe Sanders, and they were to show it around in case he showed up. He said to whoever was listening that the *gringa*—that's what he called her—lied about everything, so she was probably lying about her husband's having skipped out on her. He laughed then and said if she was his woman, she'd be barefoot and tied to the stove.

"One other thing, Mr. Snowden. Delgado was snarly mad. I say this because he cursed a lot. Very angrily. He's never done that before. He's very, very worried about Ms. Sanders. He said that before this is over, he's going to put his fist through her face and knock out all those pretty teeth of hers. That's it. Call me if you need me. I need to go home and take a bath to wash the stink off me from that place."

When Avery Snowden powered down, he clapped his hands in relief. Finally, some action. He immediately sent off an encrypted text to everyone, requesting an immediate urgent meeting. The return encrypted texts were immediate. Avery slipped his car into gear and pulled into traffic. His destination, the BOLO Building.

Ninety minutes later, the conference room was full, everyone seated as they talked among themselves. At last, a break in the mission, and it was all they could talk about.

"No time for coffee and refreshments," Snowden said as he repeated in detail what his Spanish-speaking operative had told him. "That means we all need to head to Florida. We need to get Annie's plane ready, and we need to make reservations at the Pink Pelican and do our own surveillance. Delgado and his people are driving, so we'll have the edge by flying and getting there well ahead of time."

"That won't be a problem. Annie's plane and her crew are always on standby. What time do you want wheels up?" Charles said.

"Depends if you want us to go home and pack bags. Or do you want us to buy our clothes and other gear once we get there?" Jack said. "There's more than enough money in our emergency fund for quite a bit of shopping, including for suitcases, so we don't go in empty-handed when we register. I say we go now."

The others agreed. But Maggie said she had to stay behind to keep the articles on the veterans going, as per Annie's instructions.

"Call me if there's anything that can be done by me from this end. I don't see Toby. Where is he?"

"He's with Mia, and they're having lunch with Ms. Sanders at the Blue Bell Café. Toby said she called out of the blue, all chatty and motherly, and said she wanted to get to know Mia better. That's it," Dennis said.

"Personally, I don't think it means anything other than she doesn't want to be around that scumbag who is guarding her." The others nodded that they agreed with Dennis. "Should I tell him we're leaving now?"

"Do that," Charles said, looking down at an incoming text. "Wheels up in ninety minutes. Just enough time to close up and drive to the airport. Let's move, people."

Cyrus was the first one at the door. He waited patiently for the others to open the massive door. At last, some action!

Chapter Twenty-one

"Wheels down right on schedule," Fergus said as he unbuckled his seat belt. He immediately turned on his cell phone, just as everyone else was doing. Chirping, pinging, buzzing, and musical notes filled the plane.

"Whatever would we do without these marvelous little devices?" Charles said, tongue in cheek. "Sometimes I hate them."

Dennis was close enough to hear what Charles was saying. "You know who really loves cell phones?" Not waiting for a response, he rushed on. "Men and women who cheat on their spouses. That's who."

"And we care about this . . . why?" Ted demanded.

"We really don't, Ted. I was just commenting on something Charles said. You're holding up the line. Will you please move!"

"Welcome to Miami, gentlemen," the male steward said as he looked out into the darkness. The pilot and copilot offered up salutes as the gang tripped down the portable stairs, their only luggage the rucksacks on their backs. Only Charles and Fergus carried bulging briefcases.

The time was exactly 6:50 p.m.

A man off to the side of the stairway held up a huge sign that said CHARLES MARTIN. Charles waved his hand. The gang followed him.

Jack eyed the man holding the sign. He had to be either a retired Navy SEAL or a retired Delta Force operator. Whichever he was, he wasn't someone you wanted to meet up with in a dark alley, much less in the bright light of day.

"Follow me, gentlemen. My name is Jonas Kellner. We have a few stops to make before I take you to your hotel. Mr. Snowden said to tell you, 'Welcome to Miami,' and he's sorry he isn't here to meet you."

"Wait a minute! Is Snowden here?"

"Yes, sir. He arrived forty minutes ago. He's here in Miami, but he is not here at the airport."

"How is that possible?" Jack demanded. "We all left at the same time."

"Mr. Snowden was first in line for takeoff. You were only number seven on the runway. Any other questions?" His tone clearly said there better not be any more.

"And your name really isn't Jonas Kellner, either, is it?" Jack said.

"That's right, sir. You all need to step it up. I have a schedule to meet, per Mr. Snowden's instructions."

Jack moved closer to Harry. "I think we could take this guy, don't you, Harry? Not that we would, but we could if we wanted to, right? All Snowden's guys look like this one. He must recruit each one ten seconds after they retire."

"Sometimes you are downright silly, Jack," Harry said. "The only question you should be asking is, How long would it take? Minutes versus seconds?"

Jonas Kellner stood to the side as the troop climbed into a Chevy Suburban that they all knew was outfitted in the same way as the president's.

Jack and Harry were the last to climb in. Jack had one foot on the running board when Kellner spoke out of the corner of his mouth. "I know what you're thinking, Mr. Emery. Not even on your best day! Or his best day," Kellner said, jerking his head in Harry's direction.

Harry laughed out loud. Jack shuddered. Harry rarely, if ever, laughed out loud. He turned around just as Harry put his foot on the running board. The next thing he saw was Jonas Kellner sleeping peacefully on the ground twenty feet away.

"Show-off," Jack said, a huge grin on his face. "Now we have to wait for him to wake up, since he's the only one who knows where we're going."

Cyrus barked from inside the Suburban. Action had gone down, and he had missed it.

"What the hell is our problem out there?" Ted bellowed. "Just for the record, your dog is heavy, and he's sitting on my lap."

"Nothing much. Harry was showing off. We'll be good to go in a minute, or when Harry wakes up Mr. Kellner." To Harry, he said, "C'mon. Play nice and wake up that dude. You made your point."

Harry backed off the running board and sprinted over to where Jonas Kellner lay. He reached down and yanked him to his feet. "You okay to drive, Kellner?"

Kellner let loose with a string of expletives as he stomped toward the Suburban.

Harry trotted behind, his flip-flops making slapping sounds on the tarmac. "He's good, Jack." Cyrus barked in agreement. The doors shut, and the Suburban tore across the tarmac to the exit road.

Thirty minutes later, the tanklike vehicle swerved into a long driveway that led to a prefab building that had seen better days.

"What's this place?" Abner asked curiously as he looked around.

"A beauty parlor," Kellner said through tight lips. "Go on in. I think Mr. Snowden is already inside."

The group trooped inside and was stunned to see that the inside of the ramshackle building was nothing like the outside. It was brightly lit, with overhead fluorescent lights. Everything was white or stainless steel, and it was absolutely spotless.

"What took you so long?" Snowden quipped. He looked at Jack and Harry and shook his head from side to side. Cyrus moved then to stand next to Snowden, his ears straight as arrows, the fur on his neck ruffled. He quivered in anticipation of . . . *something*.

Avery Snowden had always thought of himself as fearless. And he was, except when it came to Cyrus. Cyrus scared him shitless. He looked over at Jack. "Call him off, Jack. Please."

"He doesn't have enough meat on his bones, Cyrus." Cyrus knew what that meant: he wasn't going to be biting this guy's ass anytime soon. He backed up until he was standing next to Jack, but his eyes never left Avery Snowden.

"Gentlemen, this place is similar to Alexis Thorne's studio, where Mr. Espinosa transformed you a short while ago. We use this facility for the same purpose. It is not on anyone's radar. Except ours. We use it in order for you all to blend in here in Miami since you will draw too much attention as snowbirds recently arrived from up North. Therefore, we have to correct that, so we're going to give you all an instant suntan. We're going to bleach your hair to a degree and dress all of you like beach bums. Surfer beach bums. We've got some knocked-around surfboards and some beat-up boogie boards that you will take with you when you hit the Pink Pelican. You'll sign in, register in groups of two or a few singles. You'll all meet up in one of the beach bars.

"The Pink Pelican is part of a string of beach eateries. That's where all the lettuce and salsa are delivered. They do a monster salad and chip business. No one is looking twice at them. My people have been hard at work since I found out how this is all going to go down. We have four days to get it down pat. Charles and I have some things to go over, so follow the young man who is going to do your spray tanning. His partner will choose your clothes and your luggage. Try not to give them a hard time. It has to be this way."

No one said anything as they trudged after two buff, young beach types who were so totally ripped and bronzed that the snowbirds were jealous to a man.

"This is so neat and cool. I'm one of those people who can't tan. I burn and have to use a ton of lotion, and I still burn and peel," Dennis gushed. "I can't wait to see how I come out. Women like men with tans, did you know that? Also, you look healthier with some color. Why are you looking at me like that? It's true. I read a lot. So there!"

"Who wants to go first?" the lead guy asked.

Dennis raised his hand.

"Okay, buddy, you're up. Strip down to the buff, and I mean buff. We spray every inch."

Harry was the only one who had a problem with the words *every inch*, until Jack pinched his arm. "Not to worry, Harry. Just tell him to close his eyes when he gets to . . . you know . . . *the jools*. This is a walk in the park. Nikki and the girls do it all the time at the beginning of summer, until they build up a tan. I could never tell the difference. Nikki makes a point of never going out in the sun, so I'm thinking she does this self-tan stuff all summer long. Whatever it takes, Harry. The upside to it all is it smells good, like coconut and vanilla."

"Shut up, Jack."

Cyrus growled.

"That means you, too, Cyrus."

Cyrus looked up at Harry, then at his master as he lowered himself to slink behind Jack.

"Now you scared my dog, Harry. Not nice. One word from me, and your ass is grass. You know that, right?"

Harry leaned down to stare Cyrus in the eyes. Neither blinked. Cyrus whooped in delight, and then he was all over Harry, and Harry was loving it. Jack did his best not to laugh. It was a thing Harry and Cyrus had going that he simply was not a part of. Like Harry and the mystical dog Cooper. Some things you just had to leave alone. This was one of those things.

In the sterile great room, Avery Snowden led Fergus and Charles over to what looked like a clear Plexiglas table with matching chairs. "We need to talk. First things first. The bill for this mission is creeping higher and higher by the hour. I did warn you at the outset. Are we still good?"

"The funds are unlimited. For the most part. You have no worries," Charles said.

"I think I know how this is all going to go down. The cocaine is being shipped from all over to the Pink Pelican. They hollow out the heads of lettuce and insert a container in the middle, then pop the core on top. Voilà. The salsa is made right here in Miami by a mom-and-pop team. The mom-and-pop part is just the cover. They do make the salsa and pack it in gallon jars. They fill a quart jar, which goes inside the gallon jar, with cocaine, pour some salsa on top, and put on a screw lid, which is then sealed by machine to prove that the contents have not been tampered with. The thing is, these people have the customers to prove they eat all that stuff. Tons of it. Tons, boys.

"I can't prove this yet, and I could be wrong, but I don't think so. Whatever that guy Delgado said he's moving, you can triple it. He might be paying Sanders well, but nowhere near what he'd pay some sharp-eyed drug dealer. I doubt she has a clue."

"Why haven't the authorities cracked down on them?" Fergus asked.

"Weren't you listening to me, Fergus?" Snowden replied. "The Pink Pelican can account for the heavy orders of lettuce and salsa. When you get there, just walk up and down the beach. Each eatery is filled to capacity, and guess what they're eating! Salads and chips. My guys are not sure if any of the cocaine is being shipped in the bags of chips. They come in gunnysacks of white cotton to keep them fresh. Who can say what's in the middle of the sacks?"

"How did you find this out so quickly?" Charles asked.

"I have good people. I've had my people working this end the minute I found out the Mr. December contest was going to be in Miami instead of California."

"There's more, isn't there?" Fergus asked nervously.

Snowden stretched his lips into a wide grimace. "There is one other thing that is not going to go over well. You do realize that unless we actually catch them in the act, this thing could shut down in the blink of an eye."

"Do you have a plan?" Fergus asked.

"If you want to call it that. I made it my business to up-load all the previous pageants to see how it was all done. What they've done in the past is, after Mr. December is crowned, each dancer, including the winner, is given a gift. It's all fancied up, big red ribbon, silver paper, that kind of thing. The winner gets the biggest box, and the others a box maybe as big as a shoe box. They are told not to open them until they get back to the hotel, where the substitu-tion takes place, unbeknownst to them. The Sanders woman then takes possession of the boxes after all the pic-tures are taken, and she takes them back to the hotel for the switcheroo. She leaves the van in the hotel parking lot and takes the real gifts to the boys' rooms. Someone drives off with the van and returns it later. End of story."

"Then what happens?" Charles asked.

"The next day, they drive up to Fort Lauderdale, put on a performance, showcase Mr. December, hand out gifts, same deal. Then it's on to Palm Beach, and from there to Jacksonville, with the last stop outside Disney World. It's the end of the tour, and everyone goes home. That's all I've been able to pretty much prove."

"What's the part we're not going to like?" Charles asked.

"Your boys have to take over for the dancers. They have to actually receive the gift boxes. If you can think of a better way, tell me, and I'll listen. You hired me to snatch the Sanders woman and her husband. We lost the husband. We can still capture Ms. Sanders. What we don't want is Delgado and his people. Let the authorities handle them. That's why I said your boys have to be stand-ins. The real dancers have to be spirited away in plenty of time so as not to get caught up in the web. My people and I can take care of that end of it. Tell me, what do you think?"

"Won't that set off a red flag?" Fergus asked.

"Which part?" Snowden asked.

"Our guys taking over."

"At the last rehearsal before the big show, they throw open the doors to hold an audition of wannabes. It lasts all afternoon. That's where our guys show up. They've done it successfully for many years, according to all the taped videos I've watched. The feds aren't going to care too much, and neither will the DEA. All they want are the drugs and the goons."

Pilar was so nervous, she twitched as she walked out of her bedroom toward the kitchen. She had to walk past Santos, the baboon, and that bothered her. Her arms were full of brochures, flyers, and pamphlets that she was going to package up and send to Florida by FedEx. At least that was what she was going to indicate to the baboon. In reality, what she was going to send via FedEx was the manila envelope from the safe, with instructions to the hotel to hold it for pickup, with picture ID required when claimed.

Until last night, she had had no plan, but after hours

and hours of tossing and turning, she had finally come up with something she thought would work. It had to work, or she was a dead woman.

At three o'clock in the morning, she'd sent off an e-mail to Carlie Fisher, her business manager. It was a terse message:

Change of plans. You will be driving the van with all the gear to Miami. I have a ten o'clock flight in the morning. Arrange for a duplicate van to be delivered to the garage at 7:00 a.m. Make sure they guarantee child lock doors on all four doors. Tell them to leave the key in a magnetic box under the rear driver's side fender. I want you on the road as soon as the van is delivered. The boys fly out one hour after I do.

Pilar had then texted Toby, alerting him to her change of plans. And also to alert him to the change in hotels. She had debated about sending a text to Zuma Delgado but had decided he wasn't worth the effort. Everything was in motion now.

Her next two texts had been taken care of within minutes. She had canceled her reservation at the Mandarin Oriental Hotel and had booked a new reservation at the Ritz-Carlton. She knew Delgado would go ballistic when he found out she'd changed the reservations, but she didn't care. Enough was enough, and finally, finally, she knew what she had to do, and she was going to do it come hell or high water.

She'd rubbed at her burning eyes. If only Gabe were here. He'd be so proud of her. She'd started to cry then. So the sound didn't carry, she'd buried her head in the pillow.

It was morning now, and she knew it was the last day she would ever spend in this condo and the last day she would spend in this city. She wondered if she would miss it. Probably. She sucked in a deep breath as she stomped her way forward, knowing that the baboon was going to stiff-arm her to see what she was doing. Her own left arm shot out at the same moment. Stalemate. She showed him the FedEx box with the bright colors. He nodded. Then she showed him the stack of colorful brochures of Miami. Then she tried to make flapping motions with her hands to indicate the package had to be flown to Miami. He nodded and went back to his chair, which by now stank to high heaven, to watch the silly cartoons he was addicted to.

Pilar was so light-headed from the fact that she'd gotten away with her plan, she barely made it to the kitchen. She quickly made coffee, and while it dripped, she stuffed the manila envelope in the box and packed it tight with the brochures and flyers. She stuck on the air waybill just as the last drop of coffee plopped into the pot. She would wait until just the right moment to claim it at the Ritz-Carlton. All she cared about right now was that the manila envelope was as safe as she could make it.

As she sipped at the scalding coffee, she stared at the box sitting where the dead flowers had been. How innocent it looked. And yet it was her do-or-die destiny. She looked over at the digital clock on the Wolf range. If Avis was on time, the van should have been delivered ten minutes ago. Her cell buzzed. She looked down at the incoming text. **BMW SUV delivered on time. Key in magnetic container, as per instructions.**

She knew instantly why Avis had sent an SUV instead of a van. Vans didn't come with child lock doors. How stupid she was. She should have known that. Then again, how could she, since she didn't have children? She absolved herself. She wasn't stupid, after all.

Pilar finished her coffee and headed back to her bedroom so she could shower and dress. Her heart was beating so fast, she thought it would burst right out of her chest. She used every ounce of willpower in her body not to turn around and look at the box on the table.

Forty minutes later, Pilar was showered, dressed, and made up. She was dressed casually in a plum-colored pantsuit with a cream-colored blouse. She wore flat-heeled shoes and carried her pricey Chanel bag. A white leather duffel bag sat by the door. She'd packed it at midnight. Two pairs of black slacks, three sequined, sparkly tops, and three dressy blouses, along with her granny flannel nightgown, underwear, and makeup. Not too heavy, and she planned to carry it, not check it in baggage. She looked around to see if she'd forgotten anything. Nothing that jumped out at her.

The last thing she did was open Gabe's sock drawer. She rummaged for the only pair of argyle socks he owned, and unrolled them to reveal five thousand dollars rolled into a very tight cylinder. More than enough to get her to Florida, where she could buy whatever she needed in case she had forgotten something. She dropped it into her purse and covered it with several tissues. Done.

Pilar walked out into the living room, reached down, and pulled the plug to the television set out of the outlet. She hated the roar of outrage she heard, but that didn't deter her. She picked up her jacket and slipped it on. She carried the duffel to the front door and dropped it, along with her purse! She ran into the kitchen for the FedEx box and thrust it into the baboon's hands. She didn't care that he was texting his boss.

She opened the door to leave, but he grabbed her arm. She lashed out with her foot and gave him a good crack on his shinbone. She looked down at the text on the baboon's phone. **Stay where you are. Stay with the plan.**

Instead of saying something to the baboon, Pilar pulled her own phone from her jacket pocket and pressed in Delgado's number. The moment she heard his voice, she went into her spiel. "Do not tell me what to do and when to do it. I am leaving now. The baboon can come, or he can stay. It doesn't matter to me. Tell him if he even looks at me crossways, I will scream *rape* at the top of my lungs. I have a good set of lungs, just so you know. It's time you showed me some respect."

She shoved the phone into the baboon's hand. He was smart enough to bring it up to his ear as he leered at her. She listened to his side of the conversation, not understanding a word he was saying. Nor did she care. She did care, though, when he threw the phone at her. She was lucky and caught it before it smashed on the tile floor in the foyer. She didn't hesitate even for a second before kicking him square in the family jewels. As he doubled over, Pilar reached down for the Chanel purse with the heavy double gold chain. She wound up like a discus thrower and rapped him in the head. He toppled over, and for good measure, she kicked him in the ribs. She wasn't sure, but she thought she heard a satisfying sharp noise. She hoped she had cracked a rib. Or two. Maybe three.

Duffel in one arm, her handbag on her shoulder, the FedEx box under her other arm, Pilar sprinted for the elevator, where a white-haired elderly gentleman was holding the elevator door for her. He looked curiously over her shoulder at the baboon, who was limping down the hall and cursing in Spanish. Pilar smiled and shrugged. She was careful to position herself on the opposite side of the white-haired gentleman. She almost laughed out loud when she noticed the man sniffing and wrinkling his nose.

"What floor, young lady?" he asked genially.

"The garage level. By any chance, sir, are you going to the lobby?"

"I am. I'm taking my morning constitutional. Why?"

"Would you mind dropping this box off at the desk?

That way I can go straight to the garage. I have a plane to catch."

"Of course I don't mind." He reached for the box just as the elevator stopped at the garage level. Pilar smiled and waved as she quickly left the elevator, the baboon right behind her. Her eyes raked the parked cars. The white BMW SUV was right where Carlie had said it would be.

She walked toward it, reached under the fender, and withdrew the magnetic box and pulled out the key. She walked around to the passenger side and pressed the remote that would open the door. She took her time walking back around to the driver's side, where she fiddled with the key fob. The baboon was smart enough not to get into the car until her side opened. She had one leg up and was about to slide onto the seat when she heard the passenger-side door slam shut. Quicker than lightning, she was off the seat, the door slamming shut behind her. She ran then, dodging between cars until she found her own car. She was in and peeling rubber in seconds when she heard what she thought was the sound of a gunshot.

Damn. That was the one thing she hadn't thought of, that he could shoot his way out of the car. *Stupid, stupid, stupid. Gabe would have thought of that.*

She quickly pressed in the digits for 911. She reported a robbery in progress and said, "He has a gun, and a knife strapped to his leg. I think his name is Santos, and I suspect he's illegal." Pilar hung up before the operator could ask her any questions.

The garage came alive with sound, horns blaring, early morning risers screaming and yelling as they tried to figure out what was going on. Like she cared. She was out now and blasting down the road on her way to the airport.

She did it! She'd outwitted him! Now all she had to do was get to the airport, and it would be clear sailing. Or flying, as the case may be. She was safe. At least until she landed in Florida and met up with Zuma Delgado. She did wonder, though, if the baboon would have time to call Delgado before the police arrived.

Ninety minutes later, Pilar was thirty thousand feet in the air. She couldn't help but wonder if Santos would give up Delgado to save his own neck and what was going to go down in Florida. She leaned back and closed her eyes. She was asleep in seconds.

Chapter Twenty-two

Four o'clock at the Pink Pelican was happy hour. But then most of the guests said every hour was happy hour, especially at the tiki salad bars up and down the beach. The boys were gathered at little tables. It was hard for an observer to tell if they were all together or they were just being friendly in a relaxed atmosphere. Every table in the bar was full, and every table held dishes of salad, chips, and salsa, along with exotic-looking drinks with little umbrellas and longneck beer bottles. Chatter was loud and lively. No one paid attention to anyone else, or so it seemed.

"The Sanders woman arrived earlier, and this might surprise you, but she changed hotels. She is now staying at the Ritz-Carlton. The dancers are staying at the Mandarin Oriental, where the pageant is being held. The guys arrived around two and are in their hotel rooms, or at least somewhere on the premises. Avery said that Mia is with Toby.

"Hana, who was surveilling Ms. Sanders, said a ruckus went down in the garage, and the police were called. Three cars in total. They took her watchdog out in handcuffs. She said she saw it with her own eyes. Somehow, she managed to outwit the thug, then took a flight to here. Originally, she was supposed to drive the van with all the gear. Abner hacked into her phone and computer and found out what she was up to. Her business manager, Carlie Fisher, is now en route to Miami with all the costumes and gear. She will also be staying at the Mandarin Oriental."

"That's it?" Ted said.

"Anything on Mr. Sanders?" Jack asked.

"Not a thing."

"That's it? A dry well?" Jack persisted.

"Pretty much. The only other point of interest is every salad bar on this stretch of the beach received their salad deliveries. Double orders, I'm told. I can see why they do such a brisk business. These vegetables are so crisp and crunchy, they feel like firecrackers in your mouth. That salsa is also the best I've ever eaten anywhere, and I have been everywhere."

"I don't think anyone has given any of us a second look since we've been here. What do you want us to do going forward, Avery?"

"Nothing. Just be vigilant. I'm expecting some fire-works when Delgado meets up with Ms. Sanders. I'm still trying to figure out what she's up to. That was a pretty gutsy stunt she pulled in the garage back in D.C. Locked him in a vehicle that has childproof doors. It pains me to say this, but I don't think I would have come up with that even on my best day. And the woman doesn't even have kids. Like I said, gutsy. The idiot shot his way out, but the cops got there in time.

"He's under lock and key. He might try to cut a deal and give up his boss, but I doubt it. Still, Delgado has to be worried about that. We all need to be extra alert. I've put more men on him and his people. It's a veritable parade whenever he makes a move."

"Where is he right now? Do you know?" Charles asked.

"My people tell me he is trying to find Ms. Sanders.

He's been at the Mandarin Oriental, talking to the dancers. They are all clueless, so they have nothing to give up."

"Sounds to me like the Sanders woman is taking charge. Something must have happened. I'm wondering if somehow her husband has gotten in touch and she feels emboldened somehow. Or she got sick and tired of being told what to do by Delgado, and that thug who moved in with her might have taken a toll on her. Her payback in regard to him almost confirms it," Charles said.

Harry suddenly stood up. Dennis right behind him. Customers moved quickly as a group of men in garish beachwear entered the seating area. Delgado and his people. No one looked at anyone as they left money on the table and headed toward the beach. Dennis was the only one to stay behind. While he wasn't exactly bilingual, he understood and could converse in Spanish comfortably. He held his longneck Bud up for a refill and settled down to peck at his cell phone by sending text messages to himself. When he realized how stupid that was, he sent off a text message to Toby to let him know what was going on and to ask if he had any information. There was no immediate response, so Dennis continued to fiddle with his cell phone. He sent off messages to Maggie and to Bert Navarro, just to stay in touch.

He knew he was hitting all the wrong keys because he was concentrating on what the men were saying. Eight men, plus Delgado, who was trying to reassure them that even though Santos had been arrested, he would not give them up. The others cursed and called him a fool for believing such crap. Someone wanted to know where the woman was. Delgado said he didn't know. More curses and more name-calling. What kind of leader was he that he couldn't control one woman? Someone snapped. All of a sudden, Dennis felt like all the oxygen in the area had been sucked away. Delgado was on his feet as the men at the table continued to babble about how this would never have happened under Dito Chilo, who always controlled the trade and would never let a *gringa* get the upper hand.

Dennis started to get nervous as he wondered if the brouhaha would lead to gunplay. He wanted to leave but knew he couldn't. Instead, he gulped at the contents of the longneck beer bottle. Then, to show his complete indifference to what was going on around him, he pulled one of the chairs closer and propped up his feet. He continued to peck away at his cell phone.

"Decide now. In or out. I have no time for this stupidity."

"Me either," Dennis wanted to say, but his vote didn't count. Hardly daring to breathe, he waited to see what the outcome would be.

When all nine men got up and walked out without paying their bill, Dennis knew that greed had won out. But none of them had touched the food they'd ordered. He waited ten minutes until he felt that it was safe to leave. He literally ran down the beach to the next tiki bar, where he knew the others would be. He was breathless when he repeated what he'd overheard. "He doesn't know where Ms. Sanders is. He's hopping mad, too. You don't think he'll hurt her, do you?"

"He needs her," Charles said. "She knows that. That's why she's gotten so bold. I can't be certain, but I think before long, once she gets her ducks in a row, she'll be calling him."

"What do we do now?" Espinosa asked.

"Find a way to meet up with Toby so as not to draw attention to ourselves. Dennis, see what you can do. He's got Mia with him, so we can pretend we know her rather than Toby. Some bar later tonight where no one pays attention to anyone else. That kind of place. We should split up now. Maybe a swim, then to our rooms for a nap. That's what people on vacation do," Ted said.

A whirlwind of activity followed as everyone hurried to

do what Ted had suggested. Dennis just walked away and headed toward his room. A nap sounded really good.

He was almost asleep when his phone chirped. He read Toby's text. **Pilar is on her way here for a meeting with all of us. She sounds . . . different. More later.**

Well, there was different, and there was different. Dennis rolled over and went to sleep.

It was eight o'clock when Dennis woke to his phone chirping and a loud knocking on his door. He ran to the door to see Ted and Espinosa. He ushered them into the room, where they sat down on the bed. He read off the incoming text message from Toby. "Meet us at the Dipsey Doodle. It's right around the corner from the Pink Pelican. Nine o'clock. Something crazy is going on."

Dennis showed the message to Ted and Espinosa, then forwarded it to the rest of the team. He flapped his arms in the air. "What should we do?"

"We do what he says. We meet up at the Dipsey Doodle. We'll go now and get a table for all of us," Ted said.

"I'll meet you there. I need to take a shower and change. Do you think it's wise for all of us to be seated together?"

"Probably not, but we're going to do it, anyway," Ted said. "Take your time. You have a whole hour, and he said it's just around the corner."

Later, as Dennis lathered up in the shower, his journalistic mind wondered why Delgado was heading north with the drugs instead of to Key West and open water. If he was a drug dealer, that was what he would do. But since he wasn't a drug dealer, the point was moot.

He exited the shower, dressed in a pair of yellow plaid shorts with a white Izod T-shirt. He slipped his feet into flip-flops and was out the door twenty minutes behind Ted and Espinosa.

The team trickled in, one after the other, with Toby and Mia the last to arrive.

"We were not followed. I made sure. We're clean," Mia said. "But we need to get down to business right away, and then Toby and I are going back to party at the hotel with the other dancers, per Ms. Sanders's orders. Ten o'clock is our witching hour."

"What happened?" Charles asked.

"First of all, Pilar met with me one-on-one," Toby said. "She gave me my check for being crowned Mr. December and told me to deposit it first thing in the morning. I said okay. Then she sat me down and told me how proud of me she's always been, how she always tried to do right by all the dancers. I just listened. She handed me an envelope, and in it was the printed-out itinerary for all our airline flights. For tomorrow afternoon, after our rehearsal. I asked her what was going on, but she wouldn't tell me. Then I asked her where Gabe was. She said he'd left her, and the reasons were not important. She said she was trying to make things right. She would not elaborate. She was trying not to cry."

"So there's no contest?" Jack said.

Toby grimaced. "If we're all on a plane to wherever the hell she booked us, then I think it's safe to say there will not be a pageant. Oh, one other thing. She gave me checks for each of the guys. Fifteen thousand dollars each."

"Toby misspoke," Mia said. "When he asked her if the pageant was off, she more or less did say yes, but then she said that after the rehearsal, they always hold a contest for wannabe dancers. She said she thought this would be a good chance for the wannabes to see if they could cut it up on a stage. She said it was a sold-out house, and she had to give the ticket holders their money's worth."

"I assume you haven't told the others yet, right?" Charles said.

"We're all going out to dinner. Pilar arranged it. I'll do it then. By the way, she is not staying at our hotel. She's at the Ritz-Carlton. In case you don't know," Toby said.

He went on. "Listen, we have to get back. I know this probably won't mean anything to any of you, but she hugged me before she left and wished me luck. She hugged Mia, too, and told her she made a good choice when she picked me. Then she winked at me and said she forgives me. So I took that to mean she's known all along that she was being watched. See you all tomorrow at the rehearsal. I can't wait to see you guys perform." And then they were gone.

"Whoa. Hold on here. What did he mean when he said he can't wait to see us perform? Perform what?" Harry bellowed.

"Oh, you know, a little dance routine, a little jiggle here or there," Jack said, then ran for his life out of the Dipsey Doodle, Cyrus on his heels, Harry leaping over tables and jostling people out of the way. Once they hit the beach, it was a standoff.

"I can't dance," Harry said.

"I can't, either," Jack said.

Cyrus whined and yelped. Both men ignored him.

"Do you want to know what we're going to wear?" Jack asked craftily.

"Yeah."

"Ninja outfits!" Jack said dramatically. "We get to carry those spike things that throw off smoke. The suits are rip-off Velcro. You rip between the legs, at the crotch, and the whole damn thing just comes apart. It's like magic, Harry."

"Uh-huh."

Jack ran for his life.

The doors to the rehearsal room were locked, but the chatter and the sound of shuffling feet could be heard clearly as Pilar's dancers went through their last routine.

There were only two people seated where the audience sat, Pilar Sanders and Zuma Delgado. Pilar looked serene, and Zuma looked like a black thundercloud. When the dancers wound down and walked off the stage, Pilar turned to her drug-dealing partner.

"Satisfied? Everything is in place, so stop following me around and tell me when I'm going to get my money," she said.

"I don't trust you. You don't do what you're told. Is that why your husband left you?"

"Stay out of my personal business. Now you need to get out of here, so we can hold our auditions. This is important. We have to keep things moving and not make waves. You keep wanting to do things your way, and your way is going to bring trouble. I am not going to tell you again. Now, when do I get my money?"

"When the prizes are handed out. Your money will be in a basket of flowers. At the bottom. And I hope I never lay eyes on you again."

Pilar laughed just as the doors opened to admit the horde of young men who wanted to be the next Mr. December. Harry and Jack led the pack but took seats in the back because they had no intention of trying out a dance routine. They watched as Delgado slunk out of the room.

An hour into the rehearsal was all Jack and the others needed. He signaled that they were to leave. Outside, in the great hallway, he groaned. "That was too painful to watch one minute longer."

"My stomach is in a knot," Dennis said.

"Cyrus can dance better than most of those guys," Ted observed.

"I don't know how I kept from laughing out loud," Abner added.

They were outside the five-star hotel, looking at one another. "What now?" Jack asked, looking over at Charles.

"I guess this is what one calls free time. We do whatever we want and count down the hours till tomorrow. An early dinner would work wonders for me. I say we go back to the Pink Pelican and check out what they call fine dining around here. Avery has it all covered, so we're good for the evening."

Morning rolled around soon enough for the gang. They met up for breakfast, chatting with one another as they watched the numbers on their watches. The banks opened at eight, as opposed to nine up north. Toby would be at the bank promptly at eight. From there, he and Mia would head to the airport for the first leg of their trip. None of them knew where any of the dancers were going, not even Avery. All he would say was that Mia had resigned, had thanked him for the opportunity to work for him, but she was staying with Toby, who was happier than a pig in a mudslide, according to Dennis.

The Ritz-Carlton was just coming alive when Pilar Sanders stepped out of the elevator, dressed in blue jeans, sneakers, and a bright pink T-shirt that said THE DEVIL IS IN THE DETAILS. She carried an oversize straw beach bag with a bright bold sunflower embroidered on both sides. The bag had a zipper. She wore no makeup, and her hair was pulled back into a ponytail. Under her arm, she carried a straw hat that matched the beach bag. She stopped at one of the seating areas and leaned over to speak to Zuma Delgado.

"Don't you get tired following me around? I'm going shopping. I'll be back in two hours to get ready for tonight. I do this at each pageant, so it is nothing new. It's how I unwind. In wild anticipation of the money you're going to be paying me. Can I bring anything back for you? Chocolate, some of that shitty aftershave that you bathe in? Well, what's it going to be?"

"Two hours. If you aren't back, I'll send my people after you."

"Of course you will. Good-bye, Mr. Delgado. You have a nice day now, you hear?"

"Bitch!"

"I heard that. Bastard," Pilar called over her shoulder.

Pilar walked away from the hotel and hailed a cab. "The airport, please. The private part."

Seventy-two minutes later, Pilar leaned back in her seat and looked around the plane's interior. She was the only passenger, and she had been promised eggs Benedict when she hired the private plane to fly her to San Francisco.

"Here I come, Gabe, like it or not. I'll find you. I know I will," she whispered.

What Pilar Sanders didn't know was that when the plane landed in San Francisco, one of Avery Snowden's associates would be waiting for her. And where she was going, she would never again see Gabriel.

Zuma Delgado was a bundle of nerves as one text message after another pinged on his phone. His people were wired up, and his supplier was about to have a stroke in anticipation of what was going to go down in just a few hours. With nothing to do but answer the text messages and incoming calls, he set out to walk to the Mandarin Oriental. Watching the last rehearsal was better than sitting around here, stewing and worrying. The Sanders woman had said that the rehearsal was scheduled for ten and would run three hours. It was a little past nine thirty now. "So, I'll walk slow," he muttered to himself.

At 10:20 p.m., the fine hairs on the back of Delgado's neck started to twang. Where were the dancers? Did he make a mistake on the time? He never made mistakes. He called his people at the Pink Pelican and was told the dancers left the hotel a little before eight and had not returned.

"Who followed them?" he asked.

"No one. You did not give the order to do that. You said to wait here."

Yes, he did make mistakes. "Check their rooms." Delgado knew even as the words left his mouth that the dancers were gone. He felt the blood freeze in his veins. Sanders was gone, too. While he didn't know all that much about women, he did know enough to know they didn't go out in public without makeup, and the Sanders woman wore enough to warrant a car wash to remove it.

"Son of a bitch!"

All it took was an hour to bribe the housekeeping staff and gain entrance to the dancers' rooms, as well as Pilar Sanders's at the Ritz-Carlton. To the naked eye, it appeared that all of them would be returning. But Delgado knew otherwise.

If he hadn't been standing outside the rehearsal room, he would have missed the gang of men who shouldered him out of the way.

"Move it, buddy," Jack said. "We have a rehearsal to get under way. Hey, weren't you here yesterday for the auditions? We won! We're going to be the opening act for the real dancers. What a break, huh? Okay, one of you guys turn up the music and let's go to town. We want to make that nice lady proud of us. She said we're all going to get a prize."

"Wait a minute here. You men are dancing tonight?"

"Yeah," Jack drawled. "What's it to you?"

"I'm the guy that hands out the prizes. You okay with that?"

"Well, yeah, I guess so. Are you the guy who also pays us the thousand bucks? That's, like, each, dude."

"No, I'm not that guy. I just do the gifts."

"We gotta start practicing, dude."

"Um, yes. All right. I guess I'll see you this evening."

Charles scurried over to where Jack and the others were

standing, all flustered. "I just got a text message from one of those dancers. He said all the dancers are in the hospital because they got food poisoning early this morning. He said to tell all of you that Ms. Sanders said you will be dancing in prime time tonight. In other words, you guys are *it*."

Zuma Delgado took a deep breath and wanted to howl his rage. Instead, he backed away and bumped into Charles. *Now what the hell am I supposed to do?* "Who are you, old man?"

Charles bristled with indignation. He straightened his portly body and let loose with his best British-accented dialogue. "My partner and I represent these young men in their theatrical endeavors. Ms. Sanders has promised the contract before this evening's performance."

Delgado absorbed what he was hearing. Maybe he was wrong. He looked around. It certainly looked to him like the show was going forward. Women were crazy when it came to spending money and shopping. Every man in the world knew that. So the dancers got food poisoning. It happened. It had happened to him once, and he'd never forgotten it. To this day, he would not eat clams. He felt more upbeat as he stomped from the rehearsal hall.

"I don't think the guy is going to kill anyone just yet. We need to play some music for a few minutes, then get out of here, so they can set up the seats for tonight's show," Ted said, looking around at the stacks and stacks of chairs waiting to be set up.

"Screw the music. The guy is gone. Let's get out of here. Where is Avery?" Jack said.

"He said he was on his way to San Francisco, California, but he got a call and sent someone else. I don't know where he is right now," Fergus said.

"Uh-oh, company," Dennis said when the huge double doors opened.

A young, harried woman pushing a dolly stopped in her tracks and looked around. "Who are you people? What are you doing here?"

Jack knew immediately who she was—Pilar Sanders's right hand. And the right hand didn't appear to have a clue as to what was going on. "You must be Carlie Fisher, Ms. Sanders's assistant. We're tonight's lineup. These two gentlemen," he said, pointing to Fergus and Charles, "are our agents. I don't suppose you have our contracts and our checks, do you?"

"I don't have the faintest idea what you're talking about." She motioned to the men behind her to move forward with their piled-high dollies. "Take them to the dressing room and set it up. It's behind the stage, on the right."

"Well, here's the thing. Your dancers are all in the hospital with food poisoning, and Ms. Sanders is temporarily unavailable. In other words, we're dancing tonight. We were under the impression we were to do just one performance, but now with your men in the hospital, it looks like three performances. We want to be paid for three, not one. We need to see it in writing, like, *now*, or we're outta here. We know how show business works," Jack smirked.

"But I . . . I can't. . . . I have to talk . . . no authority . . . ," Carlie Fisher sputtered.

"Well, young lady, you better get it in a hurry or else shut down tonight's performance," Charles said.

"But I . . . all right, all right. I can write checks on the business account, but I do not have any contracts. This show has to go on," Fisher said, in full panic mode.

"I can draw something up that will cover the situation temporarily. I'm sure the front desk will be glad to help us out. While I'm doing that, you can write out six checks for three thousand dollars each. To expedite things, just leave the names blank. We can fill them in ourselves," Charles said.

"Fine, fine. I do not believe this. I absolutely do not believe this. Talk about a cluster . . . Where is Ms. Sanders?" she all but screamed as she continued to babble, all the while rummaging in her fat briefcase for the business checkbook. She scribbled, turned around, but the room was empty. She shook her head as she tried to make sense out of what was happening. She searched for her phone to call Pilar. She tried three times, and all three times the calls went straight to voice mail. "I should quit," she wailed. Instead, she sat down on the dolly and cried.

When Charles returned, waving a sheet of paper in the air, Fisher wiped her eyes on the sleeve of her shirt, reached for the one-page contract, read it, then signed her name. She handed over the checks.

"Thank you, young lady. Is there anything else I can do for you?"

Fisher shook her head. "Just show up tonight with plenty of time. You do know what to do, don't you? Ms. Sanders likes things to run like clockwork."

"Not to worry, Miss Fisher. We'll see you later."

The gang rushed up to Charles the moment he walked through the door, and they peppered him with questions. "We're dealing with dumb and dumber here, boys. There's a branch bank one street over. I suggest you all cash these checks now, but be sure to fill in your names. I didn't see any reason to expound on that. The contract only has first names. She didn't even notice, or if she did, she doesn't care. I wager she will be terminating her employment by the end of the evening," he said.

Dennis clapped his hands in glee as he fell into line for the trek to the bank. He was being paid to dance on a stage. "How cool is that?" he muttered to himself.

Their banking business finished, Charles signaled they should all split up and head back to the Pink Pelican to rest up for their performance. Dennis was the only one who was excited. Even Cyrus was glum.

On their arrival, it was obvious that happy hour was in full swing. It was wall-to-wall tourists, laughing and drinking. The scent of suntan lotion was everywhere and so intense that Jack broke away, saying he was going to take Cyrus for a run on the beach. Harry joined them. The run on the beach turned into Cyrus running off by himself while Jack and Harry plopped down on the sand.

"It's a hot mess, Harry."

Harry grinned. "What was your first clue, Jack?"

"Do you think we can pull this off? The truth, Harry."

"The truth, Jack? Too many variables."

"Yeah, yeah, that's my thinking, too. I hate saying this, but I'd feel a lot better if Snowden was here. He definitely has a feel for this kind of caper. Look around. His people could be anywhere, and we don't even know it. He keeps saying he has our backs. I hope so. By the way, what do you think about Toby and Mia going off together?"

Harry laughed. "I saw that one coming. Riding off into the sunset, or in this case the sunrise, is for the young."

"Wow, Harry. That was profound."

Harry was on his feet just as Cyrus bounded up the beach, barking his head off.

The threesome headed back to the Pelican to get ready for their evening's adventure.

Jack's watch said it was 6:47 p.m. The great ballroom was filled to capacity. Music was playing, but not loud. That would change soon. A sold-out performance. "I didn't know that Fisher was the emcee."

"I don't think she knew it, either. With no one else to do it, she stepped up to the plate. You see those presents, prizes, if you prefer. Ready to go. And Delgado has a ringside seat, front row center. It's easy to pick out his goons since the audience is all female. They stick out like tits on a bull," Ted said.

"Time to saddle up," Jack said. "This is where I give you all a pep talk that you don't need. We're oiled and bronzed. We're dancers tonight, boys. We have checks to prove it. Remember, the ninja suits rip off from the crotch, and you need both hands to do it. You fling them behind you. Then you toss that round circle upward, and a cloud of smoke circles overhead. The drumbeat kicks in, and then we . . . dance. Did I miss anything?"

"Not a thing," Dennis said. "We just wait for our cue. She goes offstage, the lights go down, and when they come back up, we're on the stage, under some blinding white lights. This room will feel like an earthquake hit it once the music kicks in." He paused. "Okay, she's winding down, get ready, boys. On the count of three, take your places. One. Two. Three! Hit it, guys!"

The drumbeat was deafening; the women in the audience screamed, shouted, and stomped their feet. Clad in black from head to toe, the line of dancers looked menacing. They stood, legs spread and firmly planted. On cue, they all tossed the circles into the air. Smoke circled upward just as the dancers reached down to release the Velcro. Ninja suits flew upward into the haze.

Game on.

The women screamed their delight as Harry moved forward, then leaped in the air. He twisted, he flew, and he gyrated to the throbbing music, showing off every martial-arts move he'd ever learned. His almost naked body shimmered under the bright lights. He did a bump and grind that almost set the room on fire. Jack and the others played backup, their moves, while not as stellar, were still earth-shattering. The women didn't even bother to wait for the end; they started tossing money onto the stage.

The following thirty minutes passed in a blur of ear-deafening sound. When the lights went down and the music stopped, the boys rushed back to the dressing room to get ready for the awards part of the pageant.

"Holy shit, Harry! I didn't know you had it in you!" Jack roared with laughter as the others clapped Harry on the back, praising his moves.

"The videos go for a hundred bucks a pop. Cash only. I ordered a dozen," Dennis chortled.

The others just stared at him.

"What videos?" Harry asked.

"The videos of our performance. The women buy them, and then they can play them over and over when they go home. Right now, there is someone out there raking in the cash in a bushel basket. Not to worry. I ordered a whole dozen. When we get old, we can look at them and laugh," Dennis said.

Jack watched Harry out of the corner of his eye. He was about to erupt any second now, and he would have, but Carlie Fisher poked her head in the door and said, "Onstage, everyone."

Jack pushed Harry forward. They lined up as the women whistled and shouted at Fisher's little speech assuring them the show would continue after the awards were given out. She again apologized for the absence of the regular dancers and got a few boo hoos from the women when she said they all were suffering from food poisoning. "And I'm sorry that Ms. Sanders isn't here, but it seems that on her way, there was a car accident, and she's being held up. But the show must go on, so without further adieu, let me introduce you to Ms. Sanders's assistant, Mr. Zuma, who will present the prizes for tonight's brief but electric performance. You understand, of course, that the dancers on the stage are accepting the awards for the dancers who aren't here."

Delgado appeared out of nowhere. He didn't say anything but reached over to the table and picked up the boot-sized box and handed it to Harry, who was first in line. Drumroll. And on down the line he went until all the gift boxes were off the table and only the basket of flowers remained. Delgado looked uncertain, until Charles walked onto the stage and said he was accepting the flowers for Ms. Sanders.

Immediately following that declaration, every light in the ballroom came on. Blue-jacketed men and women dressed in Windbreakers with the letters DEA or FBI were everywhere. Guns were everywhere. The audience, not understanding what was going on, hooted and clapped and yelled for more, more, more, knowing they were getting their money's worth from the night's event.

"Where's Fergus?" Jack asked.

"I do believe he might be outside with Avery, securing the money from Mr. Delgado's vehicle. As you know, Ms. Sanders's cut is in the bottom of this basket of flowers. I . . . ah . . . removed her portion and handed it off to Fergus the minute I got backstage," Charles whispered, so that only Jack could hear him.

"I'll take those flowers, sir," a DEA agent said.

"Of course you will, my dear. They're almost as pretty as you are," Charles said gallantly. The agent scowled at him and walked off, carrying the basket of flowers.

"Well, from the looks of things, our work here is finished. Oh, there are Fergus and Avery. They look quite happy, so I assume our coffers are once again robust," Charles said.

"How about calling the airport so we can be wheels up as soon as the officials cut us loose?" Jack said. "Where is Harry?"

"The last time I saw him, he was trying to negotiate a deal to buy *all* the videos and not having much luck."

Jack looked around at his dance companions. All wore

happy smiles. He mouthed the words, "We did good, guys. Real good."

Cyrus threw back his head and howled.

"I know, I know. Okay, the guy in the handcuffs. Go on. Bite his ass and get right back here," Jack said.

Cyrus always followed orders.

Epilogue

Two days before Christmas . . .

The armory that Myra and Annie had rented for the veterans' first annual Christmas party was a winter wonderland, with wall-to-wall fresh Christmas trees with colored lights, hanging garlands, mountains of presents lined up under the wall-to-wall trees, just waiting for the vets and their families to open them. Christmas carols could be heard playing in the background, putting a happy smile on everyone's face, especially the vets', who wore the happiest smiles that people were finally doing something for them. Not to them. All were dressed in their finest, even the children, who waited with stars in their eyes to see Santa, aka Charles, make his appearance. Not a thing had been overlooked—even Lady and her pups, Cyrus, and Murphy posed as reindeer, to the children's delight.

Tables of food were everywhere, most of it donated thanks to Annie's relentless hounding of the local businesses and the promise of free advertising in the *Post*.

Myra tactfully nudged Annie toward the door. "Something is bothering you, Annie, I can tell. Want to talk about it? By the way, everyone is here but Dennis. Isn't he coming?"

"He said he was coming, but he had the week off, said

he had some business to take care of before Christmas. I don't think he would miss this party. Something *is* bothering me, but it can wait till later. Oh, look. There's Dennis now! Great. Everyone is here!"

Dennis waved and headed in their direction, weaving his way through the crowd, but stopped when he got to Harry. They watched him smile and hand Harry a slip of paper. They looked at one another when they saw Harry hug the young reporter. Harry Wong was not a touchy-feely kind of person. Not ever.

"How did you do it, Dennis?" The relief in the martial-arts expert's voice convinced Dennis he would walk through fire for his friend Harry, if need be.

"After we got back, I went to that supper club and met with Carlie Fisher. I asked for the videos, and she just handed them over. They only had time to burn sixty-four of them. All you have to do is go to the *Post*, turn in this ticket, and Lost and Found will turn them over to you. I offered to pay for the videos, but she said no, that there was enough money in the business account to pay back all the people who had ordered them. She's hired people to help her close up the Sanderses' Supper Clubs. She told me that when she went to the office after she got back, there was a letter for her and a check for a million dollars for her years of loyal service. She was crying."

"She had no idea what was going on behind the scenes," Harry said. "The Sanderses ran a tight ship in that respect. It's over now, and we're on to our next mission as soon as Jack tells us what it is." He jerked his head in Jack's direction.

"Wonder what he and Mr. Sparrow are talking about. They look . . . *intense*. Harry, did Snowden ever find out what happened to Ms. Sanders? The last thing I heard, his associate was at the airport outside San Francisco when the private plane she had hired landed. And that when no one other than the pilot got off, he went looking for her. But she was nowhere to be found. And the pilot said that he had no idea what Mr. Snowden's man was talking about, that he had just flown the plane in from a small airfield near Denver, and there was no passenger on the plane when he got to the plane."

"Well, Dennis, that's what you get for taking a vacation and going off the grid. Two days after you left, Avery caught up with the pilot who had flown the plane to Colorado. And here is what he learned. About two hours into the flight from Miami, a message came, telling the pilot to land at that small airfield outside Denver and saying that Ms. Sanders and the pilot were to get off. Another pilot would take the plane to San Francisco. There was also a message for Ms. Sanders, to be given to her if she balked at the change in plans, which, the pilot said, she did most vociferously."

"What," Dennis asked, really interested now, "did the message say?"

"Here's what's interesting. According to the pilot, what it said was that going to San Francisco was as good as going back to that trailer in Alabama. And when she heard that, Ms. Sanders looked like she had seen a ghost. And then she started to bawl like a baby. And when she calmed down, he heard her mutter to herself something that sounded like, 'Maybe I'll get that conveyer belt yet,' which left him shaking his head and thinking she must be nuts. And, no, I have no idea what she could have been talking about.

"Anyway, the pilot landed outside Denver, he and Ms. Sanders got off, and he was given ten thousand dollars in cash and told to take a nice vacation somewhere for ten days or two weeks, preferably in South America or the Caribbean. Seems the guy had always wanted to go to Rio, so that's where he went. And Snowden's people had no idea where to look for him, so it was not until he returned home that they found him."

"Holy cow," Dennis said. "That must mean—"

"Yeah, that's what we figured, too. Somehow, someway, Gabe Sanders learned what was going on and figured that if Toby had ratted them out, there was no way that Pilar could get away by flying to San Francisco from Miami. So he set up this diversion, and, we think, the two of them probably flew off into the sunset. I guess maybe he really did love her. So, we may not have caught the Sanderses. But the mission is over. It's done, finished. We took a ton of drugs off the street. Hopefully, we managed to keep a lot of kids safer."

"I know, I know, but in the end, I think she was trying to make up for it. She could have just walked away and not paid anyone anything. Instead, she gives Carlie Fisher a cool million. She takes care of all the dancers. She forgives Toby and did not even appear to have any hard feelings. Like you said, it's over and done with. The DEA is happy, that's for sure. Man, those two look like thunderclouds. This is supposed to be a party. I'm going over there to see what Jack and Mr. Sparrow are looking so hyper about."

"Who is the present for?" Harry asked as he pointed to the gaily wrapped gift in Dennis's hands.

"It's for all these people," Dennis said, waving his arms about.

"You bought it, didn't you? You sly son of a gun! You went back to Florida. You bought the Pink Pelican!"

"Shhhh. Yeah. I did. Got it for a good price. My plan is . . . keep half for use by the public to bring in revenue and the other half for the veterans to enjoy free of charge. No one will get turned away. That's Annie's mantra these days. Lots and lots of job openings, in case any of them are looking for jobs. It's a work in progress."

"That's a great thing you did, kid. Really great. The big question is, who are you going to get to run it?"

"That's all taken care of. But until the deal is signed, I can't say a word. You're smart, Harry. Figure it out. Who *isn't* here tonight? Look over at Annie and Myra. Then look at Sparrow and Jack."

Harry turned statue still as he looked at Annie and Myra and read Annie's lips.

"Let's take this outside, Myra, and have a cigarette," she said.

"We don't smoke, Annie, and we don't have any cigarettes." Nonetheless, Myra followed Annie to the great doors that would lead them outside into the blustery December coldness.

"I know, but Sparrow does, and Jack does once in a while. They're going outside, too. We can bum one off them. Pick up your feet, Myra. Something is going down, or it already went down."

Outside, the foursome fired up cigarettes, with Annie and Myra coughing and sputtering while Sparrow and Jack drew smoke into their lungs.

"Okay. What is it?" Annie snapped. "We heard about your mission and how both Mr. and Ms. Sanders outwitted you. It happens. Remember, we lost Hank Jellicoe *twice*. Sooner or later, you'll catch them, just like eventually we'll get Jellicoe. You can run, but you can't hide forever. Now spit it out. What's going on?"

"Like you don't know," Jack muttered.

"If I knew, I wouldn't be asking. So . . ."

"Why didn't you tell us Bert Navarro resigned?" Sparrow asked.

"Because I just found out this morning, and as you can see, I've been rather busy with this party and all. He sent me an e-mail. It's not the end of the world. Macao is up and running, and his replacement is first rate. No worries.

I told him he could name his price and continue to run Babylon, but he turned me down. Why does this concern you two? It's business. No one, not even Bert, is indispensable."

"He's in town," Sparrow said. "He went by the Hoover Building this morning to see me, and my old secretary told him where to find me. He came out to the clinic. The thing is, he wasn't alone."

"You gonna make me pull it out of you, Mr. Sparrow?" Annie said.

"He had his . . . there was . . . His . . . fiancée was with him. You don't know this yet, but Dennis bought the Pink Pelican in Miami. He's turning it over to you this evening, the deed, that is. He hired Bert to run it. Bert said yes. That's all I know, and I wish I didn't know that."

They all asked the same question at the same time. "Does Kathryn know?"

Four cigarettes dropped to the ground. Four shoes stomped on them. Four people picked them up and dropped them into a trash bin by the massive doors.

"I didn't ask, but I'd say from observing Kathryn this evening that the answer is, no, she does not know," Sparrow said, holding the door open for the women to go through first.

"Just in time. Santa is about to take center stage. The military chaplains are all lined up to give their blessing. We all need to say a prayer," Annie said, a catch in her voice.

Once the prayer was over, the portly Santa waved his arms. "Ho! Ho! Ho!"

All the reindeer barked.

"Merry Christmas," everyone shouted at the same time.